OTHER WORKS

# ACCLAIM FOR THE VENUS TRILOGY

## Conquering Venus

This stunning debut novel is everything—a poetic page-turner, a wonderful mystery, and a compelling story of self-realization. - *OutSmart Magazine*

Kelley does an excellent job of taking us seamlessly into the paranormal scenes and back to reality, neither missing the proverbial beat or losing one bit of his hold on the reader.
- *New Southerner*

The writing is crisp and the novel's pace is a swift and compressed one, with finely detailed dreams, gypsy readings, hospital apparitions, undiscovered journals, and an abundance of metaphors. - *Out in Print*

## Remain In Light

Great as a standalone book, or even better as part two of a grander whole, this is the rare sequel that easily outperforms its predecessor in just about any way you can name, and it comes with a highly enthusiastic recommendation. - *Chicago Center for Literature & Photography*

Filled with what-will-they-say-next characters, a suspenseful pace, and intertwining plots *Remain In Light* is a wickedly fun read. - *Lambda Literary Review*

Collin Kelley has crafted a story that will appeal to a lot of different people for a lot of different reasons, but I can tell you this, *Remain In Light* is a first class suspense novel. - *Grant Jerkins, At the End of the Road* and *A Very Simple Crime*

# LEAVING PARIS

*a novel*

## COLLIN KELLEY

SIBLING RIVALRY PRESS
LITTLE ROCK, ARKANSAS
DISTURB / ENRAPTURE

Sibling Rivalry Press, LLC
PO Box 26147
Little Rock, AR 72221

info@siblingrivalrypress.com

www.siblingrivalrypress.com

ISBN: 978-1-943977-12-3

Library of Congress Control No. 2016931402

This title is housed permanently in the Rare Books and Special Collections Vault of the Library of Congress.

First Sibling Rivalry Press Edition, April 2016

*for*
My Father

# LEAVING PARIS

Paradise
  is defined by loss.
            Is loss.
  Is.

                 —Margaret Atwood


I'm leaving Paris for a third time… how many ways can a story be told?

                 —Vanessa Daou

THE
COMMERCIAL
APPEAL
SEPTEMBER 15, 2005

# CONTROVERSIAL MEMPHIS-BORN POET RETURNS FOR UoM READING SERIES

By Joy Lively
*Arts Editor*

Poet Martin Paige left Memphis 10 years ago under a cloud of suspicion, but will return Saturday night, Sept. 17, at 8 p.m. for a reading from his debut collection, *What Remains*, at the Galloway Mansion as part of the University of Memphis Visiting Writer's Series.

In the decade since his departure, he's lived in Paris and become a noted poet in European literary circles, but his book was met with criticism in the U.S. upon its release in the spring. *The New York Times Book Review* called Paige's verse "capable" but wondered if the confessional nature and "sexual crudeness" added anything to the canon of American poetry.

Influential literary blog site *Book-A-Whirl* questioned Paige's deal with Knopf and complained that Paige hasn't paid his dues to receive such a high profile release. In France his collection was published by Éditions Resolvere, where he works as a senior editor and is said to be close friends with associate publisher, Irène Laureux. Even French bibliophiles hinted at cronyism, but *What Remains* has met with considerable acclaim.

Paige might be better known in his native city for his connection to the River Lane High School scandal in 1995 when he accompanied a group of seniors on their graduation trip to Paris and was caught up in the terrorist bombing of a subway train and station near Notre-Dame Cathedral. Diane Jacobs, who chaperoned the trip, escorted the students home after the attack and was stripped of her teaching credentials in absentia after she fled back to Paris. One student, David McLaren, remained in Paris after the bombing and there were allegations that Jacobs was having an affair with the teenager. An investigation into Jacobs by the Shelby County Board of Education proved inconclusive and no charges were filed, since McLaren was 18 at the time. Why Paige was on the trip has never been answered and he declined comment during a recent phone interview.

Public records show that Paige's parents divorced five years ago. His father still lives in the Memphis area, while his mother has remarried and lives in Atlanta. Both refused to be interviewed for this article. Several of the poems in *What Remains* hint at familial estrangement, time spent in a mental institution and address a male lover who died. The volume is dedicated to Peter. Police records from 1992 indicate Paige was part of a botched murder-suicide plot and shot Peter Davis, 18, in self-defense. In the biography supplied by the publishing house, it states that Paige lives with his "partner," Christian Kigali, in Paris.

Paige also refused to talk about the specific names used in his poetry. "I don't dissect my work in that way," Paige said. "Despite the confessional label, my poetry is open to reader interpretation."

When pressed about his relationships with Davis and

McLaren, Paige again declined to provide any substantive information. "What I have to say about my past is in the poetry."

Paige will read with Juliette Lacombe, a French-American poet, who has become known for liberal op-ed pieces in *The Huffington Post* and *The New York Times* criticizing the Bush Administration for its policies and the ongoing wars in Iraq and Afghanistan. She accused President Bush of mass murder in New Orleans following the government's response to Hurricane Katrina and the failure of the city's levees two weeks ago. Her latest collection, *Trois* (French for "Three"), was also published by Knopf.

## prologue: Decade

September in Memphis. It is sticky hot, the humidity so thick that it shimmers in the air. Rainstorms come and go, but the heat never dissipates. He has forgotten this until now, how oppressive summer can be in the South. Hurricane Katrina has devastated the Gulf Coast; New Orleans is a drowned world. Everyone's attention is 400 miles away, but the show must go on.

Martin Paige sits at a dressing table inside the Galloway Mansion, trying to ignore the dampness he feels under his arms, the bead of sweat that rolls down his back. He second-guesses the decision he made years ago to always wear black. He wants to strip off the jacket and unbutton his shirt, but the hum of the struggling air-conditioner nearly immobilizes him. He looks at himself in the mirror. He left Memphis when he was twenty-two and now he's thirty-two. There are more tiny lines forming around his eyes, which are hidden behind glasses, and the furrow in his brow is subtly deeper. His blond hair is darker now, but he still wears bangs to cover the scar from the bomb blast on his forehead—his lasting souvenir of Paris, the summer he took Rilke's advice and changed his life.

The tattoo on his left hand—two interlocking crosses at the base of his thumb so elegantly described as a "crude prison-like carving" in *Poets & Writers*—has faded ever so slightly. Equal but opposite. The meaning of the tattoo, once a private bond, is now public knowledge. The insular world of poetry—"the bubble" as Julie calls it—is tiny, and when someone new and unvetted enters, takes up too many column inches in the literary journals and threatens to jump into the mainstream, the fragility of the bubble is exposed. *You knew the job was dangerous when you took it,* Julie singsongs to him after the publication of a bad review or inaccurate profile. She reminds him of Diane with her penchant for pop culture catchphrases and music. He wonders if Diane will show up for the reading after the angry text message she sent about the article in *The Commercial Appeal.* Then his mind drifts to Christian and Irène going on with their lives without him on rue Rampon.

Martin becomes aware of a clock ticking somewhere inside the giant house. It's a plantation fantasy come to life, a little too prim and proper for the reading he will soon give with Julie, with its massive Ionic columns and period furniture, much of it made in France. It makes him miss Paris even more. He has mastered the art of what Julie calls "smiling and nodding like you give a damn." Perhaps too well. The clock lulls him further and he has been staring into the mirror for so long that he's nearly in a trance.

He becomes aware that he is no longer looking at himself, but Irène. There is the familiar downturned mouth, the dark circles around her eyes, highlighted by her pale skin, and long, blonde hair pulled away from her face. She cradles her chin in her hands and he sees their shared tattoo. The reflecting hands, she calls them.

There is a knock on the door; both Martin and Irène turn to acknowledge it. For a moment, Martin stares at the door, hears Julie call his name from the other side.

"I'm coming. Just a second."

When he turns back to the mirror, Irène is no longer there. He pulls his cell phone from his pocket and starts to dial, but the knock comes again. It is time to go downstairs to the parlor for the reading.

He reaches out and puts his palm against the mirror, can see the deep lines etched there, streaming from the mount of Venus. This has happened before. It's a summons, a beacon, a call to return home. He taps lightly on the glass, whispers: *Paris, Paris, Paris.*

# 1 a Clock Unwound

*The dream comes in odd flashes. Men's rough hands on marble hoisted above their heads, and yet the statue seems to float above the staircase as if it's levitating. Are the men trying to stop her from floating away or forcing her to the ground? The statue has wings, shimmers in light that spills through skylights at the top of the staircase. The men are anxious, a sense of urgency palpable in the air of this familiar grand hall. Another ripple of light flashes across the statue and one of the wings beats, snaps the air like a whip, and the men look up in fear.*

When Irène Laureux woke, she was sitting at the dressing table in her bedroom on rue Rampon. It was as if she dozed for a moment, slipped into some kind of trance. On the bed, her cat, Pierre, looked at her intently. He was almost sixteen, blind in one eye and spent most of his days watching the comings and goings of the apartment from sunny patches. The strange dream was still vivid in her mind, but then Irène remembered Martin looking back at her in the mirror. Instinctively, she put her hand to the glass. The telepathy that drew them together ten years ago had subtly changed over time to become more intuitive, like that of twins. They finished each other's sentences, could often read each other's thoughts. Martin was the child she never had with her late husband, Jean-Louis, but he was also her best friend and confidante.

Irène picked up her mobile phone. It was two o'clock in the morning, which meant Martin and Julie Lacombe's reading would just be starting in Memphis. She put on her reading glasses and held the phone close to her face. She thought carrying the BlackBerry to meetings with authors and other editors made her look chic, belied her seventy-seven years, but she hated the damn thing. It took her five minutes to type in the short message to Martin, cursing under her breath as she hit the wrong letter and had to delete and start again. Technology wasn't all it was cracked up to be, she thought, but her aversion to it made her feel old and out of touch.

"You still look like you're in your fifties," Martin would say when she complained about a new wrinkle or mark.

Irène would invariably purse her lips and say, "Is that supposed to make me feel better?"

Irène finally tapped out a message and pressed send: THINKING OF YOU. BON COURAGE, MON CHER.

Almost as soon as she sent the message, there was a knock on her door. It was so unexpected that Pierre squeaked in surprise and Irène dropped the mobile. The building was secure so it had to be a neighbor or Christian coming in late from the youth center at Montfermeil.

Before she even reached the door, she heard Christian calling softly from the other side. "Irène, it is only me."

"Are you just coming in now?" Irène said, opening the door. "It's so late."

"I've tried to call Martin all evening, but there is no service out there and now my battery is dead." He hugged Irène, threw his backpack on the sofa and pulled off his scarf, all in swift motions. Christian was always moving, alert and interested, seemingly wanting to make up for the years he lost when he was living under the thumb of his father and on the streets. He was tall and lanky and even more handsome now at twenty-six than when Martin had first met him when he was only nineteen. Half Belgian, half African, his looks were so arresting that both men and women stared openly at him on the streets of Paris. He was also kind and attentive, but there was an edge to him that would never quite fade. It was those years selling drugs and his body, and squatting in other people's houses that hardened him, Irène thought. It was also that edge that gave him the resolve to return to the banlieue and try to help the immigrant kids, despite the danger. He had been mugged numerous times, attacked by a couple of youths he had tried to help, had a scar on his forearm from being stabbed with an improvised knife. He and Martin had fought bitterly after the stabbing, with Martin begging him to give up the work, or at least not to linger after dark.

Christian plugged his mobile into an outlet and began texting. "I am a bad boyfriend," he said. "Please don't mention I was so late. It was a crisis."

"I just sent him a text message," Irène said. "Tell him you are here with me and we are both wishing him luck."

Christian smiled at Irène. "I know you disapprove, too."

"My feelings are the same as Martin's, you know that. It is dangerous in Montfermeil. You are putting yourself at risk." Christian started to protest, but Irène raised her hands in surrender. "That is all I will say. I am just, once again, stating it for the record."

"Noted."

"What was the crisis?"

"There's been more police presence this week than I have seen in months. People are being detained for no reason. After dark, you are stopped and questioned about your destination or where you have been. One of the reasons I am so late is that I was stopped. They know who I am, but they do it to harass me. They ask why I want to help the scum in the banlieue."

Irène sat down next to Christian. "They are just trying to provoke you."

"I know," he said. "I have learned to stay cool, as they say. Keep calm and not show any anger or aggression, but inside I want to grab their batons and beat them to death. The police are racist and xenophobic. I think the entire force is a wing of the Front National. And there's a rumor Arnaud is going to visit. If he does, there will be a riot."

Michel Arnaud was a former inspector who had risen to become the préfet de police, overseeing all of Paris and its suburbs. He had arrested Christian for squatting at a house in Montmartre and forced him to give up information about all the drug contacts in Paris, which led to the arrest of André Sarde, the head of France's largest organized crime syndicate. The arrest put Arnaud's career into orbit, and he made no secret of his political leanings, never failing to make some controversial statement about immigrants and his desire to wipe them out of the banlieue. Arnaud was frequently challenged in the media and his resignation demanded by citizens and politicians, but he had a strong advocate in Nicolas Sarkozy, the interior minister who never failed to raise ire by dismissing the banlieue population as rabble and hoodlums. France was changing rapidly and the rise of xenophobes like Arnaud and Jean-Marie Le Pen made Irène feel like a stranger in her own country.

"Arnaud should be exposed," Christian said. "With everything you and Martin know, you could ruin him."

Irène shook her head. "But it would mean betraying

Monsieur Sarde, which I cannot do."

"But he's dead. And I know Sarde's name was really Frederick Dubois, so you don't have to keep calling him that."

"Without Freder... without André Sarde, you would still be in exile in Germany. Or have you forgotten?"

Christian sighed and folded his arms over his chest. "No, I haven't forgotten."

"I think Arnaud is a bastard. He shouldn't be a policeman, but to expose him would turn a harsh spotlight on all of us— me, you, Martin, the publishing house. Even Jean-Louis. It took thirty years to lay him to rest and I don't want to resurrect him now. If that sounds selfish, then so be it."

Irène had never regretted forgiving Frederick Dubois for seducing her husband. It was May 1968 and the whole country was in turmoil. Frederick had been recruited by the government to infiltrate the École des Beaux-Arts and rat on the radicals organizing the strikes and riots. Except Jean-Louis was not a radical, but simply caught up in the frenzy of the protests and by his unexpected attraction to his young student. They had fallen in love and when Jean-Louis was about to be arrested for sedition, Frederick had confessed that he was an operative and urged his teacher to leave the country. Instead, Jean-Louis had snapped. He shot Frederick, paralyzing him for life, before turning the gun on himself. The government had cleaned-up the garret on the Left Bank where the crime had occurred and dumped Jean-Louis' body near Notre-Dame. The police had closed the case, on instruction from De Gaulle's government, and Irène was too consumed by grief and her agoraphobia to do anything about it.

Then Martin had arrived in the summer of 1995 and they inadvertently discovered Jean-Louis' diary and a stack of letters hidden in the attic at rue Rampon. It would take Irène three years to track down Frederick Dubois, and she had been stunned to find him in a wheelchair, dying of cancer and haunted by what he had done to Jean-Louis. Frederick had spent the rest of his life avenging Jean-Louis by building an organized crime syndicate with connections deep in the government. He had politicians, police and judges in his pocket. He bought, sold and traded secrets, threatened to expose France's corruption and decades of lies. For his silence, the government allowed him to build an empire—drugs, prostitution, nightclubs, gambling dens.

In 1998, just before his death, Frederick confessed his sins to Irène and then turned himself in to the police. Frederick's arrest and death galvanized the country for months. Journalists investigating the origins of the crime syndicate all arrived at the same conclusion: André Sarde was an alias. But the collusion between Sarde's organization and the government, the charade of his arrest on live television and the deals he brokered before his death, would all remain secret. One of those deals forced Arnaud to expunge Christian's arrest record and allow him to come back to Paris to be with Martin and restart his life.

"I owe Frederick... André... whatever you want to call him... a debt of gratitude that I can never repay, I know that," Christian said.

"I prefer to remember Frederick for his atonement. The money he left us paid for your and Martin's flat, your education and saved the publishing house from closing. He repaid his debt to me—to us."

She remembered Frederick shrunken and dying in his bed at Salpêtrière Hospital, clutching Jean-Louis' diary that she had brought to him to his chest, finally at peace in the last hours of his life. Irène had started writing a memoir, but its pages were now locked up in the safe in her office at Éditions Resolvere. She would never publish the book, would burn it before she died, or instruct Martin to do so if she were unable. No, she couldn't look back.

"I am sorry," Christian said. "I should not have brought it

up again. I know you don't want to talk about it. It's just…"

She patted his arm gently. "I know."

The clock on the mantle sounded a single chime. It was half-past two in the morning. Martin and Juliette's reading would be under way. She desperately wanted to speak to him. Something was about to happen; there was expectancy in the air, like when Martin first arrived in Paris and when her dreams led her to Frederick Dubois.

## 2 Dr. Lacombe. In the Parlor. With a Dagger.

The parlor at the Galloway Mansion was, unexpectedly, full. Every chair was occupied and latecomers, mostly students, were standing around the room, while others were sitting on the floor busily texting on their cell phones.

Martin sat next to Julie Lacombe at the front of the room, uncomfortably on display for the audience to gawk at. Despite the buzz of conversation, laughter, coughs and shifting of asses in seats, Martin could feel all their eyes upon him as they waited for the reading to begin. Some of the people were genuine lovers of poetry, others were there because they read the hatchet job article in *The Commercial Appeal*, while the students were there for extra credit. Martin scanned the audience for familiar faces, but only recognized his father sitting halfway down the aisle. He wondered if David had left New Orleans before Katrina or stayed to ride it out. They'd had no contact, but Martin was curious whether David had read the book, knowing that so many of the poems were about their disastrous relationship.

And Diane wasn't there. Having her past dredged up again in the daily paper pissed her off, and she was already angry at being back in Memphis, having to deal with her meddling mother while contemplating divorce from her husband. Martin had complained about the article to his publicist at Knopf, but the damage was already done. "Controversy sells," his publicist said, dismissing Martin's complaints. "Maybe you should be a little more provocative, like Julie."

He always forgot the sudden shock of memories that flooded back when he returned to Memphis. Perhaps they were always with him, bubbling beneath the surface, but easily forgotten in Paris. Not just David, but Peter and the still missing Paul, the young man he'd met while recovering from his breakdown after Peter's death. Those days at the hospital had become cloudier in his mind, but the silent intensity of the sex he'd had with Paul, the boy's eyes when he had left him behind at the hospital, still haunted Martin. Putting the recollections down into poetry had helped dull the edges, but maybe not enough. Maybe the answer is to never come to Memphis again, Martin thought, to keep the bad memories in remission.

Julie nudged him. "I say we read our most controversial work tonight. You read all your dirty, gay sex poems and I'll read all my anti-American ones. That's what this crowd is expecting. It's what I would be expecting after that article. Although I only got one paragraph at the very end."

"Uh-huh," Martin said. "You'd have already been on the phone to your lawyer."

"Well, you did shoot your boyfriend and run off to France with a pedophile teacher," she said sarcastically. "I don't have anything like that on my CV."

"And to think, I was just starting to like you."

"You like me," she said nudging him again.

Julie and Martin had become friends as the book tour continued. She was a brilliant poet, passionate about her politics, and never afraid to speak her mind. In many ways, she was like Diane minus the crazy. Juliette Lacombe was born in Paris but moved to the States when she was still a small child. Her father had been a scientist and had gone to work with the US government. He died of a rare cancer when she was a teenager, and she longed to return to France, but her mother had quickly become Americanized and settled in Manhattan. Julie studied at the Sorbonne in Paris, but to her dismay, found herself back in America after her mother suffered a stroke and was put into a nursing home. Julie took an apartment on the Upper West Side and a job at NYU, where she remained even after her mother died.

Julie had collected a verbally abusive husband along the way, and divorced him the moment the abuse became physical. She spent ten years in a relationship with a woman, an uptight professor at Columbia, who became jealous and bitter of Julie's success.

"After lesbian bed death set in, I knew it was over," she told Martin one night over martinis in Washington D.C.

"Lesbian bed death?" Martin asked quizzically.

"Sharing the same bed, but no sex. Ever. I eventually moved into the guest room and bought a vibrator."

Since their break-up, she'd dated a few men as a palate cleanser and lost some of her lesbian friends in the process.

"I prefer women, but my sexuality is fluid," she said. "Some of my hardcore dykes were pissed off. One even called me a lesbian tourist."

Julie was petite, her auburn hair cut into a bob, and she had a penchant for tight wrap dresses, knee-high boots and, her favorite accessory, a dagger pin she wore at her throat. At forty-three, she gave off the air of a sexy schoolteacher and the men and boys at the readings usually perked up when she stepped to the microphone. That is, until she started reading the political poems.

Julie never considered America her home and, despite her dual citizenship, she was unflinching in her criticism of President Bush. Ever since the invasion of Iraq, she had received untold numbers of death threats, was told to choke on a plate of Freedom Fries by a conservative radio host, and a right-wing Republican suggested on CNN that she be deported to the communist country of her choice. Her uncompromising attacks on the Bush administration were over-the-top and bordering on libel, but as more bodies continued to be shipped home from Iraq and the debacle of Hurricane Katrina made the news, there had been more support for her opinions. She was feeling vindicated and feisty, so god knows what she would say during the question and answer session. At Virginia Tech, she had gotten into a screaming match with a religious loon who called her a whore and the antichrist before he was removed by security. There appeared to be no security at the Galloway Mansion, which Martin pointed out to Julie as the program director approached the podium to introduce them.

The program director gushed over Julie's accomplishments— prizes, fellowships, prestigious teaching gigs at Oxford and Harvard—and seemed much more excited about Dr. Lacombe's appearance in Memphis than the audience. There was polite applause as Julie walked to the podium, but the room hushed and the audience stared at her in anticipation.

"Good evening," Julie said. "I'd like to thank the University of Tennessee for having us this evening and the staff here at the Galloway Mansion for being so accommodating and for the lovely dinner. I know that everyone's minds are still on the tragedy of the Gulf Coast, so Martin and I will try to take you away for an hour." Julie's voice still retained a trace of her French heritage, which she turned up a notch whenever she read, especially if the crowd seemed hostile.

Julie pulled the dagger pin from her dress and drove the tip of it into the podium. The pin stood there, gleaming in the light. The audience shifted uncomfortably, exchanged glances. The program director was perched on the edge of her seat, hand at her throat, a look of panic on her face.

Julie turned back to Martin and winked. "This poem is about the illegal war America is fighting in Iraq."

More than a dozen people walked out of the reading before Julie finished her set of all political work. Another four left as Martin read an erotic, profanity-laced poem about the first time he had sex with David at the hotel on rue Rampon. The audience was uncomfortable with the material, but not in the same way as London or New York where they squirmed in their seats with laughter or closed their eyes as the poetry evoked some memory. Martin decided to cut his reading short, flipping to the back of the book and a short poem called "Coming." He was ready to go home.

*The goal is this:*
*touch the underside of Pont Neuf,*
*the oldest part of Paris.*
*Scrape my knuckles until they bleed,*
*leave a stain high above the water line,*
*a marker for future reference,*
*my expatriation graffiti,*
*safe from tide and wake.*
*Send photos of my scars back to you,*
*proof of life.*
*I am on the boat now.*

After the reading, the program director skipped over the

usual question and answer session. In her closing remarks, the program director thanked the poets for their "uncompromising and unsettling images."

"That's code for fuck off and get out," Martin whispered to Julie.

"I thought it was one of our best readings. Five people got up and walked out after my second poem. That's a personal best."

The program director ushered them into the main hall for the book signing.

"This doesn't look like much of book-buying crowd," Martin said. "We'll be back at the hotel with martinis in hand before you know it."

The bookseller looked despondent beside the large stack of books he had ordered for the evening; only a dozen were sold.

Martin was signing a book for a large, florid woman who was whipping a cardboard church fan back and forth across her face and neck, when he heard Julie yelp in surprise. He looked up just as Julie hurled the book she'd been signing across the table at a man who appeared to be in his late thirties, sporting an unkempt beard and a too short Allman Brothers t-shirt, a pale swath of belly fat exposed and jiggling over his pants.

"The son-of-a-bitch spit on me," Julie yelled, brushing the spittle from her face.

The man appeared ready to lunge at Julie, but two students were blocking his path. "You and Jane Fonda should be in prison for treason," the man growled, before cutting his eyes toward Martin. "We don't want you and your nigger-loving, faggot kind here."

"Someone show this redneck asshole the door," Julie ordered, pulling the dagger pin from her dress and waving it at him.

The students hustled the guy toward the door while the program director raced up to the table. "Should I call the police?"

"I think it's a little late for that," Julie said. "You might want to think about having at least one security person here. Even just for show. There are all kinds of crazies running around out there whipped up by Fox News and the fearmongering politicians."

"Uhhh... yes... I'm so sorry about this," the program director said. "Nothing like this has ever happened before."

Julie picked up her bag and headed toward the stairs. "Martin, I'll be ready to go in five."

Martin's father approached the table with a book in hand.

"Dad, you didn't have to buy another one."

"Well, I thought I'd support the bookstore guy," his father said with a note of pity in his voice. "Are you all right? That guy should be locked up."

"I'm okay, Dad. I've been called a lot worse on some of the online message boards. I've got a pretty thick skin."

Martin was glad that the relationship with his father had grown since the divorce. He rarely spoke to his mother, save for the occasional email at holidays and birthdays. She had a new life with a new husband and, like her son, had happily fled Memphis with no plans to ever return. Even for a visit. Martin's parents' marriage had never fully recovered from her affair back in the 80s, so they had finally come to the decision it was time to move on with their lives. His father had come to Paris several times in the last few years, and Martin was thrilled that he had gotten along so well with Irène and Christian.

"I'll call you tomorrow morning about meeting up for dinner," Martin said as his father prepared to depart.

"Bring along Julie, if she wants to come. She's... fascinating." His father's face turned red.

"She's a lesbian, Dad."

His father snapped his fingers. "The interesting ones always are."

Martin gathered up his notebook and pens and was preparing to go upstairs to get Julie, when he noticed a man leaning in the parlor door. He appeared to be in his late twenties, wore a white t-shirt and jeans and black hair shaved almost into a buzz cut. He was sexy and oddly familiar. There was always a pang of guilt when he felt a sexual attraction to someone other than Christian. They had been faithful for seven years, and found that absence actually did make the heart grow fonder. When Martin first toured Europe with his book, they had intense phone sex, and then Christian showed up in London to surprise Martin. They had sex in the bookstore's bathroom before the reading, and Martin thought the audience could tell by his flushed face and mussed hair. Christian sat in the front row with a grin, and every time Martin made eye contact he felt color rise to his face.

The bookseller rushed over to the table with copies of *What Remains* for Martin to autograph for the shop, hoping he might be able to recoup some losses. As Martin signed the books, he glanced back toward the parlor, but the man who had been watching him was gone.

# 3 Post-mortem

In the cab on the way back to the Peabody Hotel, Julie pulled a small, silver flask filled with gin from her bag and took a long swig before handing it to Martin.

"Despite that fat fuck tonight, this has been a pretty successful tour," Julie said. "The universities and the press picked up most of the tab. It's pissing off all the right people. Only poet laureates usually get this kind of treatment."

Martin wiped his mouth after drinking from the flask. "You will never be poet laureate. Poet laureates don't pull knives on their readers."

Julie shrugged. "If I never see Memphis again it will be too soon."

"I'll drink to that," he said and turned up the flask.

She snatched it out of his hand before he could drink the rest and drained the contents. "I want barbecue. I wonder if Rendezvous is still open."

"Jesus, how touristy of you."

"Unlike you, I have work to do tonight. I still have to write a syllabus for my class, which starts in a week. Did I mention that?"

"Repeatedly."

The cab driver, who had been watching them in the rearview mirror, glanced back over his shoulder. "Are y'all some kind of famous writers?"

"We're poets," Martin said.

"Oh," he said, disappointment in his voice. "You make any money doing that?"

Julie leaned forward. "Are you an aspiring writer?"

The cabbie grinned. "Well, I've written a few things. Mostly ideas. Like those legal thrillers John Grisham writes. Now he's famous."

Julie reached into her bag and pulled out a copy of her book and a pen. "What's your name?"

"Artie."

As the cab pulled up in front of the Peabody, Julie made a production out of signing the book with big swoops of her pen and handed it to him over the front seat along with the fare. "Hold onto it. If we ever become famous, you can brag that you drove us around one night."

"Or sell it on eBay," Martin suggested.

Artie grinned and turned the book over in his hands. "Say... what's the title? Troy, Tro-ish..."

"It's French for the number three. Pronounced 'twa.'"

Artie looked dubious. "French, huh?"

"It's a gift, Artie," Julie sneered. "Accept it in the spirit in which it was given."

She kicked open the cab door, almost hitting a hotel porter in the groin. Martin shrugged at Artie and climbed out behind her.

"That was so generous of you," Martin said, looping his arm through hers.

"It's one less book I have to pack," she said.

Martin saw that Irène and Christian had both texted him. He said goodnight to Julie and went to the lobby bar and took a small table in the far corner near the window looking out on Union Avenue. A waiter appeared almost instantly and took his drink order. Water splashed in the fountain of the atrium where the famed ducks swam every afternoon, and there was a distant sound of piano music from one of the other lounges.

Martin hit redial on his cell, and Irène answered on the first ring.

"Oh, thank god. I couldn't sleep until I heard from you," she said. "How was the reading?"

"A disaster. But that's not what I want to talk about. Right before the reading I had one of my visions."

"So did I."

"It was so unexpected. It scared me, but there was no time to call." The telepathy they shared only seemed to be active when something was about to happen or change.

"Is everything all right there? Is Christian okay?"

"Everything is fine. He's fine."

Martin felt his body relax, and he settled back into the chair. If he could just get through one more day in Memphis, he would be on his way back to Paris.

"I feel completely out of the loop," he said. "Disconnected."

"It's been very uneventful these last few weeks since you've been gone. Christian has come over for dinner several times. I believe he had another fight with his father, but he does not want to talk about it."

"Well, that's nothing new."

"How is Diane?"

"A no-show. Did you read the article I emailed you from the newspaper?"

"I thought it was cheap that the reporter had to bring up Diane and your past with David and Peter."

37

Martin sighed. "It's the South. People have long memories when it comes to petty scandals. I thought it might bring out a few extra warm bodies to buy books, but it was mostly students and book sales were dismal. Not to mention a few choice slurs from a racist asshole in the audience."

"Oh, Martin, I am sorry. Are you terribly disappointed?"

"It's poetry. Nobody reads it outside academia unless it comes in a greeting card, especially in the States. It's actually about what I expected. We got spoiled by the readings in Paris and London, and even the crowd in New York was more than I thought it would be, but the further south we go, the less people turn up."

"I can't wait for you to be home," she said. "You will try and convince Diane to return, won't you?"

"Easier said than done," Martin said.

He said goodnight to Irène and was headed to the elevator when, out of the corner of his eye, he saw Julie coming toward him with a large, greasy paper bag.

"I thought you had work to do. What is that?" Martin asked, trying to get a better look at the bag.

"Ribs from Rendezvous. I'm craving them. I was planning to eat my feelings."

"That looks like a lot of feelings," Martin said grabbing for the bag.

Julie jerked it out of his reach as they walked toward the elevators. "Hands off."

"Oh, come on…"

As Martin playfully tried to grab the bag out of her hand while they waited for the elevator, a loud beeping sounded from Julie's pocket. She pulled out a tiny black pager and checked the number.

Martin shook his head in mock disgust. "You and that pager," Martin said. "I'm still getting you a mobile for Christmas. I'm telling you, one day you're going to need to make a call and all the pay phones will be gone."

A bellhop approached them with a determined look on his spotty face. "Pardon me, Ms. Lacombe, but your agent has been trying to reach you. He says it's urgent. You can take it in the lounge."

"Nothing is ever that urgent," Julie said, shoving the bag of ribs toward the bellhop. "Can you put these in my room? 405." The bellhop looked at the bag uncertainly and nodded.

"I can take them," Martin offered.

"No, you'll eat them." She waved the bellhop on and walked toward the lounge.

In his room, Martin kicked off his shoes and stripped off his t-shirt. He flopped down in a chair, pulled his phone from his pocket and dialed Christian. There were only a couple of rings before Christian answered.

"Hello, lover," Martin said, trying to be playful and mask his weariness. "Did I wake you?"

"No, I was just reading. Thinking about you. How was tonight?"

"I don't want to talk about that," Martin said. "What were you thinking about?"

"That I would like to be inside you."

Martin felt himself grow hard. "When I get back, I want to spend the entire day in bed."

Christian was breathing heavily. "I'll make you sore. Just like you like it."

"Oh, really…" Martin unbuttoned his jeans.

"Really."

"Are you naked?"

"Naked and very hard."

Martin moved to the bed and started to pull off his jeans when there was a knock at the door. "Fuck."

"Don't answer it."

There was another knock, and then he heard Julie's voice calling his name. "Hang on, and I'll get rid of her."

Martin opened the door and stuck his head out.

"Ummm... did I interrupt something?" Julie asked.

"Sorta, kinda. I'll come down to your room in a few minutes."

"I won't be there. I'm leaving tonight. I've had some unexpected business come up."

Martin put the phone back to his ear. "I'll call you back in two minutes. I promise. I will. You know I will."

Julie scrunched her nose. "Okay, I get the picture. I'll call you when I get to New York."

"What's wrong?"

"University bullshit. Do you want all the gory details of the tenure track?"

"Maybe it's time to get out of academia."

"Maybe." Julie kissed Martin on each cheek. "Don't get too caught up in Diane's drama. She's a grown woman and should learn to act like it."

Martin smiled wearily. "I'll be sure to mention that."

"Do you want some advice? It's free of charge."

"I'd rather have some ribs."

"Cut your ties with this place. You're the most un-Southern Southerner I've ever met. You've lived in Europe for too long. America is always going to be a disappointment. No one gives a damn about poetry or literature or art in this country anymore. And once that is gone, what else is there? America is in decline, just like all the empires that came before. It's been coming for years, but Bush and Cheney are putting the final nails in the coffin. What's that old saying—get out while the getting is good?"

"Will you take your own advice?"

"Perhaps." Julie appeared to be deliberating on whether to

say something more, but then grinned at him. "Give Christian my best."

Martin hit redial and Christian picked up on the first ring. "That was two minutes and thirty seconds. I was starting to think you had abandoned me," Christian teased. "Do you still want to?"

"Yes," Martin said. "Yes to everything."

After the long day and intense phone sex with Christian, Martin thought he would fall asleep easily, but he found himself tossing and turning and unable to decompress. It wasn't very late, so he got dressed and went back to the lobby bar. He sipped a glass of bourbon, watching the tourists strolling up and down Union Avenue, until he felt someone hovering nearby. It was the young man who had been watching him at the reading.

"Hello, Martin."

There was something about his soft voice, the way he stood there before him, his intense blue eyes. Then he remembered.

"Paul?" Martin asked incredulously.

The man nodded and a smile played across his face.

Martin felt tears filling his eyes. He stood up and wrapped his arms around Paul. "I've been looking for you."

"I know," Paul said, taking Martin's face in his hands. He kissed Martin gently on the lips and embraced him again. "After I read your book, I knew I had to come and see you. Thank you for those poems you wrote... for being honest."

They sat down at the table, unable to take their eyes off each other.

"I have thought about you so often," Martin said. "Did you get the letter I sent?"

Paul reached into his jeans pocket and pulled out a folded envelope and placed it on the table. Martin recognized the address in his own handwriting. It was postmarked October

1995. He had mailed the letter to Paul just before he left for Paris permanently.

"I didn't get the letter for months," Paul said. "I had been back in the hospital and I was living with some friends. The letter went to my parents and they finally gave it to me."

"Oh," Martin said. "How are you now?"

"I haven't been back to the hospital since. The meds are finally working."

"I'm glad. I really am. I wish you'd written. I've been back to Memphis a few times and I thought about you. Where you were, how you were doing, if you were happy."

"I'm happy. To be honest, I didn't know if I could handle seeing you. I mean… I know we were only together for a few months there, but I was really in love with you."

Martin felt his throat tighten. He had a clear image of Paul in his mind, of the rough, intense sex they had while in the hospital. They would sneak away to empty rooms and stairwells, sometimes two or three times a day; avoiding the nurses and orderlies was part of the excitement. It was always the same—Martin fucking the boy relentlessly. When they were finished, Paul would whisper, "I love you." For Martin, sex with Paul was just a way to forget the pain of Peter's death, to blot out the image of his lover bleeding out after Martin had been forced to shoot him. It was only later that Martin acknowledged that he had used Paul with no regard for the boy's feelings or illness. When Martin left the hospital, he had tried to say goodbye, but Paul had become mute.

"After you left, I regressed," Paul said. "I didn't speak for about six months. I was borderline catatonic. I know I said I loved you when we were having sex because I thought you needed to hear someone say it. But I didn't realize how much I meant it until you were gone."

Martin reached out and touched Paul's face across the table.

"I'm so sorry," Martin said. "I had no idea."

Paul pressed Martin's hand close to his face for a moment and kissed his knuckles. "It wasn't your fault," he said. "It was my crazy to deal with."

"But you're really okay now?"

Paul nodded. "I have a boyfriend. He owns a vintage shop and I restore furniture there. We've been together for almost four years. I'm happy. It's a very quiet, un-stressful life, which is what I need."

Martin smiled. "I'm glad you've found peace."

"Here he is now," Paul said.

A tall, burly man wearing shorts and a tank top was walking toward them. He had a pronounced belly, furry arms and shoulders and close cropped, receding hair. He was old enough to be Paul's father.

"Mike, this is Martin," Paul said.

Martin stood up awkwardly, surprised to be face to face with Paul's partner. He stuck out his hand and Mike shook it vigorously.

"Y'all have a chance to catch up?" Mike asked, putting his arm around Paul in an almost protective gesture.

"We did," Paul said. "It was fine."

"I have to admit I wasn't too hot on the idea of Paul coming to see you," Mike said matter-of-factly. "I thought coming to the reading and seeing you might trigger him. He read your book the day it came out. It kind of knocked us for a loop that you mentioned his name. He got a little manic and thought about going to Paris, but he didn't know what to say after so many years. When he found out you were coming to Memphis to read, he said he had to see you."

There was something accusatory in Mike's tone that made Martin feel uncomfortable. "Oh," he said. "I didn't realize…"

Paul put his arms around Mike's belly and hugged him. "I told you it would be fine. I needed this. Getting closure is important."

"Yes," Martin said abruptly. This encounter with Paul had gone from joyous to unpleasant in a matter of minutes.

"Well, we'd better get going," Mike said. "We've been waiting for nearly two hours for you to come back down. Paul didn't want to go up to your room because he thought he would scare you."

Paul laughed a little too loudly. "Well, not scare. I just didn't want to bother him."

"Not at all," Martin said. "I'm so glad we got to see each other. I truly am."

Paul hugged Martin and kissed him on both cheeks. "I'll see you again soon. I'm sure of it."

"I hope so."

Martin's eyes darted to Mike, who was now standing with his arms folded across the top of his stomach.

Paul laughed. "Don't be scared of Mike. He's just being overprotective."

They said goodbye again and Martin watched Paul and his boyfriend walk out of the lounge. A moment later they were on the street and Paul waved at him through the window as they disappeared into the Memphis night.

Martin had convinced himself that he would never see Paul again when his letter went unanswered all those years ago. He had come to terms with Paul being an unsolved mystery that would reside in his poems. To see him again in the flesh was both exhilarating and unnerving. Paul would forever be the boy with curly blond ringlets of hair standing at the hospital window, brokenhearted and unable to say goodbye.

Martin felt a hand touch his shoulder and was startled out of his reverie. The waiter was standing next to his chair with a worried look on his face. "Are you all right, sir?"

"I'm fine."

"I didn't mean to wake you."

Martin laughed. "Oh, I'm sorry. I wasn't asleep. Just lost

in thought."

The waiter looked at him curiously. "Let me know if you need anything."

Martin was unfocused and hazy; it was akin to how he felt after not being able to sleep on a long flight. His phone vibrated in his pocket; he was certain it would be Christian texting to say goodnight. Instead, he found a three-word message from Diane: *mom is dead*.

# 4 Disgrace

Diane trailed behind her mother in the tampon aisle at Wal-Mart, grabbing a supersized box of maxipads and hiding them behind the jumbo pack of toilet paper in the shopping cart. She was in menopause hell at fifty-two: erratic, heavy flow, mood swings, hot flashes, cramps, the desire to eat everything in her parents' kitchen and her sex drive in park. Diane had made the mistake of trying to have a conversation with her mother about her symptoms, but her mother advised her to just suffer through it like every other woman on Earth and went back to needling her about her separation from Bernard Sullivan.

Sure, she had impulsively married him, but he was a decent man. Not her type, but wasn't having a type a luxury once you moved into your late forties? Now that she was in her fifties and drowning in her own sweat, her options seemed non-existent. She'd spent five years traveling all over Europe with Sullivan while he worked on investigations, but they always returned to Paris to spend time with Martin, Irène and Christian.

So what the fuck was she doing back in Memphis?

Her mother's angina was stable on medication, her father perfectly capable of attending to her nagging ass, but Diane had been there for nearly a month. She had made up her mind to leave after Martin and Julie's reading, although the idea of going back to Paris didn't give her any sense of relief.

"What are you doing back there?" her mother asked. "You're dawdling along like we have all afternoon. And why are you hunched over the buggy like that? You'll get osteoporosis and ruin your posture."

"I'm tired," Diane snapped at her. "We've been up and down every goddamn aisle. Can't you make a list?"

"Don't curse. Unlike you and your friends with money, I don't just grab the first thing off the shelf. I compare prices. The name brands are a rip-off. We're on a fixed income."

Diane resisted the urge to shove the cart at her mother. "You've got plenty of money and Bernard and I have given you..."

Her mother turned back and made a zipping motion across her lips. "I'm not talking about this with you in the middle of Wal-Mart. I'm already embarrassed to be seen with you."

Diane's mother had shoved a nitroglycerin pill under her tongue and clutched at her chest after she read the article about Martin in the newspaper. "You should have never gotten mixed up with that Martin. He's ruined you. Running off to Europe with a nutcase and a bunch of teenagers, disappearing for months at a time, marrying a Catholic. You're killing your father, you know that, don't you?"

"I'm fine," her father had called from the kitchen.

"No, you're not," her mother screeched. "God, why am I surrounded by apostates? What have I done?"

Diane was angry about the article, too, and had already

decided to boycott the reading before her mother's histrionics. She felt like everyone was on Sullivan's side and she was alone, yet as the hour of the reading arrived, she felt incredibly guilty for not being there. But it was too late now and she realized her mother was still kvetching over her soon-to-be ex-husband.

"I just don't know what's wrong with you," her mother said as she scanned the various bottle of antacids and gas relief pills. "I tell you to marry a nice Jewish boy and you wind up with a Catholic. You desert me and your father to go gallivanting all over the planet and get married on a hotel roof instead of a synagogue."

"Oh, you would have preferred that I got married in a Catholic cathedral? Give me a break, Mom."

"All I'm saying is that you've ruined two marriages now and you're not getting any younger."

"Wait. What? I've ruined two marriages? How conveniently you forget that my first husband was gay and fucking one of my underage students. I get the blame for that? And if I remember correctly, you're the one who called the police and had Bernard removed from the house. So, fuck you."

"Don't talk to me like that," her mother said, and pinched Diane hard on the arm.

"Owww... what the fuck."

"If you're going to act like a child, I'm going to treat you like one. Stop embarrassing yourself. I saw Esther and her daughter over on the soap aisle. She's your age and has a nice husband and kids. How am I supposed to explain you?"

"That I'm a degenerate, goyim-marrying atheist, like you always do."

Her mother made a spitting noise and walked down the aisle.

"Look, old woman, the only reason I came back here was because you called screaming that you were having a massive coronary, so here I am."

"You're welcome to leave any time you like," her mother said. "You're just trying to antagonize me and embarrass me in public. I have to live here, you know. I'm the one who everyone talks about having a mishegas for a daughter. Esther's daughter…"

"Esther's daughter is a pretzel-faced harpy."

"Shhhh! She was the victim of an unfortunate roll-over accident."

"That woman was the victim of a back alley plastic surgeon. A disfiguring car crash could only help that face."

"That's enough. You're just being mean."

Diane rolled her eyes. "Right. Okay, we'll just do the rest of the shopping in silence."

Diane's mother walked on, stopping to pick up items and complain about the prices. Diane drummed her fingers on the buggy handle until her mother either put the item in the cart or back on the shelf. Up and down the aisles they went in silence, Diane zoning out and wondering what Sullivan was doing. The big fucking oaf, she thought. And, yet, she had gotten used to him and their nomadic life together. They made a ridiculous looking pair, she knew. He was a tall, stout Irishman and she was a petite, thin-ish Jewess.

She would never have met Sullivan if it weren't for Martin and their trip to Paris so many years ago. Martin and Irène were always babbling on about synchronicity and she had finally come to believe there was some truth in the mumbo-jumbo. If she had never taken over as chaperone for the trip and dragged Martin along, they would probably still be stuck in Memphis. And Martin might be dead. Sullivan had come to Paris looking for David McLaren when he was on the run from his zealot parents and his sexuality. She had no idea where David was or what he was doing, but was glad he had been out of their lives for the past seven years. She'd heard he was living in New Orleans. Maybe he'd been drowned in the flood. Would serve him right, she thought. But David was also the catalyst for Martin meeting Christian and her meeting Sullivan in the first place, so maybe she owed the closet case a debt of gratitude.

"They've got Motrin on sale," she heard her mother call from the next aisle. "We should buy you a case."

Diane pushed the buggy and turned the corner to the next aisle. "I thought we weren't speaking..."

Her mother was laying face down in the aisle with a bottle of Motrin in her hand. Diane paused, certain her mother had slipped and fallen or was playing some kind of prank. Diane stepped toward her and then two other women appeared out of nowhere. It was her mother's friend, Esther, and her plastic surgery obsessed daughter.

"Oh my god, she's had a heart attack or a stroke," Esther shouted. "Diane, what are you doing standing there like a moron? Call 911!"

Esther's daughter had turned her mother over and was listening for a heartbeat. Diane pulled her cell phone from her purse, feeling as if she was moving in slow motion. Other people pushed past her, including a man in a white coat who appeared to be a doctor. She heard someone say her mother wasn't breathing and watched as the man in the white coat applied CPR. He pumped her mother's chest, which made her mother's stomach jiggle and her legs jerk. Diane laughed. Or maybe it was a cry; she wasn't exactly sure.

By the time the paramedics arrived, Diane knew her mother was dead. The white-coated man put his arm around Diane's shoulders and led her and Esther through a door marked Employees Only.

"I think she's in shock, Doctor," Esther said.

"I'm not a doctor," the man said. "I'm the pharmacist."

The pharmacist guided Diane to a chair in the employee break room and brought her a tiny paper cup filled with water.

"She's dead," Diane said.

"Don't say that, Diane! The paramedics will get her to the hospital. Right, Mr. Pharmacist?"

The pharmacist looked at Esther and shook his head. "She had a coronary event."

"A coronary event? What do you know? You're not a doctor," Esther cried.

"It means she dropped dead of a heart attack," Diane said.

"Oh, my god... oh, my god..." Esther muttered. "How could she do that to your poor father?"


The cab pulled up in front of Diane's parents' house and Martin hesitated before he opened the door. He didn't know what kind of mood she'd be in—angry or conciliatory. Before Diane had come to Memphis, they argued about her disintegrating marriage. Sullivan had moved out of their flat on the Left Bank and gone back to London after she refused to get marriage counseling. Diane had been separated from Sullivan for nearly six months and was sad, bored and aimless. When she wasn't restlessly roaming around Paris or haranguing the inhabitants of rue Rampon, she could be found at Café Richard drinking bottles of wine until she was snoring in a booth. Martin and Christian usually wound up putting her to bed in Irène's spare room.

Irène appealed to Euan McEvoy, Martin's ex-boyfriend, to give Diane a part-time job again at the Anglophile bookshop. She said it would only be temporary, until Diane could work things out with Sullivan, but then Diane had rushed off to Memphis after her father had called and said her mother had a heart attack.

Before Martin could ring the bell, Diane opened the screen door. She was wearing a faded, baggy t-shirt and cutoff sweatpants. Martin tentatively stepped forward and awkwardly hugged her until Diane shook him off.

"Let's not get weird about it," she said and went back into the house.

"Irène and Christian are ready to book flights as soon as the arrangements are made," Martin said, following Diane into the kitchen.

"They are made. We're burying her tomorrow morning." Diane reached into the kitchen cupboard and pulled down a bottle of Jack Daniel's. She filled one drinking glass to the rim for herself and another about halfway and handed it to Martin.

"How is that possible? She just died last night."

"It's a Jew thing. Body has to be buried as soon as possible so the mourning period can begin. We're supposed to rip our clothes, not take a bath for a week and all this other shit."

"I don't know if Irène and…"

"We don't need the international contingent. We're not burying a president."

"What about Sullivan?"

Diane drained her glass of whiskey and poured another. "What about him?"

"Did you call him?"

Diane didn't answer and went back into the living room. She sat down on the couch and propped her feet on the coffee table, resting the glass of whiskey on her chest.

"I know you're grief-stricken, or whatever you are, but at least answer me."

Diane sighed loudly. "I left a message. It doesn't matter, anyway. Mom couldn't stand Sullivan and he couldn't stand her. No love lost."

Martin sat down in a chair opposite Diane. "Yeah, but what about some support for you and your dad? Sullivan loves your dad."

"He'll live. We'll all live." She stared out the picture window and refused to make eye contact with Martin.

"You're still pissed at me? Is that why you're acting like this?"

Diane tossed a rolled up newspaper to Martin and it landed on the floor next to him.

"I was planning to come to the reading and make nice until I opened up the paper and saw my life being rehashed on the front page of the arts section. Did it help you sell a few extra books?"

Martin threw the newspaper back at her. "You weren't the only one who got screwed by that article. Do you think I wanted Peter and David dredged up?"

"Maybe you should have thought about that before you put their names in the poems or gave a reading in Memphis."

"I didn't have a choice. The publisher set it up."

"Whatever. Let's change the subject. I've heard you read all your poems anyway and I sure as hell wasn't in the mood for one of Dr. Lacombe's political harangues."

They fell silent staring at each other across the living room. "Well, what can I do?" Martin asked. "Where's your dad?"

Diane looked at her wrist, but there was no watch. "He was going to make final arrangements and now he's probably at the bowling alley knocking back a few cold ones with his buddies."

"How's he taking it?"

Diane shrugged. "How do you take the death of someone you love, but didn't particularly like? I've been trying to reach back to the good times, before mom became a horrible old cliché of the Jewish mother. She's always been a little nuts, you know, sorta like me, but after she hit menopause she kinda went off the rails. Some kind of mood disorder or something she'd never do anything about."

"Are you worried that's happening to you?"

Diane looked at him blankly. Martin went to the couch and pulled Diane into an embrace. She started to resist, but then sank against his shoulder too exhausted to cry.

# 5 the Ghosts of May

Through the open doors of the balcony, Irène could hear the sound of voices on rue Rampon. She had packed her suitcase after Martin called about Diane's mother. It would have been Irène's first transatlantic flight, and she felt guilty about her excitement. Then Martin called and said the funeral would take place before she and Christian could arrive, so not to come. Christian went to work and her suitcase still sat by the door as if departure was imminent.

Irène wandered out onto the balcony and watched the rich tourists coming in and out of the hotel across the street. Irène was devastated when the old owner died and a French conglomerate purchased the Bel Air, remodeled it and renamed it Le Admiral. Gone were the artists, travelers and students who had kept the hotel open since she was a child. There was a beautiful, and sometimes horrible, humanity about the Bel Air. She had witnessed the worst people had to offer in its shabby tourist rooms when they left their curtains open. After the name change, the drapes were always closed and the private world that had sustained her disappeared. The hotel's transformation was like a little death she mourned every day. Its history had been scrubbed clean and along with it, some of her own.

The night after the Bel Air was sold, Irène had used a key given to her by the old owner and she, Martin and Christian went inside and took mementos from the room directly across from her balcony—the curtains, bedspread, ashtray, mirror, lamp, clock, ancient television and whatever else wasn't nailed down. It was the room where she had first seen Jean-Louis and Martin. While Martin and Christian moved the furniture, she had stood looking out the window at her own apartment across the narrow street and wept. Although Martin told her it was a little crazy, she had turned her spare room into a replica of the hotel room. Rue Rampon would not be the same without the Bel Air, but at least a little part of it would always be with her.

To make matters worse, Antoine, who had run the tobacconist next door to the hotel for more than thirty years, retired and closed up shop. Irène had briefly thought about buying the business, but Martin talked her out of it. With the new fitness craze, less people were smoking and there was even talk of banning cigarettes in the restaurants and cafès in Paris. Irène was horrified by the idea. Martin had quit smoking, but she simply couldn't do it. She felt empty without her Gauloises, and the few months she tried to quit to show solidarity with Martin had left her irritable and hungry. Like her loathing of mobile phones, Irène quietly hated the changes that were sweeping the world. Nothing had been the same after the terrorist attacks in America and the rush to war. The bombing of the Underground in London earlier in the summer gave her nightmares for a week, the images on television mingling with the day Martin was caught in the bombing of Saint-Michel station in 1995. And while the European Union had existed for more than a decade, the end of the French franc and adoption of the euro had disturbed her at a base level. It was as if the country was losing its identity before her eyes. Even things at Éditions Resolvere had changed, and she wasn't sure for the better.

Irène was practically running the publishing house after Gerard's stroke two years ago. While the dear old man had recovered, he was weak and tired. Gerard came to the office once or twice week—for the regular meeting of the staff and sometimes to have lunch with Irène. The publishing house would have closed without Frederick Dubois' intervention. It was one of his lasting legacies. Soon, Martin would take over the company. He was ready to expand Éditions Resolvere and branch out into e-books and audiobooks. Gerard was greatly relieved that the company would continue despite being skeptical of the modern technology that was threatening traditional publishing.

Back at her desk, Irène tried to work on a manuscript she was editing, but an email arrived and changed her plans. Euan McEvoy announced he was selling the Anglophile and moving permanently back to London. He wanted Irène to come by the shop for lunch.

After Euan's break-up with Martin, he had sold his apartment on rue Rampon to Irène. If he was unhappy that Martin and Christian had taken up residence there, he never said so. Euan could have easily slipped out of their lives, but Irène would not leave him alone. She put him on the advisory board of Éditions Resolvere and he frequently held book launch parties for the press at the Anglophile. He'd even hosted a reading for Martin's book. Euan's bitterness over Martin's betrayal had slowly subsided and he was even friendly toward Christian, something Irène thought would never be possible. Maybe it was because Euan had a boyfriend in London. Surely that played into his decision to close the Anglophile. Even as she took a cab to the Left Bank, she was mentally running figures in her head and wondering if she could buy the shop and keep it open.

Euan served lunch in his small apartment above the Anglophile. He looked positively professor-ish in his tweed jacket, sweater and dark-framed glasses, Irène thought, but he was still quite handsome in his early forties. He had learned to relax and wasn't nearly the fussbudget he'd been at rue Rampon. Still, she couldn't fathom why she had ever thought he and Martin would be a good match.

Irène picked at her salad. "Euan, why must you sell?"

Euan removed his glasses and pinched the bridge of his nose. "I've thought long and hard about this. I didn't invite you to talk me out of it. I consider you a dear friend, Irène. You've been more generous than anyone I've ever known, but it's time to move on."

"Couldn't you just keep the store and have someone else run it?"

"That's practically what I'm doing now. I'm spending more and more time in London with the shop there, and of course with Henry. We've been together for nearly three years, and we're ready to take the plunge and buy a flat."

"That is wonderful news," Irène said.

"And I'm sure you're aware of how much the book business is starting to change. We're losing business to Amazon since it launched here, just like the shops in America. Less people are reading and now these e-books are coming along. I know Martin thinks it's the next big thing, but surely it must be a fad. Who wants to read a book on a tiny screen?"

"I don't understand it either, but Martin thinks we should start an entire division around e-books at the press. The staff completely agrees with him. Of course, they are all younger and into their electronic machines."

Euan shook his head. "I'm not sure where the book business is headed, but I think I'll be on better footing in England. Not to mention the political climate here in France. This is the last place on Earth I thought would embrace the lunatics of Front National."

"It's very disturbing," Irène agreed. "Christian is concerned about the mood in the banlieue with Arnaud antagonizing the residents with his rhetoric."

"Speaking of Arnaud, there's something I need to tell you. Now don't be alarmed…"

Irène put down her fork. "I hate when people say that. It is always something horrible."

"No, no. Nothing horrible—just curious. A journalist came by the store last evening and said he had found my name in police reports when Arnaud was investigating the break-ins at rue Rampon in 1997."

Irène's mouth went dry. "What did he want to know?"

"He said he was working on a story for *Le Monde* about Arnaud and wanted my impressions of him. I said I thought it was strange that a reporter would be digging for such small potatoes about an incident from seven years ago and that surely Arnaud must have worked hundreds of burglaries and break ins before he became police commissioner."

"And what did the reporter say?"

"He said he was writing an article about Arnaud's hardline stance against immigrants and troubles in the banlieue. It sounded like he was trying to dig up any kind of scandal on Arnaud he could find, maybe to establish a pattern. But then he asked me if you still lived on rue Rampon and if I thought you would be willing to talk on the record."

"What did you say?"

"I said I didn't live at rue Rampon anymore, so I couldn't

be of any help, but it wouldn't surprise me if you received a phone call or visit. His name is Henri Lorit. I'll give you the card he gave me."

"Merci," Irène murmured, lost in thought. The idea of a journalist digging around in Arnaud's past shouldn't worry her, but his connection with Frederick Dubois did.

Euan filled their wine glasses. "How is the tour going in America?"

"What... oh, the book tour. Not as well as they hoped. Mixed reviews, mediocre sales, a few hostile crowds because of Juliette's politics."

"I like Julie," Euan said. "She seems to have a good head on her shoulders. Direct without being so sarcastic."

Irène laughed. "Martin says she's Diane without the hostility."

"Ah, Diane. How is she?"

"Her mother died unexpectedly. Christian and I were going to Memphis, but there wasn't enough time to get there. Martin is staying a few extra days. It's very sad. Diane hasn't had a very easy time."

"Isn't Sullivan going to America?"

"No."

"So it's that bad, is it?" Euan shook his head. "Frankly, I don't know how Sullivan put up with her as long as he did."

Irène pursed her lips. "Don't be unkind, Euan. I feel very badly for them."

"Is he back in Paris?"

"Yes, he's working on a surveillance case. I need to stop by his office and say hello."

Euan went into the kitchen and brought an apple tart to the table. He sliced a piece for Irène and another for himself.

"Have you had any buyers interested in the shop?" Irène asked between bites.

"One. An American broker contacted me on behalf of a

client who wants to set up a business in Paris."

"American? That is nice to hear. Maybe some of the Francophobia is subsiding."

"Unfortunately, general xenophobia is still alive and well."

At the end of their lunch, Euan walked Irène downstairs to the sleek, beautiful shop with its hardwood floors and white bookcases. The floor was busy with customers. Students were returning to classes at the Sorbonne and École des Beaux-Arts nearby, and there were still tourists in the city.

"When will you leave?" Irène asked.

"Soon. The store is in capable hands while I'm away and until a buyer appears."

"We shall hold a dinner party for you at rue Rampon before you go," Irène said and kissed him on both cheeks.

"I'd like that. Call me if this journalist harasses you or if you need anything while Martin is away."

"I will," Irène said. "Salut."

Irène decided to walk for a while before taking a cab back to rue Rampon. She couldn't help but feel anxious about the journalist. Arnaud was a divisive figure and enterprising reporters were surely looking for any scandal to knock him off his pedestal. If the reporter knew what she knew, it could very well topple Arnaud. As she walked along rue Bonaparte, she came to the gates of the École des Beaux-Arts, where her late husband had taught graphic design during the tumult of May 1968. Where he had fallen in love with Frederick Dubois. Students and professors were coming and going, chatting at the bike racks outside the gate. Most of these young people probably had no idea what had happened here thirty-seven years ago. Irène wondered if the ghosts of May would forever haunt her.

As she walked on toward the Seine, Irène turned to look over her shoulder, sensing that someone was following her. She scanned the busy street, but no one stood out or looked conspicuous. She paused on the Pont des Arts, the lattice work of its railings now leaden with padlocks left by couples to signify their love. She searched until she found the one Martin and Christian had placed there, their names etched into the metal, before throwing the key into the Seine. Irène sat down on a bench in the middle of the bridge as the golden afternoon light shimmered off the water. To the west, the top of the Eiffel Tower peeked above the trees, while to the east the towers of Notre-Dame were just visible above the trees on Île de la Cité—the island where Martin almost died, where two lights burned for her parents at the Holocaust memorial, where Jean-Louis' body had been found. And just across the bridge was the Louvre where the Venus de Milo and Winged Victory stood in silent vigil. For a moment, she felt oddly stateless, like a tourist in her own city. As if all of these familiar landmarks and her time there were transitory.

# 6 in the Banlieue

Christian's commute from rue Rampon to Montfermeil took an hour or more each morning: first by train to Gare du Raincy and then by bus to Avenue Paul Cézanne and the youth center near les Bosquets. Every day, there seemed to be more graffiti spray-painted on the walls, more abandoned cars with their windows smashed and tires missing, more aimless, sullen youth in track suits lounging in doorways and congregating on the expanses of broken and dirty sidewalks. Christian had been one of them. Although he had spent years there before escaping, it still tightened his gut to return to the youth center.

From a distance, the hulking apartment buildings of les Bosquets looked abandoned, but as the bus drew near, there were people hanging laundry on balconies, leaning out windows, moving around the scrabbled, trash-strewn grounds. Many windows were boarded up, while others were ringed in scorch marks from kitchen fires and dropped cigarettes. Hundreds, possibly thousands, of immigrants and poor lived in these buildings, including Christian's father. Like his son, Olivier Kigali was a stubborn man. He had scraped together enough money doing odd jobs to open a newsstand on rue de Courtais selling beer, candy and cigarettes to the locals. The newsstand had become a point of pride and survival for Olivier, the only thing he had left after losing his Rwandan homeland, his wife to cancer and his godless, homosexual son. Olivier's anger had subsided over the years, but his religious zealotry had only deepened as he tried to ensure a better life in the afterworld.

When they were still living in Belgium before Christian's mother died, Olivier had managed a market and was a quiet presence in their house. But afterwards, he drank too much and stupidly agreed to invest in a business scheme with Rwandan cousins in France. The business went belly up in a matter of months and they wound up living in les Bosquets. It was a surreal nightmare to wind up there, like moving into a war zone with no defined enemy. Olivier's shame and grief overwhelmed him and his son's burgeoning sexuality only added to the despair.

Christian's father had physically thrown him out of their squalid apartment after he was caught having sex with a boy in an empty flat. Olivier had beaten his son, leaving him with a broken nose and bruised face. Christian had vowed to drum his birth name, Baptiste, out of his head and never return to the banlieue again. And, yet, he returned their every day to work with immigrant kids like himself who desperately wanted to escape les Bosquets. Christian hoped to steer them away from the route he had taken once he had left Montfermeil. The fact that he survived on the streets of Paris for so long selling drugs and sex amazed him. If it hadn't been for Martin, he might be dead.

Like Irène, Christian was sad about Diane's mother's death,

but secretly excited to see Martin in America. Martin would be coming home in a few days, and Christian planned to take the rest of the week off to be with him. The idea of spending the day in bed with Martin aroused him and made him feel giddy, as if it was going to be their first time. He had worried that their attraction to each other might dim, but it had only grown. Christian wanted to marry Martin, spend the rest of his life with him, and the idea of their future made the dreariness of Montfermeil fade for a moment.

Martin wanted Christian to work in the city, argued that there were runaways and kids who needed his help there just as much, if not more, after they had escaped places like Montfermeil. But Christian worried that his new life, where money wasn't an issue and creature comforts easily lulled one into complacency, dulled the survival instincts that he taught himself on the streets. One day those skills might be needed again.

The bus stopped briefly at the corner of rue de Courtais and Christian was the only one to exit. The weather was already turning colder, and he pulled the hoodie over his head. He always made sure to never bring his iPod or anything of real value with him to Montfermeil. The hoodie covered a sweater worn over a nice shirt and tie, made him blend into the neighborhood. He even modified the way he walked into a lackadaisical slouch as he approached his father's newsstand. Christian stopped there every morning to say hello, to buy a drink and candy bar—any excuse to say hello to Olivier.

Olivier's shop was a niche cut into the wall of the building. Newspapers, umbrellas and other goods were underneath a pop-up canopy, while just inside the door were old coolers, mostly filled with sodas and beer, and a few shelves filled with snacks and candy. Inside the enclosure where Olivier sat all day were cigarettes, a few bottles of cheap wine and condoms. Kids from other neighborhoods had robbed Olivier a half-dozen times in the last few years, twice at gunpoint. The denizens of les Bosquets and Montfermeil respected Olivier, especially his willingness to fight back against intruders with a large metal pipe and his solidarity against the police who were harassing the locals.

As Christian approached, he saw his father sitting behind the counter, a cigarette dangling from his bottom lip, staring at nothing in particular. When he sensed his son's approach, Olivier stood up and stubbed the cigarette out in an ashtray. Olivier was tall and thin, although he had developed a belly from all the beer he drank. He was bald, but sported a beard slowly fading to gray. His skin was dark and taut over high cheekbones, much like his son's.

"Bonjour, Papa," Christian said.

"Salut," Olivier said, the ambivalence he felt toward his son palpable even in one short word.

Christian entered the small store, pulled a Coke from the cooler and a Balisto bar from the shelf and approached the counter. He already had the correct change in his hand so his father could toss the euros in the till.

"Ça va?"

Olivier's shoulders lifted almost imperceptibly. "More police last night."

"Was there trouble?"

"There was no trouble except the usual trouble. They were harassing young people leaving the mosque."

Olivier had converted from Catholicism to Islam after losing touch with his religion following his wife's death. He liked the strict doctrines, the formality, the prayer and, although he would never admit it, Islam was good for business in Montfermeil, which was dominated by North Africans and Algerian immigrants who were devout Muslims.

"I am sure I will hear much about that today at the youth center," Christian said.

"And what can you do about it?" Olivier asked. "When the trouble begins, you have returned to your nice home with your tapette friend."

"You know I don't like that word, Papa. It is just as ugly as négro."

Olivier visibly bristled at the slur. "Then do not come back to my shop."

Christian smiled. "I will come back. You are my Papa, after all, and I love you even if you do not love me."

Olivier waved his hand dismissively, not looking at his son. "Go to work. I have things to do."

"I will stop by again on my way home."

"I may close early. There is a meeting tonight I must attend."

"What kind of meeting?"

"Nothing that concerns you," Olivier said testily.

Christian realized he had already pressed his father enough this morning. He said goodbye to Olivier and walked toward the youth center. He turned to look back and saw his father watching him, but Olivier quickly averted his gaze and made himself look busy behind the counter. Perhaps persistence was paying off, Christian thought.

Despite being funded by the local council, le centre social—as the placard by the door read—was a hole in the wall. The year before, they had been forced to ban teenagers over age sixteen after repeated fights, refusal to follow the center's rules and abuse of equipment and staff. Christian thought it defeated the purpose because it was the older teens who were most at risk. They came to the youth center adrift, having dropped out of school, often living in volatile homes and with little hope for employment. Most of the immigrants existed on La Sécu, France's version of social security, which allowed children up to age twenty to stay on the dole. Fraud was rampant in the system and immigration laws made it difficult for those trapped in the banlieue to find stable, permanent work. Marooning the immigrants in Montfermeil and other towns like it, with no easy access to transportation or jobs, was an issue that France's politicians had no answers for, so it was swept under the rug.

The youth center was, essentially, a day care center for those who did have menial jobs. The young ones plopped in front of the TV in the main room while others went back to sleep. Parents or older siblings appeared a few hours later to collect them. After school, there would be an influx of older kids who wandered in to play table football or get a soda from the vending machines. Occasionally, a kid would sit forlornly in front of Christian's co-worker, Marie, at the "job desk" hoping to find something to supplement the family's income. And, every now and then, a kid would just want to talk—and that was Christian's department. In his years there, he had heard stories that under any circumstances would have made him cry, but he had learned to keep his emotions in check as children reeled off stories of parental abuse, bullying at school, unwanted pregnancies, sexual confusion and general despair over their future in Montfermeil.

Marie was a tall Algerian woman in her late thirties who liked to wear colorful headscarves and flowing robe-style dresses. She reminded Christian of Grace Jones. Marie was chatty and friendly under most circumstances until a kid would test her patience. "I am having none of your shit," she would bellow and the center would go quiet. Riling up Marie was never a good idea, and neither was banishment from the youth center. Marie and Christian knew every child who came through the door by name. For just a few hours, there was calm from the chaos that lay just outside on Avenue Paul Cézanne. The kids who came there regularly knew the youth center was an oasis, so most had learned to temper their behavior to have a place of safety.

When Christian arrived that morning, Marie was a study in maroon, her scarf and robe apparently cut from the same cloth. She was seated behind the job desk and the center seemed under-populated for a Tuesday morning.

"Where is everyone?" Christian asked her.

"Trouble brewing," she said quietly and stood up, beckoning him to follow her to the office.

Marie and Christian stood in the hallway where they could keep an eye on the dozen or so kids playing and watching cartoons, but out of earshot.

"Tension very high this morning," Marie said. "Police were harassing people leaving the mosque last night. Arrests were made. That Arnaud was on television this morning heating things up even more. He's coming here next week. There have been meetings among the leaders in Montfermeil."

"My father said there was one tonight, but would not tell me where or what the meeting was about."

Marie lowered her voice even more. "Protest."

"Against Arnaud?"

Marie nodded. "And perhaps rioting and violence to make a statement."

There had been riots in the banlieues before, usually triggered by police brutality—real or perceived—which meant a night of youths running wild, breaking car and shop windows, looting and vandalism. The rioting became less about the police incident and more about raging against their plight and letting off steam. An organized response to Arnaud's visit to the banlieue would be something else entirely.

"The mood reminds me of Algiers," Marie said. "Like civil war."

"That is a step too far, isn't it?"

"How do civil wars begin? They are not spontaneous. They begin with small, secret meetings in secret places."

"What should we do?"

"Remain calm and vigilant. I will go out today and talk to some of my people," Marie said. "Talk to your father."

"Easier said than done. And then what?"

"What can we do? We can warn the kids to avoid the streets. If word gets back to the council that there is trouble, they will close the center. If there is serious trouble, this place will probably be burned to the ground."

"We should call..." his voice trailed off.

Marie finished his sentence. "Call someone? Who do you call? The police? The government? Montfermeil would explode."

Christian knew she was right, but he felt helpless and, perhaps, a little afraid. He flashed on his father injured or in jail. For all the anger and hurt that had passed between them, Christian did not want trouble to come to his father.

Marie put a hand gently on Christian's shoulder. "Fight the urge to do something. Nothing can be done at this moment. Remember, our first charge is to help the children who come to us."

"Will you go to the protest?"

Marie watched the children, but seemed to be looking through them. "I wasn't interested in the protests and politics in my country. And when I had the opportunity, I escaped to come here. After I left, my entire village was massacred. Pregnant women had their stomachs sliced open. Children were hacked to death with machetes. Men had their limbs cut off—sometimes all of them."

"You were lucky to get out when you did."

Marie nodded. "Yes, I should feel that way. But there is also guilt that I am alive and all of my people are dead. And that I said nothing."

She reached into her pocket and pulled out a business card and handed it to Christian. It was for a reporter named Henri

Lorit at *Le Monde*.

"A journalist was here?"

"Yes, waiting outside when I arrived to unlock the doors. He wanted to talk about Arnaud's visit and the mood in Montfermeil. The mood—as if it's a restaurant."

"What did you say?"

"I refused to speak with him, but he said he would be back."

Christian ran his finger over the raised font on the card before putting it in his pocket. Journalists rarely visited Montfermeil unless they believed that trouble was on the horizon.

The youth center was unusually quiet for the rest of the day. When school let out, a dozen or more kids normally arrived shortly thereafter, but only three came in. Marie had gone out during lunch and said there were more police in the area, as if they were expecting something to happen. Christian left early, hoping to catch his father before he closed the newsstand.

As he approached rue de Courtais, Christian saw his father pulling the metal door down over the front of the shop as a black Range Rover approached and came to a stop. Olivier got inside the SUV, which pulled away quickly from the curb. All the windows were blacked out and Christian only caught a few numbers of the license plate before it made a sharp turn and disappeared.

He reached into his coat to pull out his phone, then remembered Marie's words: *Fight the urge to do something.* Christian realized there were other people on the street. Youths in doorways and leaning on balustrades who were also wondering what a fancy car like that was doing in the banlieue. Wondering what Christian's interest might be. Christian flipped up his hoodie and walked toward the bus stop, the slouch returning to his shoulders, the gait of his walk casual. He blended once again to his former surroundings. Just another banlieue kid on the streets waiting for something, anything, to happen.

# 7 Kaddish

Diane struggled to remember the kaddish at her mother's funeral. She and her father, Abraham, sat closest to the grave with the other mourners breathing down their necks. Diane stole a glance back at Martin and his father, who both looked ridiculous wearing yarmulkes. The wind had blown Martin's askew and it hung from the side of his head like a deflated balloon. She almost laughed out loud, but bit down hard on her bottom lip and refocused on the rabbi's words.

Diane and her father threw handfuls of dirt onto the casket as it was lowered into the earth. Abraham looked incredibly old in his black suit, and he stood a little too long at the grave. Diane could see Esther, her hatchet-faced daughter and her mother's busybody friends, giving disapproving glances. When the service ended, the mourners stood in two rows, creating a path away from the grave. Diane and Abraham walked hand in hand back toward Martin's rental car as the mourners intoned *Ha-Makom yenahem etkhem b'tokh sha'ar aveilei Tzion v Yerushalayim*—may the Omnipresent comfort you among all the mourners of Zion and Jerusalem.

Once at home, Diane immediately broke tradition and took a shower. She hadn't even given it a second thought, until Abraham wagged his finger at her.

"Hurry up," he said, going downstairs. "I need a drink before those yentas get here."

Chief yenta Esther and the women of the chevra kadisha had arrived at the house before dawn and moved all the chairs into the guest room, brought in pillows and footstools, covered the mirrors with cloth and rolled the television into the coat closet. "If she thinks I'm missing *Judge Judy* for seven days, she's out of her mind," Abraham had whispered to his daughter as Esther fussed around the house.

Diane tried to explain to Esther that she and her father did not worship and they preferred to have a private mourning period. Esther's face twisted in horror and she could barely contain her rage. "You should be ashamed. You ruined your mother's life with your behavior and now you want to ruin her death? What kind of daughter are you? Your mother was at synagogue every week. She was a faithful wife and devoted to you and your father and you repay her like this? Meshumad!" Esther spit on the floor and stomped out of the house, followed by the other women who clicked their tongues in disgust.

"What did she call me?" Diane called to her father, who was hiding in the kitchen.

"Meshumad—the destroyed one," he said.

As Diane and her father sat at the kitchen table emptying a bottle of whiskey before the mourners arrived, Diane suggested they either lock the door or leave town all together.

Abraham shook his head. "I still have to live here. I'd never hear the end of it. Besides, your mother would want it. She liked all these old customs and having the biddies around to fuss over her. We'll just have to suffer through it." He filled Diane's glass again and they both drank.

"This might not be the right time, but I really want you to think about going back to Europe with me."

"To Paris?"

"Yes. I want you to be near and I might even fix you up with Madame Laureux." Diane winced, wishing she hadn't said it so soon after the service, but her father laughed.

"She might be a little too old for me. I'm looking for a young thing, someone in their sixties."

"I'm serious, Dad. I want you to think about it."

"What does your husband have to say about it?"

Diane slumped back in her chair and crossed her arms over her chest.

"You look like a little girl when you do that," he said. "You always turned up your nose and crossed your arms when you weren't getting your way."

To his credit, Abraham had not pestered her about Sullivan. When she had returned to Memphis, he made some passing comment about a break doing them both some good and left it at that. Her mother had never shut up about it, constantly needling, working herself up into a state and clutching at her chest. Diane knew she would have plenty to regret regarding her mother in the future, but telling her to "drop dead" during one of their heated arguments would surely rank at the top. Especially after her mother had unceremoniously did exactly that at Wal-Mart a few days later.

"Whatever problems you and Bernard have is your business," her father said, taking her hand. "But you are a miserable kalba when he's not around."

"Sullivan seemed to think I was a miserable bitch when he was around. I even called him a hatichat harah once. See, I still remember a little from Hebrew school."

Abraham waved his hand. "The bottom line is that Bernard

loves you and you love him. But you have to stop trying to control everything in the relationship. You don't have to go on every case with him, do you? No. You have to let the man have his career or you emasculate him. Go with him sometimes. Stay at home sometimes. Find something to do to keep you busy that doesn't rely on your friends. Go back to teaching. You're an independent girl; you've always done exactly as you please and it troubles me to see you turning into a nagging old housewife like your mother became. You're going to have to learn to give a little. Compromise. Sometimes a sign of strength is being able to swallow your pride. And maybe—and I'm not saying you need it—but maybe get on some pills."

Diane looked at her father across the table, her mouth hanging open. They'd had serious talks before, but she couldn't remember him ever being so direct. Abraham turned his glass around, sloshing the whiskey, looking a little embarrassed for being so forthright. Irène and Martin had told her, basically, the same thing, but hearing it so concisely from her father made it clear and undeniable.

The doorbell rang, the first mourners arriving for shiva, and her father cleared the glasses and bottle of whisky while Diane straightened her dress. Abraham walked over to his daughter and pulled her into a tight embrace. They let the doorbell ring, made their way slowly to the door, hanging onto each other for support.


After the mourners left for the night, Diane went into her old bedroom and shut the door. She put on headphones and cranked Led Zeppelin until she thought "Gallows Pole" would burst her eardrums. The silence in the house all day had driven her nearly mad. Part of shiva was to quietly reflect on the dead, but Diane's mind had wandered to Sullivan. She left a message on the answering machine at his office near Place Monge, not expecting a return call, but still pissed off that one hadn't come.

They'd had five good years, traveling all over Europe as Sullivan worked cases, but always returning to their little family of friends in Paris. Sullivan said they were like a modern day Nick and Nora Charles, which Diane found ridiculous and, secretly, a strange comfort. Every time he came up with some off-the-wall theory about a simple case he was working, Diane would mock by calling him the "Un-thin Man." Rarely did Sullivan take cases that might put them in any danger, but once or twice there had been some hairy moments that made her second-guess her reasons for being with him. For the first year, the travel and b-grade intrigue was fun and exciting, but then waking up in some cheap hotel near an airport in Antwerp, Berlin, Madrid and Geneva began to wear on her. The terrorist attacks in America made travel more of a hassle and the cases Sullivan took started to drag out. While she assisted Sullivan with research and surveillance, Diane often found herself alone in a hotel or wandering around a strange city. She should have played tourist on the clients' dime, but it reminded her too much of 1995, when she had returned to Paris to force David out of hiding and admit his feelings for Martin—her grand triumph which had almost instantly turned to ruin—and then set off on a journey around Europe in a bid to "discover herself." She had grown stronger, more resilient, but she had run out of money and been forced to move back in with her parents. She was terrified of always winding up back in Memphis, as if the gravitational pull of the place was inescapable.

Diane thought of the night Sullivan proposed to her at Windows on the World. They had wrapped up an embezzlement case in Manhattan and decided to stay few extra days to see a show and visit some landmarks. Sullivan secretly booked a table at the restaurant, and when they were getting ready to go out, he told her to put on something nice. He was wearing a linen suit she had bought him that was actually slimming and made him look dapper.

When the taxi pulled up in front of the World Trade Center towers, he had jumped out and held an umbrella for her as thunder rumbled overhead. She had already begun to guess that this wasn't going to be an ordinary dinner.

Sullivan had booked a window table, and looked disappointed that the low cloud ceiling and rain obscured what was usually the best view of the Manhattan skyline. Diane was unimpressed by tourist traps, but as the rain cleared, the dazzling glow of the city from one hundred stories up left her giddy. Or maybe it was all the wine they were drinking over good steaks and Sullivan's stupid jokes. When the waiter brought dessert, he placed two champagne flutes on the table. At the bottom of hers was an engagement ring.

"You corny fuck," Diane said, picking up the glass and draining the contents until the ring clicked against her teeth.

"Is that a yes?"

Diane dumped the ring into her palm and offered it to him with a smile. "If I must." After he slipped the ring on her finger, Sullivan stood up and pulled her into one of his crushing, bear hugs, lifting her off the ground and swinging her around while couples at the other tables applauded them.

By the time they had woken from their hangovers, the World Trade Center towers were in ruins. They sat on the edge of the bed watching as CNN played the footage of the planes striking the towers over and over again. They were only fifty blocks away, but it seemed like the terrorist attacks were happening somewhere else. Their phones started beeping and chirping with delayed messages and texts from Martin and her mother wanting to know if they were okay.

"I'll never be able to take you back there for our anniversary," Sullivan said mournfully. "Maybe it's a bad omen."

"Do you want the ring back?" Diane asked, pulling it from her finger.

Sullivan looked at her stunned. "Of course not! Don't be foolish, woman. It's just sad to think about that beautiful place and that view no longer existing."

They had married the next spring on the roof of the Bel Air Hotel on rue Rampon, which seemed only fitting, but it wasn't long until she and Sullivan were back on the same treadmill of innocuous hotels and penny-ante cases that bored her to tears. There was resentment on both sides, petty arguments and a big blow-up in Lyon when some photos she took of a husband and his mistress leaving a hotel turned out dark and unusable in court. After the argument, Diane packed her bags, got on a train and went back to Paris. As the TGV streaked through the French countryside, she couldn't help but wonder if Sullivan had been right and their marriage would be just one more casualty of the terrorist attacks that had unraveled the world.

# 8 Unfinished Business

Irène walked with Christian to the metro station at Place de la République, sidestepping debris left over from a demonstration that had been held there the night before. Crude signs denouncing America and its supporters for invading Iraq littered the pavement and still hung from the plinth holding the statue of Marianne, the goddess of liberty. The charred remnant of an Israeli flag was draped over the handrail of the steps that led down to the station. Diane had predicted that anti-Semitism would increase after the invasion of Iraq despite France's rejection of the war, and she was right. In the past year, bombs had been thrown into a Jewish pastry shop in Sarcelles, a Jewish teenager had been beaten by a group of Muslim youths on his way home from school and headstones had been smashed in Jewish cemeteries.

"This sickens me," Irène said, carefully folding up the remains of the flag and placing it on the steps.

"If you heard what the kids said at the youth center, you would be horrified," Christian said.

"I hope you call them out for it."

"I do... for all the good it does," Christian said, giving her a peck on the cheek before rushing off to catch his train to Montfermeil.

There was a chill in the air, the first hint of autumn. Irène buttoned her sweater and readjusted the shoulder bag holding the manuscript that still needed an edit. She walked down Avenue de la République toward Café Richard, her favorite place to work when she wanted to get out of the apartment. The café was her haven, and had been since it opened and Jean-Louis took her there. The old proprietor, Claude, would shoo away anyone who might be sitting in the back booth to make room for her to drink coffee, smoke her cigarettes and work. If she were still there at noon, he would bring her a sandwich and a glass of wine without even asking.

As she walked, Irène noticed that a man on the opposite side of the street was keeping pace with her. He was average height, late thirties or early forties with thinning blond hair, wearing a blazer and jeans with what appeared to be a camera bag slung over his shoulder. He could be a tourist, Irène thought and decided to test him. She paused at a jewelry store to window shop, lingering to admire the display of watches and rings. In the window's reflection, Irène could see the man also pause, but he kept walking toward the corner of rue de Malte before dashing through the crosswalk to reach her side of the avenue.

Irène turned from the window as the man approached and confronted him. "May I help you, monsieur?"

The man blushed a deep red and looked at the pavement. "My apologies, madame. I hope I did not alarm you. I was just hoping to take a moment of your time. My name is Henri Lorit."

"Ah, oui, the journalist."

The man seemed taken aback. "I did not realize my byline was so well-known."

"It's not, Monsieur Lorit," Irène said, and reached into her pocket for her packet of Gauloises. "I understand you have been asking questions of my friends about ancient history on rue Rampon."

Henri fumbled for a cigarette lighter in his blazer pocket, but she was already blowing a plume of smoke toward him.

"I am working on a story for *Le Monde* about Michel Arnaud. I am trying to get impressions from those who dealt with him while he was a police inspector. Your name came up in several files I requested through the documents administratif office."

Irène summoned a thin smile. "Monsieur Lorit, I do not know how I can help you. Inspector Arnaud investigated a burglary in my apartment and another at the tobacconist across the street that I happened to witness. My interactions with Arnaud were brief. My impression of him was that he was a policeman handling a routine case. Now, if you will pardon me, I really must go. I have work to do."

Irène walked toward Café Richard, but the journalist trailed behind her. "I am sorry to trouble you, but I just found it curious that someone at Arnaud's level in the police would be handling what you call a routine series of petty burglaries."

"Perhaps you should ask Arnaud."

Lorit caught up with Irène and walked alongside her. "Please, Madame Laureux, just one more question: How did you know André Sarde?"

Irène fought to hold her composure, not give anything away with a shift in her countenance. "André Sarde? The gangster? Oh, Monsieur Lorit, you truly have me confused with someone else."

She walked into Café Richard, breathing heavily and feeling as if one of her panic attacks might be setting in. She plopped down in her usual booth, but saw Lorit was standing silhouetted in the doorway. A waiter rushed up to her table and she ordered her usual coffee. Irène busied herself pulling the manuscript from her bag, but she sensed Lorit standing near the booth. She looked up at him and slammed her pen down on the table.

"Really, monsieur, this is harassment. I cannot imagine the newspaper would approve of these tactics. I cannot help you, so please leave me alone."

Lorit reached into his bag and pulled out a piece of paper and placed it on the table in front of Irène. It was a bad photocopy, but appeared to be a log of names on lined paper. She pulled her glasses from her bag and put them on. Highlighted on the page about halfway down were two names: Irène Laureux and Martin Paige.

"Arnaud did an excellent job scrubbing and redacting information from his files, but he did not know about this. It's a log of visitors kept by one of the officers guarding André Sarde's room at Salpêtrière Hospital in 1998. Arnaud confiscated the official log, but the officer felt something was amiss so he secretly wrote down all the names. He said there were all sorts of people in and out of Sarde's room before he died that surely had no business being there. Including you and your friend, Martin Paige."

Irène felt a drop of sweat roll down her neck. She was trying not to have "one of her moments," as Martin called them, which would eventually mean passing out. "I have nothing else to say to you, Monsieur Lorit," she said. "Again, I ask you to please leave me alone."

Instead, Lorit sat down in the booth and leaned conspiratorially across the table. "I know you are afraid. Arnaud is a powerful man with many connections, but you know as well as I do that the truth about Sarde has never been explained. There was collusion between Sarde and the police to cover up something much larger, more involved. Now that Arnaud is the prefect, the truth must come out. Arnaud has used the arrest and breaking up of Sarde's operation as the triumph of his career and his dedication to ending organized crime in France. But we all know Sarde is a myth. Who was he really, Madame Laureux?"

"I have nothing to say to you," Irène said, lighting another cigarette with trembling hands. She was giving herself away.

"The story will be published," Lorit said, an aggravated tone in his voice. "I will use the list of names, including yours, and more journalists will call on you and investigate your friends and the publishing house."

Irène pulled the lit cigarette from her mouth and tossed it into Lorit's lap. "Don't threaten me, Monsieur Lorit, or you will find out who my friends really are," Irène hissed as he scrambled to brush away the cigarette.

Claude approached the booth and tried to sound authoritative. "Madame Irène, is this man troubling you?"

"He was just leaving," Irène said. "Weren't you, monsieur?"

Lorit stood up and glared at Irène. He started to speak, then turned and stalked out of the café.

"Are you all right, Madame Irène?" Claude asked, putting a hand on her shoulder.

Irène used a napkin to blot her face and forehead. "I know it is still early, Claude, but I think I could use a glass of wine now."

Claude went to the bar to fetch her drink, and Irène pulled her mobile phone from her bag. She scrolled through the contact list until she found the number she was looking for: Bernard Sullivan.

Sullivan had taken over the office that once belonged to V. Hugo, the detective that had helped Irène track down

Frederick Dubois. After Dubois had died and things had settled at rue Rampon, V. Hugo had returned to the humdrum investigations—divorce cases and loan dodgers. After the adventure looking for Dubois, he told Irène that everything else seemed pedestrian and unworthy of his time. So he had retired and written a mystery novel with a detective who was nearly indistinguishable from its author. Éditions Resolvere had published V. Hugo's first book—which even he admitted was a flop—in the 1970s and Irène felt she owed V. Hugo another chance. With good editing and marketing, his second book had sold modestly well in France and a few other territories. V. Hugo was currently writing a third book and occasionally helped the publishing house with research and copyright issues. He'd happily turned over his list of sad sack clients to Sullivan, along with the key to the office.

The tiny office was just around the corner from Place Monge metro station, and Sullivan and Diane had rented a flat near there while they were still together. Sullivan had spent more time out of Paris since the breakup, taking more lucrative cases in England and Ireland. Sullivan was also the liaison between Irène and Geoff de Courcy, who now ran the syndicate Frederick Dubois created as André Sarde. While Arnaud claimed to have busted the syndicate, de Courcy had intimated that the syndicate still held vast amounts of money and power, although the "business" had been streamlined and become less conspicuous in Paris. Irène preferred not to know what that meant, since under Frederick it had meant espionage and drugs, but she assumed it was more of the same. Irène had only seen de Courcy twice in the past eight years, and even then it was just about finances concerning the publishing house.

As Irène climbed the stairs to Sullivan's office, she considered asking him to contact de Courcy about the sudden appearance of Henri Lorit, but wondered what would happen if she did. Frederick had made it no secret that he had the power to make people disappear. Would the journalist suffer the same fate at de Courcy's hands? Irène understood Lorit's desire to expose Arnaud, but where that exposure might lead frightened her. She was tacitly complicit in Frederick's underworld, but she also understood its beginnings and purpose. Frederick's desire to avenge Jean-Louis's death in 1968 had driven him until the end of his life, and while his methods were abhorrent, she was at a loss on how to extricate herself from it. Or if she even wanted to. Insulating Jean-Louis' memory, protecting her little family on rue Rampon outweighed any moral objections she might have.

Sullivan seemed happy to see her and pulled her into one of his bear hugs. She always forgot how tall and wide Sullivan was until he was crushing her against his chest. He pulled a handkerchief from his pocket and made a show of dusting off a chair for her.

"What brings you all the way over here, Madame Irène?" Sullivan asked, settling behind his desk, the wooden chair squeaking and cracking under his weight. "You know I would have been happy to come to rue Rampon. I don't have very much on my plate." He gestured at his empty desk and spread his arms wide.

"Have you spoken to Diane?"

Sullivan mopped at his brow with the handkerchief and stuffed it back in his pocket. "She left a message on the machine. It didn't seem to require a return call. Obviously, she didn't want us there. Especially me. Is that why you came here?"

"Of course not. I wanted to see you, Bernard. It's been ages. You know I'm very fond of you, and I do hope you will work things out with Diane. I think you are good for her."

Sullivan laughed. "She would beg to differ."

"The reason I've come is that I have a job for you," Irène said.

"I take it this is a job outside of the business of the

publishing house."

"Yes. I need information on a journalist named Henri Lorit."

"Have you tried Googling him? Private investigation has lost some of its thrill now that any sod can access the Internet."

"Of course, I did. There was just a very brief bio at *Le Monde* and bylines in some magazines. I need... well... everything. His entire history."

Sullivan leaned forward in his chair. "Is the bastard bothering you?"

"I cannot say at the moment. I just need you to do this for me quickly and quietly and without asking why. It may be nothing."

"I'm on it. Give me a day or two."

"You are a dear. When Martin returns from America, you must come to dinner."

"I never turn down a free meal."

As she was pulling on her sweater and preparing to leave, she casually asked if Geoff de Courcy had been in contact.

"I can't even remember the last time we spoke. Do you need to reach him?"

"No. I was just curious."

Sullivan studied Irène, who stood smiling innocently at the door. "You will tell me if something is wrong, won't you?"

"Of course. And remember, quickly and quietly," she said and put a finger to her lips as she left Sullivan's office.

# 9 Departures and Arrivals

Martin's flight to Paris was uneventful. There had been no delays in Memphis or New York, except the new hassle of post-September 11 security: removing laptops, taking off shoes and belts, being randomly felt up by surly TSA agents. Prior to 2001, you could show up thirty minutes before a flight, breeze through the metal detectors and have your loved ones see you off at the gate. Now, it involved arriving hours ahead of time, standing in line and far too many questions at customs. Every time he left France, he wondered if his carte de séjour would be revoked. Martin's residence permit had been arranged by Frederick Dubois before his death, and he had lived in France long enough to become a naturalized citizen, but he had yet to formally renounce America. Julie was right—he no longer thought of the United States as home. It seemed like a foreign country.

Diane had driven him to the Memphis Airport and was noncommittal about when she would return to Paris. She had broken another of the shiva commandments by leaving the house and was spoiling for a fight with her mother's old cronies.

"Promise me you'll come home in a few weeks," Martin said at the curbside as he pulled his baggage from the trunk. "You've got to patch things up with Sullivan."

"Yeah, yeah, yeah. I've already had this conversation with Dad. We've got some things to figure out. I'll email you."

A security guard approached Diane's car and told her to move along as she hugged Martin goodbye. "Give me a fucking break. Do we look like terrorists? Goddamn it." She got back in her car, revved the engine a few times and then peeled away from the curb.

The security guard looked at Martin suspiciously. "Her mother just passed away," he said. "She's very upset."

Martin tried to settle in and watch a movie on the plane, but the selections were uninteresting. He read half of Joan Didion's memoir, *The Year of Magical Thinking*, but it made him think of Irène's advancing age. Even the music channels were playing nothing to make him zone out. He stared out the window at the layer of broken clouds over the Atlantic until he began to doze. The dream came almost immediately.


*Martin walks down a long, ornate hallway. The ceiling is impossibly high and the walls are covered in art he does not recognize. At the end of the corridor is a set of tall double doors, which swing open as he approaches. Beyond the doors is a grand salon, flooded with light that shimmers and prisms from chandeliers. Martin shields his eyes against the brightness, but he can see there is a figure standing in the middle of the salon. As he reaches the threshold, the figure comes into focus: the Venus de Milo, incongruous in her surroundings outside the Louvre. Beyond the statue, there is another figure—someone crumpled on the floor. He runs toward the person, his body heavy and his feet weighted down. The body lies in a pool of blood. Martin kneels and turns the body over. It is Peter. The blood begins to move backwards, seep back into the healing wounds, until Peter sits up with a gasp. He touches Martin's face, tenderly, leans in for a kiss.*

Martin woke with a start to find a flight attendant standing next to his seat.

"Having a little nightmare?" she asked in clipped British accent. "Would you like beef or chicken?"

"Uh, no… nothing for me."

The flight attendant moved on and Martin tried to make sense of the dream. His nightmares about Peter Davis had ended long ago, so it made Martin feel anxious that his dead lover had made an unexpected appearance. He tried to chalk it up to being back in Memphis, reading the poems about Peter and running into Paul. After his vision of Irène in the mirror before the reading, the feeling that something was about to happen was strong. He leaned forward in the seat, as if doing so might make the plane fly faster toward Paris.

Christian was waiting behind a rope barrier in the arrivals hall at Charles de Gaulle Airport holding a small white card with Martin's name on it. Martin fought the urge to push his way down the escalator. The desire to run into Christian's arms made him tingle. It never failed to amaze Martin how beautiful Christian was, especially after they had spent time apart. His smile was dazzling and the tight sweater and trousers he wore showed off his slim body to perfection. As he approached the crowd of limo drivers and those waiting for their friends and loved ones, Martin dropped his bags on the floor and Christian picked Martin up and lifted him over the barrier into his arms, oblivious to the stares of onlookers and security.

In the parking garage, Christian pulled Martin under the stairs and pushed him against the wall, their mouths finding each other's in the cool darkness. "I want you right here," Christian whispered in his ear. Martin unbuttoned Christian's trousers and worked his hand inside, finding his lover's cock hard and wet with pre-come.

There were voices and footsteps above them and approaching from the terminal. As Martin's eyes adjusted, it wasn't quite as dark as it had seemed. An older couple passed by and openly stared as Christian and Martin made love against the wall. Martin's cheek rested against the concrete as Christian entered him roughly, the initial jolt of pain becoming pleasure.

"We're going to get caught," Christian said as he kissed the back of Martin's neck.

"Good," Martin panted.

As Christian neared climax, he slipped his hand into Martin's jeans and jerked him off, the tugs matching the rhythm of his thrusts. Martin moaned and he felt Christian's hand slip over his mouth as he brought them both to orgasm. Martin thought his knees might buckle as Christian collapsed against his back, gasping for breath.

They hurriedly fastened their trousers and arranged clothing, giggling like teenagers. Christian grabbed Martin's bags with one hand and put his other arm around Martin's waist and pulled him close as they walked toward Irène's red Mercedes convertible. Martin and Christian drove the classic car more than Irène did now, as she was afraid she would have an accident in the increasingly hectic Paris traffic. Christian babied the car as if it were his own, keeping it gleaming and pristine, looking just like it did the first day Jean-Louis had presented it to Irène back in the sixties.

Inside the car, Christian and Martin continued to kiss and grope each other. "I want to do it again," Christian said.

"I'm glad that my ass has put you in better spirits," Martin teased.

Christian held Martin's face in hands and kissed him softly. "I'm more in love with you than I ever thought possible."

Back at rue Rampon, they made love for hours until Christian fulfilled his promise of making Martin sore all over. They settled into a hot bath together. Irène was preparing a midnight dinner for them across the hall and Martin was eager to put his arms around her, to reconnect, to see if their proximity shed any light on the dream he'd had on the plane.

Martin rested his head against Christian's chest as they soaked in the bath, the bubbles starting to break up and their skin to wrinkle. Christian's slender, strong brown hands massaged Martin's shoulders, relaxing him even more.

"How are things at the center?" Martin asked.

"I would like to say good, but nothing changes."

"And your father?" Martin could feel Christian's body tense.

"You know… my father is my father. Some days when I see him we get along, some days we do not."

"Did you have another fight?"

Christian hesitated. "You may not have seen it on the news or read about it while you were in Memphis, but there has been trouble in Montfermeil. More police agitation, threats of rioting. Olivier is going to community meetings and getting mixed up in it."

Martin had met Olivier once five years ago in a greasy little restaurant near Gare du Nord. Christian did most of the talking, a cheery stream of chatter about anything and everything, while Olivier stared at Martin with a mixture of contempt and, perhaps, horror. After half an hour, Olivier had stood up, said goodbye and walked out of the restaurant. He never said a word to Martin.

"I'm sorry. I know you hate fighting with him. I wish there was something I could say or do to make it better."

Christian kissed Martin's forehead. "All I want is for you to be here."

"I'm here, and I think it's time to make it permanent."

"Becoming a citizen?"

Martin nodded. "And maybe we should talk more about that other thing, too. We've had a very long engagement."

Christian put his arms around Martin and held him tightly. "You make me happy."

Martin remembered their first few years together as Christian struggled to fit into his new life. Christian found that he missed the clubs, the energy of the streets, the thrill of breaking into other people's houses. He was determined to give it up because all he wanted was Martin, but he was often restless and unfocused—unsure of what to do with his life. It was Martin who had suggested they enroll in school together, and Christian found that he liked the formality of the schedule, knowing he had somewhere to be and someone to come home to. He had to finish lycée, the equivalent of high school in France, to obtain his diploma, which was both frustrating and embarrassing, but Martin had stood by him. When it was time for university, Christian decided to focus on counseling and, to be closer to Martin, he minored in English. He read more books in four years than he had in his entire life. Christian felt like he was at last on equal footing with his partner, and that gave him a sense of peace. When Martin second-guessed using real names and scenarios from his past in the poems of *What Remains*, Christian had encouraged him.

"Your poems are why I fell in love with you," Christian said. "Don't change a word."

Of course, their relationship wasn't perfect. They fought about little things that long-term couples usually argue about. They said things they didn't mean. Once or twice, one of them had slept on the sofa, but breaking up never entered their vocabulary. Nothing was unfixable, Martin said, as long as love remained.


Irène cooked pasta, Martin's favorite, and the smell wafted into the hallway making his mouth water. She flung open the door at first knock and pulled Martin into her arms. She pushed him away, holding him at arm's length to look him up and down, then pulled him close again. They took each other's hands, thumbs finding their shared tattoos and momentarily caressing them. It was their private check in, as if the power of their shared telepathy emanated from the little crosses.

"I am so happy you're back," Irène said, kissing both of his cheeks.

"Me, too. I want to be a homebody for awhile."

"Have a seat and I'll bring in dinner," she said, heading toward the kitchen. "I can't wait to hear everything. You look well."

Christian leaned down and whispered in Martin's ear. "Well fucked."

Martin grinned. "Mmmm-hmmm."

Martin kissed Christian quickly on the lips as he heard Irène heading back into the living room. "To be continued."

Martin and Christian ate ravenously, which delighted Irène. Over a second bottle of wine, Martin hit the highlights and lowlights of his tour with Julie, the debacle of the Memphis reading with the homophobic, racist redneck threatening them, the funeral for Diane's mother and the odd appearance of Paul at the hotel. As he told the story, Martin saw the change in Christian's body language, the way he flared his nostrils and wouldn't make eye contact. Jealousy. It had been rare that Christian ever displayed that side of his nature when it came to Martin, because it was usually Christian who was being flirted with or ogled in the street. When Martin's book had come out and the moody black and white publicity photos appeared in newspapers and magazines, boys and men flocked to his readings and all eyes were on Martin instead of Christian. It had been a subtle balancing of power in their relationship. They had both acknowledged it, but Christian didn't like to talk about it. Martin knew that when they had sex again later, it would be more intense, and he secretly liked it.

They talked until nearly three in the morning before Martin suggested it was time to turn in. Jet lag was catching up with him and he was feeling slightly tipsy from the wine. He and Christian planned to sleep late and watch movies all day.

As they were leaving, Christian pulled the keys for the Mercedes from his pocket and put them on a little hook by the door. Irène was cleaning off the coffee table when she noticed Pierre pawing at a piece of paper on the floor.

"What is that, Pierre?" Irène asked, carefully picking up the cat and nuzzling his neck before putting him on the sofa. She bent back down and picked up what appeared to be a business card. It must have fallen out of Christian's pocket when he hung up the keys. Irène put the card on the pedestal by the door, the one that held the statue of Venus, and was about to turn out the lights, but the name on the card caught her eye: Henri Lorit.

# 10 Gutter Ball

After the mourners had left for the night, Diane and Abraham snuck away from the house and drove to the Belle Isle Lanes bowling alley. It was her father's favorite place to hang out and have a beer, and they served kosher hot dogs.

Earlier, Diane had been banished from the living room by Esther and her gaggle of yentas and was sitting shiva in the kitchen. She quietly drank herself into a stupor while her father's bathroom breaks grew longer and longer.

"The Jew bastard who came up with shiva didn't have to sit with Esther," Diane said as her father drove them. He was avoiding the usual roads in case someone recognized the car. They came to an empty four way stop, but Abraham hesitated, looking in both directions.

"What is it?" Diane asked.

Her father seemed to snap out of a daze. "Oh, sorry. I just don't usually go this way and for a minute, I was lost."

Thankfully, the bowling alley wasn't busy, with just a group of teens goofing off at one of the lanes, making fun of each other's missed strikes. Diane and her father sat at the bar and the owner, Bubba, came to take their order. He was a squat, fat man wearing a stained apron and sporting one of the thickest southern accents she'd ever heard. Maybe she'd lived in Europe too long, but she could barely understand a word he said. Abraham didn't seem to have that problem, and the two fell into conversation about one of their buddies being in the hospital for a gall bladder operation as Bubba pulled beers from the tap.

Diane hadn't been inside the bowling alley in more than a decade, but it looked and smelled the same—smoky, greasy and like a million feet. A young woman working the shoe rental counter was chewing gum and reading *National Enquirer*, obviously bored. There was something familiar about her. The woman sensed that Diane was staring at her and looked up from the magazine. Diane turned back around to the bar just as Bubba was bringing the hot dogs and relish tray.

"Sorry to hear about your mama," Bubba said to Diane. "A real shame. My mama died of a heart attack, too. It's a mercy when they happen real fast like that."

Diane had just taken a bite of her hot dog and could only nod at Bubba's attempt at sympathy. She felt relish run down her chin and hit her t-shirt. Without looking, her father handed over a stack of napkins. As she dabbed at the stain, someone sat down on the barstool next to her. There's a whole goddamn empty bar and they have to sit next to me, Diane thought. She glanced out of the corner of her eye and saw that it was the woman from behind the shoe rental counter.

"Oh, my god. You're Ms. Jacobs, aren't you?"

"I plead the fifth," Diane said, avoiding direct eye contact.

"You are her. I thought it was you. I'm Beth Gilroy. I was on the trip to London and Paris, remember?"

Freak girl Beth. She'd been in a heavy goth phase then, with too much white makeup, heavy eyeliner, piercings and an illegally-gotten tattoo in London that became a bloody, infected mess. In Paris, she had disappeared one night on the Champs-Élysées and went into an expensive jewelry store and asked them to pierce her clit. After the terrorist bombing, her parents had unsuccessfully sued the Shelby County School System and threatened a civil suit against Diane, as if the bombing had been her fault and their daughter wasn't a disciplinary nightmare.

"How could I forget?" Diane deadpanned.

"God, it's been—what—ten years ago?" Beth said. "Are you still teaching?"

Diane laughed. "Yeah. I'm educator of the year."

"Oh, right. I forgot all that shit that happened when we got back. Well, anyway, it's weird to see you here. I'm just working nights right now. My husband works construction during the day and I stay home and watch the kids, but we needed the extra cash, so…"

Diane turned to properly look at Beth. She was now in her late twenties, a little overweight, hair dyed black. Her face was pockmarked, which was maybe why she had worn all the goth queen makeup. The piercings were all gone except for a tiny stud in her nose. Diane suddenly felt old.

"I don't live in Memphis anymore. I'm just visiting."

"Oh, hey, you are never going to believe who was in here the other night. David McLaren."

At the mention of David's name, Diane felt a shiver pass over her. He was the last person she wanted to run into.

"He's up here staying with his folks after Katrina. He said the bar he was managing got flooded or whatever. And get this—he said he was engaged. I asked what the guy's name was and he got all defensive and said it was a girl. He's so fucking gay. Not that there's anything wrong with that."

Diane was dumbfounded. "Wait, did you say he was marrying a girl?"

"See!" Beth exclaimed. "He's gay. He was totally fucking that friend of yours who was on the trip with us. Martin, right?"

"Uh, yeah…"

"See, that's what I told everybody. I remember there was that rumor going around that you and David were having some kinda Mary Kay Letourneau affair, and I was like, no he's not—he's totally gay."

Diane realized that her father and Bubba had both been listening to the entire conversation. She wanted the floor to open up and swallow her.

"Beth, get back to work and let these people eat," Bubba said, flicking his dishrag at her. "You got shoes to clean."

"Right. Well, it was cool to see you, Ms. Jacobs. Maybe I'll see you at the twenty year reunion." Beth laughed at her own joke. "Oh, and tell Martin that David is on MySpace. There are all kinds of pictures of him and this chick he says he's marrying. She must be a total dumbass if she can't tell her husband is a rope smoker."

Diane watched Beth go, bewildered by the encounter, and then turned and looked at her father. He popped the last bite of hot dog into his mouth, picked up his beer glass and clinked it against Diane's.

"You're right," Abraham said. "Maybe we do need to get out of Memphis."


After her father went to bed, Diane went into the spare bedroom where her parents kept the computer she had bought them. Save for emails and her dad looking up news or sports scores, they had rarely used it. Abraham had learned some computer basics before he retired from an accounting firm and frequently emailed her, but her mother continued to nag by phone. I won't have to worry about that anymore, Diane thought, and felt a momentary pang of guilt.

Diane found MySpace and made up a fake account. After twenty minutes of trying to figure out how to navigate the clunky site, she finally found David McLaren's page. His profile picture showed him shirtless in a swimming pool, wearing sunglasses and a backwards baseball cap. He was raising a beer can in salute at whoever was taking the picture.

"Still a drunk douche," she said aloud.

David was still thin and had a decent looking body, but something about his face had changed. He had lost that pretty boy appeal and, despite being only twenty-eight, he looked older. In many of the photos he was over-tanned and it looked like he was bleaching his hair, which she noticed was starting to recede at the temples.

She clicked through the pictures in his photo album: scenes of Mardi Gras in New Orleans, dark, grainy ones of him working behind a bar and others of him mugging for the camera with drunk revelers. There were a dozen or more photos of him with a girl who was tagged with the name Miranda. In one, they were outside the Super Dome before a Saints game. He was wearing one of those hats with beer holders and straws attached and she was wearing tight cut-off shorts and a football jersey. She was vaguely pretty with short, curly dark hair. In another, the girl was sitting on David's lap next to a Christmas tree. There was one that appeared to be at some formal occasion where he wore an ill-fitting suit and she was wearing an ugly dress, and David had his arm around her waist. And in another, they were in a hammock together, cuddled up like lovers. Maybe it was her own bias, but Diane thought all the photos had a staged quality about them. As if David was trying to prove something to himself and others.

Diane had predicted this kind of future for David long

ago, but more along the lines of him marrying some clueless sorority girl and knocking her up with a few kids all the while sucking cock in the public parks or the back rooms of gay bars when he was supposedly out with buddies. David's rightwing, religious parents would be thrilled he was marrying anyone with a vagina and could continue to live in denial.

The last picture was the one Martin took of David standing in front of the Eiffel Tower. Diane was there when Martin took the photo. He's grinning at the camera, arms crossed over his chest, wearing tight jeans and the top of the tower is shrouded in mist and clouds. It was David's one nod to the past, to his true self, when he was young, beautiful and his life was before him.

# 11 the Origin of Fire

Irène liked to occasionally take the metro, despite her history of agoraphobia and panic attacks. She considered the subway trains the ultimate test— being jammed into a hot, enclosed space, possibly tucked under someone's armpit, and forced to endure it. Martin told her she had proven her point and why risk an episode, but she insisted, and so they rode from Republic Square toward the Left Bank and a meeting at the publishing house.

Irène sat hemmed in a corner next to Martin and tried to focus on the newspaper. She was reading an article about the government discussing a smoking ban in cafés and restaurants. The more she read, the angrier she became. She elbowed Martin and shoved the paper in his face.

"Did you hear about this?" she demanded. "They want to ban smoking in the cafés now."

"Yes, it's been on the news."

Irène wadded the paper up and threw it on the floor. "What is happening to this country? What about our liberties?"

"Smoking isn't sexy anymore."

Irène cut her eyes at him. "I liked you better when you were addicted to nicotine."

"I wouldn't worry about it. Café culture would collapse if they banned smoking. It won't happen."

It was a sunny afternoon and the 6th arrondissement was lively with students and tourists. The Éditions Resolvere office was on rue des Canettes, a narrow street lined with restaurants and shops, near Saint-Sulpice church. The publishing house occupied two of the floors above a Greek restaurant and Irène had been negotiating to take over the third so that the staff would no longer have to double up in offices. Gerard had maintained a meticulous library on the second floor with copies of every book Éditions Resolvere had published over the last fifty years and a sizeable collection of newspaper and magazine clippings about the press that two staffers were working to digitize and free up space.

Although Gerard hadn't kept regular office hours in years, he still popped in at least once a week to check on things. Irène couldn't help but notice the look of anxiety that passed over Gerard's face when he would see the changes being implemented by Martin and the younger staff members. When they ordered new office furniture, ripped up the carpet and refinished the hardwood floors, and given the office a new coat of paint, Gerard had cried. He was adamant that the archive of reviews be preserved, and offered to pay for a storage locker himself after the digitization was complete. And while he recognized the changing trends of readers, he told Irène over one of their lunches that Martin's plan to start an e-book division kept him up at night.

Irène insisted Gerard be allowed to sit in on staff meetings despite his penchant for telling rambling stories of the publishing house's past.

"He means well," Irène said, "and, after all, it's still Gerard's house until he decides to give it up."

"From his cold dead hands," Martin muttered.

He loved the old man, but Gerard was completely out of the loop on modern publishing and the stroke had left him emotional when it came to business matters and the need to change with the times. Martin had suggested clearing out Gerard's office to make more room, and it was one of the few times he had quarreled with Irène.

"Are you trying to finish him off?" Irène asked angrily. "Imagine showing up to the business you built for fifty years and finding your office gone? No, I won't allow it."

Martin and Irène shared a big office at Éditions Resolvere, their desks pushed together in the center of the room just like they were at rue Rampon. They could easily pass manuscripts back and forth, although Martin had begun editing more work on the computer. And also like at the apartment, her desk had piles of books and manuscripts, while Martin's was neat and tidy.

As they settled into the office to check emails and read correspondence before the weekly meeting, Gerard shambled in, leaning heavily on a cane. The stroke had aged him considerably and he had taken to wearing large cardigans and vests because he was always cold. He seemed much smaller than the robust, jovial man Martin had met a decade before.

"Madame Irène," he said gravely. "Is the spring catalogue not ready?"

"We're finalizing it today," she said. "That's the topic of the meeting."

Gerard looked unhappy. "It's almost October."

"The titles and cover art are all on the website..." Martin offered.

Gerard tapped his cane so hard on the floor that it made both Irène and Martin flinch. "Booksellers expect a catalogue and it is going to be late. Not everyone uses a computer. Éditions Resolvere is known for its catalogue!" He was on the verge of having a breakdown.

Irène stood up and looped her arm through Gerard's. "I am starving, Gerard. Take me to lunch. I have some very exciting manuscripts to discuss with you."

"But the catalogue…"

"The catalogue will be complete and ready to send to the printer today," Martin said. "You have my word."

Gerard looked from Irène to Martin uncertainly for a moment. "I could do with a bite."

As Irène led Gerard out of the office, she winked at Martin.

*Thank you*, Martin mouthed to her, relieved that Gerard wouldn't be there to disrupt the meeting.

He had just turned on his computer when there was the sound of a distant explosion. The concussion made the building shake. Martin flashed on the bombing of the RER station at Notre-Dame, of David almost losing his life, of all the bombs that had gone off around the world since then. Irène appeared in the doorway, her face ashen, unable to speak. Many of the staff had already rushed out of the office to see what had happened and Martin and Irène followed them. Gerard was sitting in a vacant chair at someone's desk mopping his face with a handkerchief.

As they walked out onto rue des Canettes, Martin could see dark smoke billowing from the end of the street at Saint-Sulpice. The smell of petrol and burning metal was already filling the air.

"Oh, my god," Irène said. "Have they bombed the church?"

The ambiguous *they*, Martin thought. Was it Al-Qaeda? Algerians? Homegrown radicals with an axe to grind and a martyrdom complex? People ran past them with panicked faces while a crowd of onlookers craned their necks to see something just out of view. Irène grabbed Martin's hand and they walked toward the flashpoint as the wail of sirens filled the air.

Three burning cars sat at strange angles in the middle of the wide avenue in front of Saint-Sulpice. One of the cars was fully engulfed in flames; it must have been the gas tank exploding they had heard at the publishing house. On the sidewalk outside a mobile phone store, a policeman and what appeared to be tourists had three dark-skinned boys pinned on the sidewalk. The trees along the sidewalk had caught fire and burning leaves wafted slowly down, crackling in the air before flaming out on the pavement. A phalanx of armored police vehicles, fire trucks and ambulances came roaring into the intersection. Riot-geared officers poured out of the vans with guns at the ready.

"Qu'est-ce qui s'est passé?" Martin asked a man who was filming the incident with his mobile phone.

"Those three kids broke windows in some of the shops and tried to steal phones," the man said, never taking his eye from the screen. "Then they broke out the car windows and set them on fire. Some of the pedestrians moved the cars into the street because they were afraid the explosion would destroy the buildings. They had just moved that Peugeot when it went up. You think I can sell this footage to the news?"

The police were forcing people back onto the sidewalks, even as firemen poured extinguishing foam on the cars and aimed their hoses at the burning trees. Martin pushed his way through the crowd so he could get a better look at the boys surrounded by armed policemen. The boys were sitting on the ground with their hands on top of their heads, two with defiant looks on their faces, another grinning as the chaos unfolded around them. An officer kneeled in front of the boys and shouted questions at them.

The grinning boy reminded Martin of Christian with his mixed African and European coloring, tight curls and lanky body. This boy was no more than fifteen, but he already had an edge to him that Martin still occasionally saw in Christian.

Irène had shouldered her way through the crowd and was standing next to him. Her breathing sounded labored and she had all the telltale signs of a panic attack. Martin put his arm around her.

"You okay?"

"I will be fine. This has brought back so many unpleasant memories."

The police were putting plastic flexicuffs on the boys' wrists, and they complained they were too tight and cutting off their circulation.

"Oh, they are so young," Irène said.

A young waitress moving damaged tables and chairs from the sidewalk café overheard Irène's comment. "Don't feel sorry for those little terrorists. They are more banlieue scum ruining this country."

"Be quiet! No one asked your opinion!" Irène shouted at the waitress' retreating back. "What is wrong with people?"

The officer continued to barrage the boys with questions: where were they from, what were their parents' names, were others involved, why had they set the cars on fire? The boys exchanged looks with each other and laughed, then the grinning boy's face turned into a sneer.

"C'est le seul début de l'incendie," the boy shouted and spit in the officer's face.

*This is only the beginning of the fire.*

# 12 La Guerre

The door was locked when Christian arrived at the youth center. He knocked twice, thinking Marie or one of the kids had accidentally bolted the door, but when no one answered he fished a ring of keys from his pocket. As he was turning the key, the door cracked open and Marie motioned him inside.

Rather than her flowing robes and headscarf, Marie was wearing black jeans, a black sweater and her head was covered in a knitted beanie cap.

"What is going on?" Christian asked, as Marie locked the door behind him. "Where is everyone?"

"We've been closed."

Christian looked around. "Is there someone else here?"

Marie shook her head and motioned for him to follow her back to the conference room. As they passed her desk, Christian saw two small, bulging suitcases on the floor.

There was the stale smell of cigarette smoke, and empty Styrofoam cups and McDonald's hamburger wrappers littered the table in the conference room. The old boombox they kept on a side table was dialed in to a reggae station.

"Did I miss some kind of meeting or party?" Christian asked, trying to keep the rising tension out of his voice.

Marie went over and turned up the music on the radio. "Did you notice how quiet it is this morning?"

He had noticed it. There was hardly anyone on the streets and those who were kept their eyes down. No one was loitering in doorways or corners. His father was at the newsstand, but the canopy was down and Olivier's presence seemed more like pretense. He had shooed Christian away with even more gruffness than usual and returned to reading the newspaper, which he held in front of his face like a shield.

"Why are we closed?"

"I got a phone call at home first thing this morning. Closed until further notice."

The reggae music was loud and throbbing in his ears. He went to turn it down, but Marie touched his arm, pointed at the ceiling and made a circling motion. Christian looked at her quizzically, and she made the strange gesture again and pointed at her ear. Someone was listening.

Christian moved closer to Marie and whispered. "What happened here last night?"

Marie stared at Christian, as if she was trying to decide what to say, then she whispered in his ear. "Some of the community leaders wanted a quiet place to talk and asked if they could come here."

Christian drew back. "Are you crazy?"

"Perhaps it was a mistake."

"Is that why we're closed? Because the council found out there was a meeting here?"

Marie shook her head. "There have been threats of violence. Some cars were vandalized last night and arrests made. And

Arnaud is still planning his visit."

"Were you at the meeting? What did they talk about?"

Marie put her hands on Christian's shoulders. "My advice is for you not to come back here. There is going to be trouble. More trouble than you can imagine."

"And you're leaving. I saw your bags."

"I thought I would stay and fight. Maybe I am a coward. But I was in bed last night and realized this is not my country. This is not my home. I do not want to die in a French prison."

"What are you talking about?"

"I am leaving France. You won't see me again, Christian."

"What happened here last night?"

"You should talk with your father," Marie said. "Perhaps he can return to Belgium or even to Rwanda. Things are better there now..."

Christian grabbed Marie's arm, digging his fingers into her flesh. The look of surprise and fear on her face made him feel ashamed, but he was frightened and Marie was not making any sense. He pulled Marie close and spoke harshly into her ear.

"What does my father have to do with this?" He flashed on his father getting into the Range Rover.

Marie tried to break free, but Christian tightened his grip. "I cannot tell you. I cannot."

"You must."

"Please let me go." Marie's steely facade had completely crumbled. Her face was a mask of fear.

Marie brought up her knee and tried to kick Christian in the groin, but he twisted just in time so that she missed his testicles. In a swift move, Christian took Marie to the floor of the conference room and pinned her there. She muttered some kind of prayer, her eyes clenched shut.

"I know you are afraid, Marie, but you have to tell me. If my father is in trouble, I must know."

Marie whispered something, but Christian couldn't make

it out. He put his ear to her lips. "La guerre."

War.

"What do you mean?"

Marie opened her eyes and looked at Christian. She brought up her knee hard enough to topple him and scrambled toward the door, but Christian caught her by the leg and yanked her back.

"Tell me, Marie, and then we will leave here together. I will go with you to the station and make sure you are safe. I won't ask where you are going. I will say nothing else or mention you to anyone. But you must tell me what they are planning to do."

Marie lay on her belly, breathing heavily. She pulled herself into a sitting position and buried her face in her hands.

"Tell me."

Marie motioned for him to come closer, and Christian warily knelt in front of her. She flung her arms around his neck, almost knocking him off balance, and whispered in his ear. "A militia is being formed to fight the police. Guns and weapons are being brought in. Bombs are being made."

"When?"

"For Arnaud's visit."

Christian and Marie left by the back door. There was a woman waiting in an old Citroën to pick up Marie and take her to the train station.

"We'll give you a lift," Marie said, offering Christian the backseat.

"I'm going to see my father."

Marie got into the car and rolled down the window. "You need to get out of here and not come back. Don't be foolish, Christian. Go home and live your life."

Marie waved goodbye, tears flowing down her cheeks as

the Citroën pulled away from the curb.

Christian felt exposed on the street and tried to walk as casually as he could back to his father's newsstand. The neighborhood was still eerily quiet. He saw people in windows looking out at him. Cars sped past dusting up debris in the cool morning air. Christian hadn't been this afraid in years, not since his first days on the street.

Olivier had left the newsstand. The doors were padlocked and there was a note scrawled in hasty French: fermé aujourd'hui. Closed today. If Christian was going to see his father, he would have to walk to les Bosquets. It was a short journey, but it seemed like miles and he was sure unseen eyes were watching him from behind dark windows. He wanted to run, but that would have attracted more attention.

Christian was relieved to see a few more people on the street as he approached the high-rise complex of buildings, but they all seemed to be in a bigger hurry than usual. Women in hijabs with groceries in one hand and pulling children by the other, a youth here and there on a skateboard keeping close to the perimeter of les Bosquets. Usually the streets would be teeming at this hour.

Laundry hung from windows or off the edges of tiny balconies filled with clutter or furniture that wouldn't fit inside the apartments at les Bosquets. Even before entering the building, there was a smell that combined sewage, old cooking oil, petrol and musty damp. Christian had almost forgotten the scent of the place, but it came rushing back and made him gag.

Graffiti covered every wall and staircase in the maze of walkways leading to his father's building. Gang symbols, words in languages Christian did not recognize, *fuck the police* in big bubble letters. Scraggly trees and grass fought for oxygen and sunlight amid the trash and long shadows cast by the other high rises. Christian was amazed at how quickly the feeling of anxiety and despair descended upon him again, as if he had never left. How could his father, how could anyone, continue to live here? Was this kind of living better than death? Christian wasn't sure.

Once inside, the hallway was dim and fetid. Olivier often picked up the refuse discarded in the hallway, resenting having to act as a janitor for the floor and yet resigned to it as well. "Garbage attracts more garbage," he often told Christian as he bent down to pick up an empty soda can or crisp packet.

Olivier's door was one of the few in the corridor that was not scarred or marked with remnants of graffiti. Many of the kids and teens were afraid of Olivier, while others gave him grudging respect for running a business that would sell them beer and cigarettes although they were underage.

Christian knocked twice, softly, and called his father's name. He put his ear to the door and could hear his father's feet on the creaky floor. "Papa, it's Christian."

He could picture his father hesitating, his hand hovering over the locks. Then there was the sound of the three heavy bolts sliding back. Olivier stuck his head out, an angry frown on his face.

"Why are you here? You should be at work."

"You and your friends have closed my work."

Olivier's eyes widened, then he opened the door and motioned his son inside. The apartment was tidy, but falling apart. There were ancient water stains on the ceiling that had been badly patched. The fake wooden floor, full of gaps, shifted underfoot. There was a faint smell of his father's brand of cigarettes—something he imported from Africa.

"What have you heard?" Olivier asked, not offering his son a seat but standing with arms folded in the middle of the living room.

"Everything."

"I do not believe you."

"Arnaud."

Olivier dropped his arms and seemed to slump. "You must go."

"I saw you get into the Range Rover and today I heard you were at the meeting at the community center. I have ears here as well."

"It was that meddling bitch, Marie," his father growled. "She needs to be taken in hand."

"Marie is gone and will not return. Papa, listen to me... you must untangle yourself from this. It is not your fight. This is not your home."

Olivier jabbed his finger at Christian. "No, no... this is not *your* home. You made your choice. You live your rich life in the city with no thought but of your own sinful ways."

"You threw me out, Papa. That was not my choice."

"Your aberration was a choice."

Christian did not want to rehash the old argument. He had to reason with Olivier and keep the conversation on track.

"What will war accomplish? You will be caught and sent to prison or die on the streets. The police and the government will destroy this community."

"They are already destroying this community. No transport, no jobs, no education, no opportunity. Arnaud and his kind want to dismantle the banlieues. He wants to stop people from coming here who are fleeing for their lives. We will stand and fight. If Arnaud dies, all the better. After what he did to you, I would think his death would be welcome."

"I do not care about Arnaud, but I care about you."

Olivier looked away. "Keep your sentimentality."

"Papa, listen to reason..."

"It is too late. I would rather die or go to prison instead of sit and do nothing. I fled one country. I will not leave another without a fight."

Olivier walked to the window and peered out, haloed in weak light filtering through the dirty curtains.

Christian swallowed hard. His mind reeled with disbelief that he was even having this conversation with his father. He thought of his mother. She would have been able to talk Olivier down, make him see reason.

"Who was in the Range Rover?"

"You should go now," Olivier said.

"Answer me."

Olivier grabbed his son by the arm and hauled him toward the door. Christian was surprised how much strength his father still possessed; even as he tried to pull himself away, he could feel his father's bony fingers pinch deeper into his bicep.

"Papa, please…"

"Do not come back here. Go back to your life. This is not your fight any longer."

And just as he had so many years ago, Olivier pushed his son into the hallway and locked the door.


Christian was lost in thought as he walked toward rue Rampon from the metro station. He had run scenarios in his head for the hour it took to get back to central Paris from Montfermeil, and he couldn't help but wind up in the darkest place: his father dead or rotting away in some government cell. He would have to tell Martin and Irène; perhaps Geoff de Courcy could intervene. Christian always thought Irène and Martin were paranoid about their secret connection to Arnaud and Frederick Dubois, but now he realized their fears were justified.

On rue Rampon, Christian noticed a man wearing a blazer and jeans standing in the doorway of Le Admiral. The man openly stared, and Christian wondered if he was a john. Christian automatically sized the man up, a holdover from his days on the street when he might have sucked the man off for quick cash, but sensed this wasn't a tourist looking for a fumble in an alley. There was a whiff of cop about the clothing and

114

haircut, the way he stood there trying too hard to look casual. Had the police already found out about the plot?

Christian crossed the street, pulling his latchkey from his pocket. As he opened the street door, he sensed that the man was behind him. Christian whirled, grabbed the man by the throat and slammed him against the wall of the apartment building.

"Can I help you?" Christian asked.

The man struggled to speak and Christian loosened his grasp on the man's throat. "I'm sorry, I'm sorry," he sputtered.

"Sorry for what?"

"I should have... I should..."

"You should know better than to sneak up on people," Christian said. "I could have killed you in self-defense."

"I'm not a thief or the police," the man gasped.

A voice from overhead startled them both. "He's worse than a thief or the police—he's a journalist," Irène said, leaning over her balcony. "I warned you to leave us alone, Monsieur Lorit."

Christian looked from Irène to Lorit. "You're Lorit? You were at the youth center." He grabbed Lorit by the jacket and pulled him close. "Why are you following me?"

"I know there is trouble in Montfermeil and that Arnaud is stirring the pot by planning to make an appearance. Maybe something else."

Christian tightened his grip on Lorit's lapels. "What else?"

"Talk to me and find out."

Irène came downstairs and opened the street door. "I won't warn you again, Lorit. Christian, come inside. Say nothing more."

Christian shoved the journalist against the wall and raised a fist as if he intended to punch Lorit, but Irène pulled him inside.

Christian felt lightheaded and his body trembled as he

leaned on the credenza in the lobby to try and regain his composure. No one had rattled him like that in years. Irène held up Lorit's business card.

"This fell out of your pocket the other night. I was worried that Lorit might have gotten to you."

"He left the card at the youth center. What's going on, Irène?"

Irène put her arm around Christian's shoulders and maneuvered him toward the stairs. "I've called Sullivan and Martin is on the way from the publishing house."

Irène's mobile chimed that a text message had arrived, but there was no message, only two photo attachments of black and white images shot with a camera phone. The images were of Jean-Louis and a young Frederick Dubois taken from the 1968 yearbook at the École des Beaux-Arts. It was perhaps the last image of Frederick before he became Sarde. She and Martin had found it a decade ago, and now Lorit had, too.

"Are you all right?" Christian asked. "What does the message say?"

"That my worst fear is coming true."

# 13  Around Midnight

Shopping at midnight was a strange experience, Diane thought as she pushed her cart through Wal-Mart. There were only a handful of customers in the store, which meant walking up and down aisles and never running into another person. Other than humming florescent lights, there was an almost apocalyptic emptiness about the place. She had driven to the Wal-Mart in Bartlett to avoid running into any late-night wandering Jews who might admonish her for breaking shiva, plus she wasn't ready to return to the store where her mother had died. But she realized that this store looked almost identical to the one near her parents' house, and the memory of the argument and seeing her mother dead on the linoleum floor came back to her.

There was a conspicuous amount of junk food in the cart—potato chips, soda, Hostess cupcakes, pudding and a tub of chocolate cake frosting that Diane had already opened for a taste. The sugar jolt made her feel better for a moment. She needed to buy a new pair of jeans and some shirts, and dreaded trying on anything, but she'd rather be doing it when others weren't around to judge her growing midsection or dealing with some meth-faced, trailer park girl who thought she was hot shit because she worked in women's clothes at Wal-Mart.

Diane was in the shoe aisle trying on a pair of cheap sandals when she heard two indistinct voices a few aisles over. As they moved closer, their conversation became audible, like a radio antenna picking up a signal. It was two women talking about a fight one of them had with a boyfriend or fiancée.

"His parents think we're at a late movie," one of them said.

"Where is he?" the other one asked.

"Getting drunk, I'm sure."

"Are you sure you want to marry him?"

"Don't start that again. I'm marrying him. We love each other. It's just been weird being up here and having to stay with his parents and not knowing when we can go back. He's under a lot of pressure."

"Have you heard anything about the bar?"

"There wasn't any flooding, but there's wind damage and the power's still out. They're talking about opening the Quarter back up next month, but David's tired of waiting. He wants to sneak in."

"That's a good way to get shot."

At the mention of David, Diane turned to look through the boxes of shoes to see if she could sneak a peek at the women on the other side of the shelving unit. She saw two sets of tanned legs—one in cut-offs and the other in some kind of silky basketball shorts.

"Tell me about it. His dad is all for it. Wants to load up some guns and head down there. He's such a right-wing freak."

"What about his mom?"

"Oh, she's fine. Really sweet."

Diane quietly stood up, trying to get a glimpse of their faces. She shifted a box of cheetah-print heels a couple of millimeters and could see the women. The one in basketball shorts could almost have been mistaken for a lanky teenage boy. Her dark hair was close-cropped and she wore a loose, faded Joan Jett and the Blackhearts t-shirt that hid any figure she might have. Total butch. The one in cut-offs also had short, curly dark hair and was wearing a Saints jersey. It was David's fiancée, Miranda.

"Did they say anything about that shit in the paper?"

Miranda's face clouded. "No. It's really embarrassing for David and his whole family."

"Well, yeah, but that is some serious stuff. Terrorist attacks, the teacher going back there to see him and the homo poet."

"It's just the media making shit up," Miranda said brusquely. "That was ten years ago. It's ancient history."

"But was he banging the teacher?"

"God, no. She was old enough to be his mom and a total psycho bitch. He told me the whole story—the real story—and I believe him."

The girl in basketball shorts leaned close to Miranda. "Maybe he was fagging out."

Miranda pushed the girl away. "No, that's you. Stop creeping on me. You know I hate when you do that."

"You liked it that one night," the butch girl said, backing Miranda against the shelves.

"Kari, stop. You're freaking me out. That was years ago and I was drunk. I thought you were Clint."

"Another homo. You're always hooking up with the gay boys."

"David isn't gay. And neither am I."

Miranda ducked under Kari's arm and walked off down the aisle. A look of dejection passed over Kari's face before she sprinted after Miranda. "Hey, wait up. You know I'm just playin' with you."

Uh-huh, Diane thought. Butch girl was totally in love with Miranda, and had been for years. Miranda was either a closet lesbo looking for a beard or, more likely, she had a fatal attraction to gay boys. God knows Diane could identify with that after her first husband and her crush on Martin. At least she knew Sullivan was straight.

Diane saw movement on the other side of the aisle—another shadowy face staring between shifted shoeboxes. Then their eyes met. Diane drew back, feeling heat rising in her face. She crammed her feet back into her shoes and pushed the cart quickly down the aisle. She made a sharp turn to the left and ran head-on into a pimply-faced stock boy, who was looking back over his shoulder.

"Sorry, sorry," Diane mumbled.

The kid grinned, a mouthful of braces catching the fluorescent lights. That's when she noticed he had an erection poking through his khakis.

"I love working here," the stock boy said giving Diane two thumbs up before sidestepping her cart and walking away down the wide, empty aisle whistling "God Bless America."


Abraham was sitting at the kitchen table in his bathrobe, chin against his chest and dozing, when Diane got home. She put the shopping bags on the table and put a hand lightly on his shoulder. He jerked awake so violently that it gave them both a start.

"Didn't mean to scare you," Diane said.

"Where have you been?" There was an angry tone in his voice.

"Uh, Wal-Mart. Remember?"

"It's two in the morning."

"I told you I was going to the one in Bartlett."

Abraham looked at her strangely, then his face softened. "Oh, right. I guess I fell asleep and lost track of time."

"They had those cupcakes you like on sale," Diane said, pulling two boxes from the bag and setting them on the table in front of him.

His eyes lit up and he opened the box and pulled out one of the cupcakes, tearing open the plastic wrap with his teeth.

"Someone called while you were gone," her father said as he licked the cupcake filling from his lips.

Diane was putting the junk food in the pantry. "Who would call this late? Was it Martin?"

Abraham didn't answer. He was opening up another cupcake. "Earth to Daddy. Was it Martin?"

"What? Oh, yes… it was Martin."

Diane came to the table and looked down at her father. "Have you had a little nip? You are totally out of it. What did Martin want?"

"I don't remember!" He was belligerent. "He woke me up. I was half asleep. Call him back." Abraham crumpled up the plastic wrap from the cupcakes and tossed them on the floor.

Her father pushed back from the table, stood up, smiled and patted her on the cheek. "Don't stay up too late. The hens will be back bright and early."

Diane watched her father leave the kitchen and picked up the cupcake wrappers off the floor. She checked the whiskey bottle in the cabinet and it didn't look like any was missing from the last time she'd poured herself a drink. He was just addled from being up so late past his usual bedtime, she thought, but then remembered her mother making several off-hand remarks about her father forgetting little things. "I told you three times already to take out the trash, Mr. Alzheimer's," her mother would nag.

Diane pushed the idea of her father succumbing to Alzheimer's out of her mind. She pulled the whiskey from the cabinet and took a swig from the bottle. Her mind wandered back to the butch girl kissing David's fiancée. Sullivan loved girl-on-girl action and would have no doubt been turned on by what she had seen. He would have probably tried to take photos and high-fived the stock boy for their great luck. Her thoughts flitted to the sweaty sex she had with Sullivan, indulging in the fantasy for a moment, before she grabbed a spoon from the drying rack on the counter and headed to the pantry to eat the rest of the tub of chocolate frosting.

# 14 Collateral Damage

Irène sat in a café on rue Falguière just up the street from *Le Monde's* offices in the 15th arrondissement waiting for Henri Lorit. She sipped from a cup of tea and pretended to read a book. The café was almost empty except for a young woman sitting in the back working on a laptop and a man in a hat and coat with his back to her at the next table. A barista slowly dried cups and saucers, gazing out the window with a look of boredom on her face.

Christian had wanted to meet Lorit to try and ascertain what the journalist knew about the plan in Montfermeil, but Sullivan had vetoed it immediately.

"You're too emotional and volatile," Sullivan said as they huddled around the coffee table at rue Rampon. "He might not even show up for the meeting after you attacked him in the street. This little operation will have to go like clockwork."

"If he thinks I have information, he'll show," Christian said. "My father could be killed. You have to let me. I can do it."

"I'm sorry, lad. It's got to be Irène."

Christian had slammed out of the apartment with Martin on his heels, trying to calm him down.

Irène heard the door to the café open and close. Henri Lorit came in and scanned the café before sitting down across from her. He shrugged off his jacket and let it drape over the back of his chair. The barista appeared and Lorit ordered an espresso, then turned his attention to Irène. There was something smug about the look on his face that irritated her.

"I must say I'm surprised you've decided to talk, Madame Laureux. What changed your mind?"

"Perhaps curiosity, monsieur. To find out who you really are. I took the liberty of launching my own investigation. Your name is not Henri Lorit. It's as if you sprang to life fully formed."

The smugness flickered away and was replaced by a blank look, but Irène knew that she had him worried.

"Who am I?"

The waitress returned with the espresso and the cup and saucer slipped from her fingers, hitting the table and splashing the hot liquid onto Lorit's shirt and lap.

"Fuck," Lorit shouted and half stood up.

As the waitress mopped at the table and dabbed at Lorit's shirt, bursting into tears as he continued to swear, Irène saw a hand reach into Lorit's jacket and remove his mobile phone. It was the man, wearing an overcoat and hat, sitting directly behind Lorit. He stood up and walked nonchalantly toward the toilets at the back of the café.

After the barista cleared up the mess and retreated behind the counter to prepare another espresso, Irène stared Lorit down.

"This isn't quite your day, is it?"

"On the contrary, Madame Laureux," Lorit said and reached back for his jacket. For a moment, Irène thought he was going for his mobile phone, but instead he reached into the other pocket, removed a folded up piece of paper and tossed it onto the table.

She picked it up and turned it over in her fingers before unfolding it. Printed on the paper were pictures photocopied from the École des Beaux-Arts yearbook from 1968 that he had texted to her. Irène felt her chest tighten again, but tried not to show the discomfort.

"I did not want to drag your husband and his unfortunate past into this, but I will."

Irène folded up the piece of paper and ripped it into pieces. "Any information you have about my late husband is dubious at best and libel at worst."

"Frederick Dubois was an operative for the government and was assigned to spy on your husband and his communist friends at the École des Beaux-Arts. But they fell in love and your husband killed himself rather than being taken into custody. Does that sum it up?"

Irène had always known this day would come. She had predicted years ago that some journalist would continue to dig into the past and discover the truth about Jean-Louis' death and eventually about Frederick Dubois.

"It was almost forty years ago, Lorit. Are you going to publish a story about an art professor who no one but his lonely old widow remembers? Do you actually believe threatening me with that will make me tell you anything? And what does that have to do with Arnaud?"

Lorit ignored the question. "What I find more interesting is that Frederick Dubois seems to have disappeared after 1968. No tax records, no death records. But then André Sarde appears, as you said, fully formed."

Irène feigned boredom. She picked up her cold tea and swirled it in the mug, watching the tiny leaves float at the bottom. "So you believe Dubois is Sarde? Is that right? I wish you luck trying to prove that." She summoned up a smirk and shook her head at Lorit. "This is quite a fishing expedition you are on, monsieur. For someone who has likely changed their own name and erased their past, you seem to have no problem delving into the lives of others. You won't mind if I do the same. We will see who arrives at the truth first."

The man who had taken the mobile phone returned from the toilet and sat down again. He was tall and patrician with tiny spectacles perched on the bridge of his nose. Irène saw him slip the phone back into Lorit's jacket just as the waitress returned with another espresso. "I don't want it," Lorit snarled at her, and she scurried away.

Lorit stood up and pulled his jacket off the back of the chair. "You're playing a very deep game, Madame Laureux, but you have no idea what is really going on. Protecting Arnaud may seem noble, but he will make you collateral damage for his own purposes."

"What do you mean by that?" she asked. "Does it have something to do with Montfermeil?"

"Now who's on the fishing expedition?"

Lorit walked out of the café and up the street toward the newspaper's offices. Irène saw the man who had taken Lorit's phone chatting with the barista before handing her a one hundred euro note. The girl smiled, kissed the man on the cheek and pocketed the money. V. Hugo turned to Irène and tipped his hat.

While Irène kept the journalist talking, V. Hugo had cloned the SIM card, allowing him to check Lorit's voicemail at anytime.

"He's figured out that Frederick Dubois and André Sarde are the same person. Once he has proof, he will publish the story," Irène said as they walked back to V. Hugo's car parked around the corner from the café.

"Finding poof will be difficult," V. Hugo said.

"We walked into the bureau of records and found out in a matter of minutes," Irène recalled. "Surely Lorit isn't that stupid."

"There is no file. It was removed after you found it in 1995," V. Hugo said. "Monsieur de Courcy told me that Dubois had left it there wondering how long it would take you to find it."

"Of course he did," Irène sighed.

"Let's go to my… I mean Monsieur Sullivan's… office and meet the others. I will show you how to access his mobile."

"Did you hear what he said about Arnaud making us collateral damage? He was going to say something else, but he caught himself. It makes me wonder if there is more to this than Lorit is telling us."

V. Hugo started the car and looked at Irène. "I have found that when it comes to you, Madame Irène, there is always something more."

Once they were at his old office, V. Hugo tethered a small, black box to a laptop computer. Irène, Martin and Sullivan were crowded behind V. Hugo in the tiny office as he entered commands on the keyboard, hunting and pecking his way slowly, but surely. Christian stood at the window with the blinds cracked to make sure the old detective and Irène had not been followed. He'd agreed to come along, but he was still brooding about not being allowed to meet Lorit.

A tiny hourglass spun over and over on the laptop screen while the contents of the box were read. After a moment, an icon for France Télécom appeared on the desktop.

"Now, if we click the icon, it should give us access to the mobile," V. Hugo said.

The screen filled with tiny icons, and V. Hugo clicked one marked voicemails, but the folder was empty, as was another for text messages. V. Hugo moved the mouse to a folder marked photos. Inside were the images of Jean-Louis and Frederick that Lorit had sent to Irène, along with grainy images of Martin and Irène leaving the apartment, Christian going into the youth center at Montfermeil, Euan arranging books in the stalls outside the Anglophile, Sullivan and Diane having dinner at Café Richard and Arnaud speaking at a press conference.

"He's been following us for at least a year," Sullivan said. "That dinner with Diane was before we… well… before the unfortunate break-up."

Martin pointed at another folder marked photos. "What's in

that one?"

There was one photograph—a scan of a black and white studio portrait that was at least forty years old. It showed a handsome man in a tailored suit with a young boy sitting on his lap and a smiling woman, perhaps his wife, standing by his side.

"Anyone recognize the happy family?" Sullivan asked.

They all studied the photo, but the people were unknown. "Send that to my phone," Sullivan said. "I'll track it down."

"There's one more file," V. Hugo said.

The folder opened to reveal a series of thumbnails of the exterior of an apartment building. "Anyone recognize this place?" Hugo said enlarging one of the photos so it filled the screen.

"There's a plaque next to the buzzer," Sullivan said. "Can you zoom in?"

V. Hugo typed in a command and everyone leaned forward to try and read the address. "It looks like 25 rue…," V. Hugo said, putting his nose almost on the screen. "There's a shadow. I can't quite make it out."

"25 rue Civigni," Irène said in a strange, strangled voice. "Near the École des Beaux-Arts."

"Does that address mean something to you?" V. Hugo asked.

Irène looked away from the screen. "It's the street where Frederick Dubois had a flat in 1968. Where Jean-Louis died."

# 15 Rue Civigni

The four-story building where Frederick lived had been transformed into luxury apartments. Once lined with poorly maintained student lodgings, rue Civigni was now one of the most expensive streets on the Left Bank.

Irène had never wanted to see this place, not after Frederick's story of what had happened there in 1968, and she felt anxious as they drove slowly past the building.

"If we see Lorit or anyone suspicious, I'll text you," Sullivan said to Martin as he parked the car around the corner from the building. "Put your mobile on vibrate and keep it in your pocket."

"I think I should come with you," Christian said.

Martin leaned over the seat and kissed him. "We'll be fine. I promise."

Martin and Irène walked back down rue Civigni and up the steps to the building. Irène rang the buzzer for several of the apartments until a man answered his intercom.

"Bonjour, my name is Irène Laureux. I used to live in this building and I was wondering if I could show my grandson my old flat."

"Just a moment," the man said.

"Your grandson?" Martin asked.

"I am improvising. Play along."

A bespectacled, middle-aged man opened the door. He looked annoyed. "What do you want?"

"I lived in the garret of this building in the 1960s when I was attending the Beaux-Arts school. I just wanted to show it to my grandson. Do you know who lives there now?"

The man regarded Irène and Martin suspiciously. "No one lives in the garret. It's storage for the tenants."

"Oh, what a shame," Irène said. "It was a tiny space, barely big enough for one person, much less storage."

The man seemed to relax. "Yes, it is quite a useless space. If you want to see it, I can take you up there."

Irène smiled, batting her eyelashes. "That is very kind of you. What is your name, monsieur?"

"I am Patrick," he said. "The building supervisor."

The man quizzed Irène about her education and her time at rue Civigni as he led them up the steep stairs.

"Were you here in 1968?" Patrick asked.

Irène paused. "No, I had already graduated by then."

"There has always been a rumor that a student was killed in the garret during the riots," Patrick said nonchalantly, "but no one has ever been able to find out any details."

By the time they reached the landing, Irène was out of breath. "I had forgotten just how steep these stairs are," Irène said.

Patrick produced a ring of keys from his pocket and unlocked the garret door. It swung open to reveal an orderly collection of boxes, furniture and other disused items. The late afternoon sunlight barely penetrated the window. Irène tried to imagine the room as Frederick had described it, with a writing desk, narrow bed and sofa. It was much smaller than she had imagined.

"Go inside," Martin encouraged her.

Irène tentatively put her foot over the threshold and stepped into the garret. Once inside, she noticed that shelves lined the walls and held old appliances, toys and toolboxes. She walked haltingly to the other side of the room until she was standing in front of the window. There was a desk underneath and she wondered if it was the same one Frederick had mentioned in his story. She ran her hand along the surface, stirring up dust that shimmered in a burst of sunlight that illuminated the room. Irène felt a chill run through her entire body.

Irène turned back to look at Martin and the building manager. She could see them standing in the doorway watching her, faintly hear Martin calling her name, but they became transparent before fading away all together. Instead, she saw a young man sitting on the landing, his face battered, clutching a wound in his stomach where dark blood oozed and formed a pool around him. It was Frederick Dubois.

Irène walked toward the door, felt as if her feet weren't quite touching the floor, but floating just above its surface.

She looked down at Frederick on the landing and he pointed back toward the garret. Jean-Louis was in the doorway, the gun awkwardly aimed at his chest. She called out Jean-Louis' name, moved toward him.

"Tell Irène I'm sorry and that I love her," he whispered and pulled the trigger.

Irène reached for Jean-Louis, as if she might be able to catch him before he fell, but his body passed through her arms like a ghost before hitting the floor with a thud. She felt a strange detachment watching Jean-Louis' death, as if her emotions were muted somehow.

Irène heard Frederick call her name. He was bleeding out

on the landing, already paralyzed by Jean-Louis' bullet.

"You've stumbled through the looking glass," Frederick said, a weary smile darting across his bloodied face. "We meet again… No, that's not right. We meet in the middle."

"How is this happening? I feel like I am here and not here at the same time."

"Time is constantly folding and unfolding, like a wave crashing in on itself. I will tell you when we meet in thirty years that there is some kind of magic around you. You will call it synchronicity." A ragged laugh escaped his throat. "Perhaps this is quantum entanglement. Have you read Einstein? Or it could be retrocognition, or retrocausality or a paradox. The wood between the worlds."

"I don't know what you mean." Irène knelt down and reached out to Frederick, brushed his cheek with the back of her fingers. She was so startled to feel his soft skin that she stood up and stumbled backwards away from him.

"They say—I don't who *they* are, exactly—there are soft spots where past and present intersect."

"It's 2005."

"Am I dead?"

Irène nodded. "Will you remember this when we meet? Will this change something in the present?"

"I don't know. I guess we—you—will find out soon enough. But you have come here seeking an answer and that answer is behind you."

Frederick looked past Irène, a twisted smile on his face. She sensed someone was behind her and looked over her shoulder. Irène was startled to see a man wearing a trench coat and holding a gun.

"Yves Dennis," Frederick said. "He has a son."

Irène immediately recognized Yves Dennis as the man in the family portrait they had found on Lorit's mobile phone. He went inside the garret, stepped over Jean-Louis' lifeless body, and returned with two suitcases. After he closed the door, Yves pulled a walkie-talkie from his pocket.

"Can you see me?" Irène whispered, waving her hand in front of Yves' face. "You bastard."

The walkie-talkie made a strange squealing noise and the words Irène had just spoken were repeated. Yves' put the radio to his ear.

"I know what you've done," she said.

Yves snatched the radio from his ear and held it at arm's length, fear in his eyes.

"I think you got his attention," Frederick said with a weak laugh. "Vous êtes fantastique!"

The landing began to spin and Irène's knees buckled. She closed her eyes and felt arms around her, easing her to the floor. When Irène opened her eyes, Martin was holding her while Patrick looked down at them with a worried expression. Their voices sounded like they were underwater, muffled and indistinct.

"Should I call an ambulance?" Patrick asked.

"I think she'll be okay," Martin said. "We've had a very long day and no lunch. I think climbing those stairs finally did her in."

"Are you American?"

"Yes," Martin said hesitantly, gently patting Irène's face. "Time to wake up now, grandma."

Irène came to and Martin helped her sit up. "Oh, merde…" she said rubbing at her temples. "How long was I unconscious?"

"Just a few seconds," Martin said.

"Who is Frederick?" Patrick asked. "You called out his name just before you fell on the floor."

"Did I?"

Martin helped Irène to her feet and started walking her toward the stairs. "I'm sorry for the trouble," he said. "You were very kind to let us in."

Irène could feel Patrick's eyes boring into the back of her skull as he followed them down the stairs.

"Merci beaucoup," Irène said and limply shook Patrick's hand.

Irène looped her arm through Martin's to steady herself as they walked down the steps.

"He's still watching us. Don't look back," Martin said through clenched teeth. "Are you really all right?"

"When I was up there, I seemed to phase out of this time and into the past. I saw what happened in 1968. I saw the man who recruited Frederick to spy on Jean-Louis. Yves Dennis— the one who covered it all up and had Jean-Louis' body dumped at Notre-Dame."

"I'm not following you," Martin said.

Irène tightened her grip on Martin's arm. "I believe Henri Lorit is Yves Dennis' son."

When they turned the corner, Sullivan and Christian were standing on the curb next to the car having a heated argument.

"What are you doing?" Martin snapped at them. "We need to go."

"Show them the message," Christian shouted. "We have to go to Montfermeil."

"What message?" Irène asked bewildered. "Get in the car. Everyone!"

Christian snatched the mobile from Sullivan's hand, explaining that V. Hugo had intercepted another message from Lorit and held it up for Martin to see. Lorit was trying to arrange a meeting with Olivier.

# 16 at Beale and 3rd

Diane has been craving a burger from Dyer's for a week. She remembered her parents taking her there as kid before it moved from a shack of a place on Cleveland Avenue to the tourist trap of Beale Street, which had resurrected itself from a rundown row of mostly boarded up businesses. They would sit at the counter and her father would say what a damn shame it was that the city was knocking down historic buildings all around Beale in the name of urban redevelopment. Her mother would keep her purse on her lap, afraid that someone might snatch it. Typical. But it was worth it. The burger, deep fried in ancient grease and surrounded by French fries, would arrive on wax paper in a plastic basket along with a gargantuan Coke float. Even as a kid, Diane liked her burgers nearly raw, and the wax paper would be soggy in bloody red juice. That's when restaurants would still cook the meat extra rare.

"You're going to get food poisoning and die," Diane's mother warned her. "How can you eat that?"

Her mother had been dead for almost three weeks, and the days after shiva floated by in a haze of errands put off during mourning, dealing with insurance and boxing up her mother's clothing and possessions for donations to the synagogue. Abraham was unsentimental about possessions and only wanted a few photos and pieces of jewelry as remembrance. He said the rest could go, or maybe Diane could figure out how to sell it on eBay.

She quickly boxed up her mother's floral dresses, ancient pantsuits she insisted were still stylish and sensible shoes to donate to the Jewish center. Diane went into the bathroom to clean out the medicine cabinet and saw that her black mourning dress was still in the trashcan.

When the last of the mourners had been ushered out the door on the final day of shiva, Diane ran upstairs, peeled off the dress she'd been wearing for a week, wadded it into a ball and threw it in the garbage in her mother's bathroom. She thought about setting it on fire and watching it burn in the bathtub, but her father already thought she was a kook, so she settled for watching it sink into the metal can as the plastic shopping bag her mother used for a trash bag puffed out and covered the dress like a shroud. The dress had belonged to her mother, probably the most sensible thing she owned, and since Diane had put on weight, nothing else that fit seemed appropriate.

Diane perched on the edge of the toilet looking at the dress before pulling it out of the trash and holding it to her nose. It mostly smelled of her sweat and funk, but there was still a trace of the perfume her mother wore embedded in the collar. Yves Saint Laurent Parisienne—the closest her mother would ever get to Paris. It screamed old lady perfume, but it was the scent she most associated with her mother. Diane folded the dress neatly and put it underneath a stack of towels in the linen closet.

She stood in the middle of her mother's bedroom, arms folded tightly across her chest, the ticking clock on the nightstand loud in her ears. Her parents had stopped sleeping in the same room after she moved out for college. She vividly remembered coming home one weekend during her freshman year and, after saying goodnight to her parents, watching them go into separate rooms. The next morning, she had tried to casually mention it over breakfast.

"I need more space," her mother said, flipping pancakes at the stove.

"She snores," Abraham said. "Sounds like a foghorn."

Her mother didn't turn around, but Diane saw her square her shoulders. "It's our personal business, anyway. We don't ask who you're sharing a bed with at school."

That comment, that moment, might have been when the relationship with her mother soured. She had wanted Diane to go to college in Memphis, but even then, Diane couldn't wait to get the hell out of there. She'd thought about going to Tulane or Brandeis, but decided to stay in Tennessee and go to Vanderbilt. It was two hundred miles from home, but seemed like a world away. She'd partied too much, her grades were below average and she'd discovered sex in a big way. It was almost as if her mother could smell it on her.

Nothing Diane did after she went away to college was good enough. Her first apartment, her first teaching job in Shelby County, her first husband, everything that came after her first husband, her move to Europe, her second husband. Diane's mother seemed to morph into a caricature, fulfilling every Jewish stereotype to the letter.

"Your mother grew up in a stricter time," her father had said. "She's jealous of your freedom. She swore she wouldn't raise you like her parents raised her, and we didn't, but now she sees what that actually means. You have independence and she never did, and now she's a little resentful."

Diane was never sure what to do with that revelation and she never brought up to her mother. It would be the space between them until the day she died.

It was a Saturday night on Beale Street and the place was crawling with drunken tourists and college kids with fake IDs. She had to park way down the street and hike back toward Dyer's. It was still hot, and she was sweating by the time she got there and found a line snaking out the door. The glowing hexagon letters spelling out the restaurant's name and the black and red striped awning made her nostalgic. She walked up to the window and saw every table was full. There was one open seat at the counter. The harried hostess let Diane in, but the din of children screaming, frat boys laughing and chattering voices was more than she could take. She ordered a double to go, but they refused to cook it rare.

Back out on the street, she wandered across to W.C. Handy Park, where a jazz band was playing. The park was full and there was nowhere to sit, so she kept walking west, eating the burger out of the wrapper. She caught her reflection in a souvenir store window and didn't recognize the person staring back at her. Who was this woman in a sleeveless shirt, shorts and sandals? She realized that she was starting to take on her mother's shape: not fat, but wide and kind of dumpy.

Beale was closed to traffic and people wandered—and staggered—on and off the sidewalk. Like her father, Diane thought it was a shame that a historic avenue known for its music had become a second-rate Bourbon Street. Too many bars, too many junky tourist shops and too many assholes crammed into a short mile.

Diane sat down on a windowsill to finish her burger, felt the juice running down her chin. Even overcooked, the burger was heaven. She should have ordered two. As she popped the last bite in her mouth, a gaggle of young women stopped in front of her. One of them was wearing a bridal veil with a tank top and booty shorts. They were reading from a piece of paper, and from the excited screams, Diane realized they were on some kind of bachelorette party scavenger hunt. The next item was to get a guy to give them his underwear. They all shrieked at the prospect and started asking every reasonably cute guy that walked by if he would donate his boxers.

Eventually, a twentysomething guy with a military buzzcut and his buddies sauntered by and the girls propositioned him. Without even blinking, the buzzcut unbuttoned his jeans and danced around on one foot trying to pull them off. He tossed the jeans to a buddy and mooned the girls before peeling off his boxer briefs and twirling them around his finger while shaking his rather impressive cock. The guy's buddies egged him on, while the girls screamed and hooted as he danced around like a stripper. A policeman on horseback trotted by and didn't give the x-rated tableau a second glance.

Diane walked on until she was at the corner of Beale and 3rd Street and decided she needed something to drink. The humid air seemed to ripple with music pouring out of the doors and windows of clubs, competing with the cacophony of voices on the street. She went into a bar and found people three deep waiting to order. A frat boy with tousled blond hair and wearing no shirt offered to get her drink order to the bartender.

"Jack and Coke," she yelled in his ear.

"You got it, mama," he yelled back and winked at her.

Mama? Great.

Diane stood near the door and soon the frat boy returned with a plastic bucket running over with alcohol.

"What the hell?"

"It's a diver. You won't need a refill anytime soon. Be careful, mama, they are lethal." He winked at her again and didn't bother to take the ten-dollar bill she held out to him.

It took both hands to hold the bucket and she felt faintly ridiculous walking out onto the street with it, but then realized every tourist in the intersection had one. She sat down on the concrete ballast that supported the fading buttresses holding up what was left of the old Gallina Building. The famous old saloon and hotel had burned in 1980 and all that was left was the facade, which needed supports to keep it from crumbling into the street. There had been plans to rebuild it, but twenty-five years had passed and the buttresses had become a landmark on Beale. When the city floated the idea of hiding the buttresses behind the facade, there had been an outcry.

As Diane sipped on whatever concoction was in the bucket, it certainly wasn't whiskey and Coke, she began to cool down and people watch. There was a breeze blowing in from the Mississippi, just a few blocks down Beale. Before she realized it, half the bucket was gone and she had a definite buzz. Fuck. She'd have to leave the car and take a cab. Oh, well…

As she continued to drink, she became aware of a voice in the street that kept shouting "harder." This was followed by a crack of leather so sharp it sounded like a gunshot. Lightheaded from the alcohol, Diane turned and saw a guy in jean shorts, a t-shirt and baseball cap bent over in the street. He had apparently taken off his belt and was letting people whip him. She couldn't see his face, but there was something familiar about his voice, which was begging people to take a whack at his wiggling ass.

"Dude, you are too drunk," a guy standing on the sidewalk said. "Put your belt on and let's go."

There were a couple of girls, too, and they laughed nervously and told the guy in the street it was time to go. A small crowd had formed and was watching this drunk—maybe he was a Navy cadet from the base at Millington or another frat boy—and they were egging him on to take a few more lashes.

People were coming out of the crowd to take the belt and each blow to his backside seemed harder than the one before it. Yet he kept begging for more.

"Come on," he slurred. ."Hit me."

Even in her almost drunken state, the voice finally clicked in Diane's head. It was David McLaren. She stood up to walk away, but sat back down heavily on the ballast, her head swimming from all the alcohol.

A cop was sitting on horseback a few feet away watching David's antics, but didn't seem interested in breaking it up. One of the girls said, "We should just fucking leave him. I hate when he does this shit."

Diane reached into her pocket, pulled out her cell phone and fidgeted with the buttons until she found the video camera. Who would she show it to? Martin, David's parents, maybe email it anonymously to that dim bulb of a fiancée?

A guy in Navy whites delivered a blow so hard that David's knees buckled. He screamed out in a mixture of pain and delight. From the assembled crowd, there was a cheer both derisive and dangerous. Out of the corner of her eye, Diane saw a scrawny redneck in a muscle shirt take the belt. His thin lips turned into a sneer as he curled the belt in his hands and cracked it over and over.

Diane flinched as the redneck reared back and brought the belt down. The thwack reverberated through the air and David, who had been laughing just seconds before, urging the redneck to "punish him," fell headfirst into the pavement.

"Fucking faggot," the redneck said, throwing the belt onto David's prone body before sauntering away.

The gathered crowd quickly dispersed, the fun and games suddenly not so entertaining. The mounted cop never intervened, but sat watching with a contemptuous grin on his face as David's friends picked him up. His baseball cap had fallen off, and as he struggled to stand up, he made eye contact with Diane.

She quickly stopped filming and shoved the phone back in her pocket. She was sure he hadn't recognized her with his glassy eyes and face contorted in pain, but she averted her gaze and concentrated on the sweating bucket she clutched in both hands.

"Guys, he's bleeding a little," one of the girls said. "Maybe we oughta take him to a hospital."

"You stupid fuck," the guy said in a weary voice, as if he'd seen David in similar situations before. "Good luck explaining this one to Miranda."

David didn't respond. He swayed a little and the guy caught him under the arm and started walking David down Beale with the two girls following. They had left his baseball cap in the gutter.

Diane poured the rest of the alcohol into the street and left the bucket on the ballast. She walked over and picked up the hat. It was faded blue, sweaty to the touch, and embroidered with the name of the bar David managed—The Blue Parrott, New Orleans—along with a colorful bird logo.

She dropped the cap onto the pavement and walked away, then turned around and picked it up again. What was she going to do with it? Return it to him? Fuck no! Ten years later and David was still a drunken, closeted mess. She wondered if his delusional parents were still making excuses for him, and had a good mind to call up his mother. Diane remembered holding David's crying mother in the parking lot at Starbucks after he went missing, when she was begging for help to find him. "I don't care if he's gay," his mother had sobbed into Diane's shoulder. But she did care, and David's father—the Bible-thumping whackjob who had, no doubt, voted for Bush twice—cared most of all. He had told Diane he'd rather see his son dead and buried than be gay.

Diane walked by the mounted cop and gave him the best

eat shit and die look she could muster.

The cop grinned at her. "You have a good night, too, ma'am. Don't drink and drive."

Back at her car, Diane sat behind the wheel and watched the shaky footage she had shot on her phone. It was grainy, but David's face was clearly visible. She debated on whether to send the video to Martin. Would he even want to know? Martin had immortalized David in poetry, but had long since moved on. She thought again about the synchronicity doublespeak Martin and Irène were always going on about. Surely they would have pointed out the un-randomness of Diane running into freak-girl Beth at the bowling alley, seeing the fiancée at Wal-Mart and witnessing David's drunken, public masochism. These were more than coincidences. As she ran her fingers over the raised-relief of the embroidered parrot on the cap, she was overcome by the feeling that a run-in with David was inevitable.

"Fuck," she said and tossed the cap into the back seat before starting up the car and driving home. Whether she was or not, Diane felt sober and wished she hadn't dumped the rest of the bucket onto Beale Street.

# 17 Surveillance

Sullivan procured a Renault, boxy and faded navy blue with heavily tinted windows, for the surveillance operation. It was made in the 1980s and would fit right on the streets of Montfermeil, Christian thought when Sullivan picked him up at rue Rampon. He didn't want to spy on his father, but Olivier—and Lorit—had left him no choice.

Sullivan's attempts to find information about Yves Dennis and his family had proven impossible. The Dennis family seemed to have been scrubbed from public records. The detective had tracked down Lorit's address in Porte de Vincennes on the city's eastern periphery by chatting up a secretary at the newspaper, but Lorit had vacated the tiny flat the week before, according to the building's manger.

Christian had returned to Montfermeil determined to make his father confess, but Olivier refused to answer any of his son's questions. He sat smoking behind the counter at his shop and, later, when Christian followed him back to les Bosquets, had refused to let him in.

"Don't speak to Lorit," Christian shouted through the door. "You do not understand what is happening."

Why Lorit wanted to meet with Olivier was a mystery. Was it an intimidation tactic to try and make those at rue Rampon talk? Was Lorit milking Olivier for more information to use in an article? Or had Lorit discovered the plot in Montfermeil? Sullivan said old-fashioned gumshoe detective work, like surveillance, was the only way to find out.

"Diane and I used to sit in cars for days waiting to photograph or follow someone," Sullivan said as he drove them to Montfermeil. "Once in Istanbul we sat on the same corner for a week. Diane and I wanted to murder each other when that one was over."

Christian had never been to Montfermeil by car before, and was distracted as the scenery changed from the vibrant streets of Paris to an urban landscape of gas stations, garages and old high-rise apartment buildings. The outskirts of Montfermeil weren't so terrible, with neat little houses packed together, but then the shabbiness of the town began and they were on the familiar bus route Christian took every day when the youth center was open.

Sullivan parked the car on rue de Courtais not far from Olivier's newsstand. They were in the shadow of one of les Bosquets buildings and just like the week before, the streets were empty. It was so early that Olivier hadn't arrived to open for the day.

"It's like the zombie apocalypse," Sullivan joked, opening a tall thermos and pouring them both a cup of coffee. "Settle in, lad, we're in for the long haul."

Between sips of coffee, Sullivan fiddled with what looked like a small radio and kept adjusting the tiny listening device crammed in his ear. "I don't even hear the drink coolers running. Are you sure you switched it on?"

"Yes, I turned it on and put it under the edge of the counter just like you said. Perhaps it's your cheap equipment." Christian was sure his father was going to notice him planting the tiny listening device, but his father had been flustered and, as was his custom, wouldn't look up from his newspaper.

"This isn't cheap… oh, wait. There it is. A little frequency interference."

A half hour later, Christian saw his father walking up the boulevard. He involuntarily crouched down in case his father looked in their direction.

"Unless your dad has X-ray vision, he's not going to see us," Sullivan said.

Olivier raised the metal door, arranged some magazines and took his seat behind the counter, where he remained for the next eight hours. Besides interactions with customers and a bathroom break, Olivier sat reading a newspaper, then a magazine, followed by staring into space.

Christian found himself dozing for twenty or thirty minutes, waking to find Sullivan still alert, gnawing an unlit cigar and checking his email. He had never spent any real time alone with Sullivan in all the years he had known him, so it felt unexpectedly awkward to be cooped up in the Renault. Their small talk eventually drifted into silence, broken by occasional pings from one or the other of their mobile phones. Martin texted a couple of times just to make sure they were okay, and Christian was glad his boyfriend was putting on a brave front despite his fear. Martin and Irène were keeping up appearances in Paris, going to the publishing house, the market and carrying on with their lives as if nothing was amiss.

If Lorit were Yves Dennis' son, there was no evidence of it. Anywhere. Sullivan had called in a favor at Interpol and had them run variations on Henri's name, but there had been no solid leads.

"I'm not saying Irène's vision—or whatever she calls it—is

wrong, it just seems strange Lorit has waited all these years to come forward," Sullivan said to Christian as the first day of surveillance wore on. "The whole crusading journalist in the name of the father bit. It's too convenient, too pat."

For two days, Sullivan and Christian arrived in Montfermeil every morning and watched Olivier's same routine unfold. The Renault got a couple of looks from some teens who had noticed it parked in almost the same spot, but when Sullivan cracked the window and scowled at them, the teens looked away and kept walking.

"They think you're a cop," Christian said.

"Let them," Sullivan said. "As long as they don't touch the car. I promised to bring it back in the same condition."

"You borrowed this heap?"

"Tut-tut, Christian. Don't let its age and appearance fool you. What matters is under the bonnet. Just in case we need it."

"What's the most exciting case you've ever been on?"

Sullivan pondered the question for a moment. "Well, all that business with David McLaren would be right at the top. Very memorable because of you and Martin and Irène. And Diane."

"I'd never been so glad to see anyone when you and Diane came to collect me in Berlin."

"That's when I convinced Diane to fall in love with me."

"Did she need that much convincing?"

Sullivan roared with laughter. "Oh, did she ever. We hung around a few days in Berlin to make sure you settled in, we told you that. After that we went by train and car to her father's old village in Poland where his family is buried. What was left of them after the Nazi bastards were done at Auschwitz. He wanted Diane to put stones on the graves—that old Jewish custom. Keeping out the demons or more permanent than flowers, whatever it's for."

Sullivan said it took them several days to reach the village in Poland. They shared a bunk on the train, and she had allowed him to hold her, but refused sex.

"Diane is not what you would call affectionate, but she was trying hard to be nice," Sullivan recalled.

He kept up a steady stream of jokes and compliments, buying her dinners and little gifts until one night over dinner in the only café in her father's village, Diane leaned across the table and kissed him while he was mid-sentence. Sullivan had told her he was thinking of relocating to Paris and she got a little misty-eyed, as he called it, and then she was kissing him.

"I was never very smooth with the ladies. Always been a big man, and most females want the slim and debonair type. That was never going to be me. I come from big Irish stock and even when I lose a few pounds, I'm still big. I'd dated a few women in my life, fallen in love a few times, had some flings. I was beginning to think I was going to be a bachelor forever until Diane turned up. I knew it from the moment I started following her for David's insane parents. She would be a challenge and a handful, but I knew she was the one."

"Is she still the one?"

"Oh, yes. She'll come around. Eventually."


On the second day of the stakeout, Sullivan received a long text message full of phone numbers from V. Hugo. The old detective had gone through Lorit's mobile at Sullivan's request and compiled the list.

"That's a big list," Christian said.

"We have to cover all the bases," Sullivan said, dialing the first number on the list. "Like we have anything better to do."

There were more than one hundred numbers and Sullivan eventually split up the list with Christian. Many went straight to voicemail with no greeting, some had been disconnected, others went to various desks at *Le Monde*, takeout restaurants, a mechanic's shop and several to Café Victor Hugo, a touristy coffeehouse on the city's west side. Sullivan made a note to follow up with that one later.

On the third day of the stakeout, Sullivan parked across the street in an empty spot closer to the newsstand, and Christian saw his father look directly at the car several times.

"I feel like he knows we're here," Christian said.

"He can't see us."

"It's still unnerving."

The night before, he had sat up with Martin talking until dawn. They tried to have sex, but neither could focus. It was a first, and that too was unnerving.

"It doesn't matter," Martin said, kissing him gently.

"Do you still want to marry me?" Christian didn't know why he had asked the question, but it came out sounding fearful and urgent.

Martin pulled him closer, their legs intertwining under the sheets. "Yes. The question is will you still want to marry me if I become tabloid and gossip fodder. Or go to jail."

"You won't go to jail," Christian said, dismissing the idea. "You'll be given immunity."

"They might deport me."

"Then we'll leave Paris and go somewhere else."

Christian was turning the conversation over in his mind, staring blankly at his father's newsstand, when he saw the Range Rover approach on boulevard Bargue. It was just after lunch.

"That's the same Range Rover I saw before," Christian said.

"Maybe this isn't your father's first meeting with Lorit," Sullivan said.

Olivier pulled down the metal doors, locked the shop and quickly got inside the SUV.

"Oh, shit!" Christian started to open the door, but he felt

Sullivan's hand on his shoulder.

"Sit still. It's covered."

One of the teens who had been checking out the Renault a few days before sprinted up rue de Courtais and crossed the street behind the Range Rover. The teenager flung a small, shiny object at the back of the SUV as it pulled away from the curb and kept walking. As he passed the Renault, the teen gave a thumbs up to Sullivan.

"What the hell was that?" Christian asked.

"Magnetic tracking device. Click and throw."

Sullivan switched on the sat nav attached to the dashboard and punched in a code. The street grid of Montfermeil appeared and a tiny blue dot was moving up the boulevard toward the edge of town.

"We can follow at our leisure." Sullivan patted the sat nav. "All right, let's see what kind of fine mess your father's gotten himself into."

They followed the Range Rover back into central Paris, staying a half-mile back or more. The SUV made its way through a circuitous series of side streets before coming to a stop near Place Victor Hugo on the western side of the city.

Sullivan turned down a narrow street and they saw the Range Rover wedged into a tight space between two cars. Just ahead of them, the street opened onto the traffic circle at Place Victor Hugo with a leaping fountain at its center. The side streets were lined with shops and apartments, lively with afternoon shoppers and people lingering over long lunches at the cafés.

"What's the plan?" Christian asked as Sullivan illegally parked on a corner with double yellow lines.

Sullivan leaned over Christian's lap, opened the glove compartment and pulled out a camera. "I want to get that license plate number and see if we can get a look inside the Rover." He slung the camera around his neck and reached into the back seat to retrieve a cap that read, "Paris is for Lovers" along with a long leather case. Sullivan unzipped the case to reveal a series of slim jims for unlocking cars.

"That looks like a 2001 model," Sullivan said, selecting the next to longest metal pick. "You know how to use one of these?"

"I preferred to smash windows, but yeah, I know," Christian said.

"I'll get the tracker, you open the door and we'll have a quick scrounge around."

They got out of the Renault separately—Sullivan slowly walking up the street and taking photos of everything like a tourist. Christian put his messenger bag over his shoulder and pulled out the battered paperback of Joyce's *Dubliners* that Martin insisted he read. He easily passed for a student.

Sullivan stepped off the sidewalk to retrieve the magnetic tracker but reappeared almost immediately and shot Christian a worried look.

"The tracker is gone," Sullivan said as Christian walked past him.

"We're parked outside the café Lorit has been calling from his phone. They must be inside."

"I'll check it out and try to create a little diversion while I'm at it."

Sullivan lumbered off toward the café, clicking photos with a silly grin on his face, playing up the fat tourist. There was the sound of a crash as Sullivan backed into a table and sent cups and plates flying.

Christian popped the lock of the Rover in seconds and opened the door. "Fuck," he said.

The magnetic tracker was sitting on the passenger seat on top of a white paper napkin which had been inscribed with a message in flourished English: *Nice try*.

# 18 the Proprietor

*Martin stands at the doorway of the grand salon. Venus stands at the center, glowing in the fading light. There is a strange, distant roaring sound that he cannot identify until he looks out the window. Water is rising, sinking the salon into darkness. Martin goes to the window, can hear the sound of the casing starting to give, panes of glass cracking. The whole room will be flooded. He turns to run, but there is a face in the water, pressed against the glass. David McLaren screams in silence, pounds on the window causing more cracks to form, calls Martin's name. David puts his hand flat against the pane of glass, his eyes imploring. Martin is transfixed, walks toward David's floating body, and presses his hand against David's through the window. At his touch, the window gives way and a wave of water lifts Martin off his feet and washes him back into the salon. Venus remains rooted to the floor despite the deluge, and Martin catches her by the neck and holds fast. The water is rising toward the ceiling, will drown him if he can't get out. Water gushes into his mouth, splashes into his eyes. But it doesn't taste like water. The coppery taste is familiar. Blood. There's a chandelier over his head. Martin spits the bloody water from his mouth, reaches for the fixture and dangles from its lower rung of lights. Then he realizes that the salon's ceiling is gone. Instead, there is a vast, star-filled sky. The chandelier hangs from nothing. Something brushes past his leg. He feels fingers wrapping around his ankle and when he looks down, there is just enough starlight to reveal David standing on the shoulders of Venus pulling Martin back underwater.*

When Martin woke from the dream, he was soaked in sweat and had a throbbing headache. His mouth tasted of blood and he realized he'd bitten his tongue in the night. Christian had already left for Montfermeil with Sullivan, so Martin stood under the hot shower for nearly half an hour trying to wash the image of David's ghostly, drowned face from his mind.

Irène was sitting at her desk and talking on the phone when Martin came into her apartment across the hall. He sat down at his own desk and switched on his laptop just as the phone slipped out of Irene's hand, landing on the desk with a thud. He could hear Euan calling Irène's name through the receiver.

"Euan, it's me," Martin said after he picked up the phone. "I'm guessing you sold the store?"

"Yes, hello… yes, I was hoping both of you might be able to stop by on your way to the office. I'd like you to meet the new proprietor. I think you'll be pleasantly surprised. Is Irène all right?"

"She's fine, just being dramatic. We'll drop by."

Irène sat down at her desk, stacked and unstacked several manuscripts before finally slamming one of them down. "I am feeling overwhelmed. Too much is happening at once. I feel like we are—what is that saying? Going through the motions."

"That's because we are," Martin said.

Christian and Sullivan were on their third day of surveillance in Montfermeil. The detective didn't seem ruffled by sitting in

153

a parked car in the middle of one of France's most infamous housing projects day after day. Christian, on the other hand, was keyed up and tense when they returned with nothing to report. Martin was worried every morning when they left, but Sullivan had privately taken Martin aside and said he would keep a close eye on Christian, reminding him that his boyfriend used to live and work there and had survived on the streets of Paris for years before Martin came along.

"He can take care of himself," Sullivan said. "Just because he's gotten used to the finer things doesn't mean he's gone soft. He's a bloody good little actor, which I'm sure you remember."

Martin hadn't forgotten Christian's past, but it seemed hazier as the years passed. Christian had become the man he pretended to be when they first met and, rightly or wrongly, that was the Christian he knew. When Christian would tell stories about dealing with the kids at the youth center, his voice would slip into a less formal, more slang-laden cadence. His body language changed. The old Christian who had grown up in les Bosquets and sold drugs and hustled on the streets would emerge momentarily, then recede. Irène had seen it firsthand when he attacked Lorit on rue Rampon, and Martin was almost sorry he'd missed it. Christian was so gentle that seeing him get angry and physical with someone was a curiosity. Martin felt slightly guilty for eroticizing the idea. Their sex life had been in park since the revelations, replaced by over-analyzing until the wee hours.

Irène threw manuscripts into her giant over-the-shoulder bag, grumbling under her breath, while grinding out a cigarette in the ashtray on her desk and fanning the smoke away.

"I hope this new owner is a gay man," Irène said.

"What difference would that make?" Martin asked.

"Gay men love me," she said as they went out into the hall. "I can bend them to my will."

When they arrived at the Anglophile, it seemed busier than

usual with groups of two and three standing in corners or in the aisles talking in low tones. A notice posted at the counter said a book club was meeting to discuss *The Da Vinci Code*, the bestseller about the Holy Grail buried underneath I.M. Pei's glass pyramid at the Louvre.

"We need to find a book like that and publish it," Martin said. "A bestseller to really put us on the map."

"It's preposterous and poorly written and edited," Irène said, yet she hadn't been able to put it down.

They started upstairs, but Euan met them halfway. He wore a dazed look and his forehead was sweaty. "It's official, we just signed the papers. I no longer own the Anglophile."

Irène let out a disappointed sigh. She had secretly hoped the deal would fall apart at the last minute. "You want us to meet him, I presume."

"Her," Euan said. "It's a woman. As I said, I think you'll be pleasantly surprised."

"That remains to be seen," a voice called from the top of the stairs. Julie Lacombe appeared on the landing, a Cheshire cat grin on her face.

"Juliette, what are you doing here? Martin said you'd gone back to New York..." Irène's voice trailed off as the realization set in.

"You've bought the Anglophile?" Martin asked incredulously.

Julie came down the stairs and draped her arms around Euan's shoulder. "Surprise!"

"So was this the unexpected business?" Martin asked.

"Yes. It was too good to pass up. I wanted to tell you, but I wasn't one hundred percent sure I would go through with it until I met with Euan. And you were the one who suggested I get out of academia. So... et voilà!"

Julie looked at Irène, whose face was a storm of emotions. "I hope you're not too angry with me, Irène. I know you had considered buying the shop yourself."

Irène came up the stairs and tried to hug Euan and Julie simultaneously. "This is a wonderful relief."

"I've never run a shop before, so I might need a little help. I was a library assistant for a semester and worked at a cinema concession stand for two weeks one summer when I was seventeen. I was fired after the owner caught me kissing a girl in the projection booth."

"We're happy to help any way we can," Martin said. "Just let us know."

"I have to go back to New York and tie up the loose ends at school and pack up my apartment, but I thought that Diane might want her job back as manager."

"I advised against that," Euan chimed in, and Irène gave him an icy glare.

"I'm not sure when she's coming back," Martin said. "She was noncommittal."

"We'll play it by ear."

Irène kissed Euan on both cheeks then embraced Julie again. "This is even better than a gay man."

Julie laughed uncertainly and looked at Martin.

"Smile and nod, Julie, smile and nod."

A beeping sound emitted from Julie's jacket and she reached inside and pulled out her pager.

"I did not know they still manufactured those," Irène said.

"More reliable, more secure. Call me old-fashioned." Julie tossed the pager playfully in her hands a couple of times before putting it back in her pocket. "I have an appointment I can't miss. I'll see you both soon."

Once they were back on the street walking toward the publishing house, Irène seemed to have more spring in her step, and Martin commented on her sudden change of mood.

"This is a positive sign," she said. "One less thing to worry about."

For a brief moment, Martin had forgotten what was looming over them. As they approached Saint-Sulpice, Martin saw that the smashed windows of the shops had been replaced. A maintenance crew had partially blocked the street and was trying to pressure wash the pavement to remove the scorch marks from the exploded car.

The roar of the pressure washer's engine and the splashing of water brought the morning's dream back. Martin's entire body shivered, like someone had walked over his grave. He had dreamed of Peter and now David. And Venus was there, the constant marker in his life. He could still see David's face staring up at him through the water, desperate to pull him under.

# 19 In France They Kiss on Main Street

Diane sat at a small table at the back of Starbucks, a latte with a heart swirled into the froth cooling before her. An acoustic version of Alanis Morissette's "Ironic" piped over the stereo. It seemed like an appropriate song for the moment, Diane thought. The table was behind a tall rack with all sorts of teapots and overpriced knick-knacks, hiding it from the windows. In the middle of the afternoon there were a few college kids nursing drinks while working on their PowerBooks. When the first Starbucks had opened in Paris a year ago, she had silently despaired. They would wind up on every corner supplanting the lively little coffee shops around the city, and even Euan had floated the idea of trying to put a Starbucks inside the Anglophile. She had threatened to burn the store to the ground if he ever brought it up again. Martin texted that Julie Lacombe had bought the bookstore and she deleted the message without answering it. The idea of returning to Paris seemed to slip further away.

The last time she had been in this Starbucks, Diane had been preparing to go back to Paris, flush with the blessing of her father and the cash he had loaned her to start her life anew with Martin and Irène. That excitement had been tempered by running into David McLaren's parents in the parking lot. They had been desperately searching for David, who had gone missing in Europe. Diane's return to Paris had been fraught with the idea that David would show up at rue Rampon and jeopardize the fragile stability Martin had found. If it hadn't been for David's disappearing act, she would have never met Sullivan, who had been hired by the McLarens to track him down, but now that she and the detective were headed for divorce, it renewed her hatred for the McLaren family.

Sipping the latte, Diane regretted sending the video of David's antics on Beale Street to his mother. She had been drunk when she hit the send button, but now that she was sober, her instinct was to run. Getting herself mixed up again with David's closet case routine and his crazy parents was a terrible idea, but just as she made up her mind to leave, Diane looked up and saw Kathy McLaren approaching the table.

Diane remembered David's mother as athletic, petite with short hair. The woman sitting down at the table with a large mocha frap had put on seventy or eighty pounds and wore her silver hair in an unflattering bob. Kathy's face glowed with moisture and exertion from her short trip from the parking lot to the coffeehouse. Diane was too dumbstruck to say anything, and the two women stared at each across the table before Kathy finally spoke.

"How did you get my cell phone number?" she whispered.

"My husband is a private detective. I've learned a few tricks of the trade."

"Oh," Kathy murmured.

"That's beside the point, isn't it? I thought you should

see the video. It was disturbing and, trust me, I've seen some disturbing shit."

Kathy looked at the table. "Please don't interfere. David is marrying a wonderful girl and has been doing well in New Orleans since..." her voice trailed off.

Diane rolled her eyes. "Since he snuck back into the country with a fake passport and didn't bother to contact you for nearly a year?"

"It was a very difficult time for my family," Kathy conceded. "Things are better now."

Diane snorted loudly. "Really? Should I play the video for you again?"

Kathy appeared to be on the verge of tears. "Please keep your voice down."

"Let's be clear about something. I didn't go looking for David on Beale Street. I haven't thought about him or you or your batshit husband in years. I thought David had sobered up and come out of the closet by now, but he seems to be in worse shape than he was ten years ago."

Kathy dabbed at her face with a napkin. "You don't know how much stress our family has been through. My husband is not well. I have high blood pressure. It's taken a toll on all of us. These last few years have been the most peaceful we've known and it's because of Miranda and David being together."

"Oh, my god. Are you serious? You know your son is gay and yet you're going to allow him to marry some girl who doesn't know any better so he can ruin her life, too? So *you* can have a little peace?"

Tears were coursing down Kathy's cheeks and she was shielding the side of her face and trying not to blubber. "I beg you, Ms. Jacobs, please just leave us alone. David and Miranda will be going back to New Orleans soon. We're just trying to get through this."

"Oh, I get it," Diane said, unmoved by Kathy's tears. "Out

of sight, out of mind. Well, I guess that's one way to deal with it."

"You don't understand how much David has suffered. He's never been the same since that trip to Europe. The fact that he has a steady job and fiancée is more than we could have hoped for."

"He needs an intervention."

"He's tried to get sober. He really has been better about it since Miranda came along. I know you won't believe that, but it's true. The hurricane and having to move back up here has thrown him for a loop. And then Martin Paige's book came out and that article in the newspaper. His father is so angry he wants to sue."

"Good luck with that."

"Why did Martin have to write that book and stir it all up again? The newspaper said he had a boyfriend or partner, and yet he's still writing about David. Didn't he think about how devastating this would be for David?"

Diane narrowed her eyes at Kathy. "So, by devastating do you mean David's emotions or do you mean the McLaren family reputation?"

"Both," Kathy sputtered.

"Ah, well, there's the crux of it. Remember the afternoon we were in this very same parking lot and you were begging me to help find David and didn't care if he was gay? Has all that evaporated or have you just put the blinders back on to save face?"

Kathy's lower lip trembled. "I don't want to talk about this. Please."

"That's the whole, ever-lovin' fucking point isn't it, Mrs. McLaren? You and your husband have never wanted to talk about it, and look what's happened. David was begging those men to whip and punish him. He needs therapy or counseling or… something. How can you sit back and just let your only child go down this path?"

Kathy covered her face with both hands and was making a low moaning sound that quickly turned into something between a scream and a roar. She stood up, catching the small table with her stomach and it hit the floor with a gunshot-like bang. Their drinks exploded like tiny bombs, coffee and ice spraying across the hardwood floor. Kathy's face was mottled with color; her entire body heaved as she manically ran her fingers through her hair.

Out of the corner of her eye, Diane saw the customers and baristas staring at them with horrified looks. One of the students had pulled his headphones off and held them in mid-air as if he was frozen. The place was dead quiet except for Joni Mitchell's "In France They Kiss On Main Street" playing over the speakers. Diane laughed out loud. She couldn't help herself. The irony of the song playing at that moment was just more of the weird synchronicity that Martin and Irène had cursed her with. Diane thought she must look as crazy as Kathy McLaren, who was ripping at her hair and hyperventilating as if she might pass out.

"Stay away from us!" Kathy screamed. "If you come near my family, I'll get a restraining order against you!"

Customers were leaving the Starbucks, hurriedly stuffing laptops into bags or collecting purses, and one of the baristas was on the phone, surely calling the police. Kathy stormed away, but slipped on a melting piece of ice and fell hard against the counter. A college student moved to help her, but Kathy pulled herself up and barked, "Get away from me."

"Well, fuck you, fat bitch," the student said.

Diane laughed uncontrollably, a hand covering her mouth. It was the opposite kind of hysteria of David's mother, but just as inappropriate.

Kathy fled the Starbucks, hurling her weight against the door before tumbling out into the parking lot. Diane righted the table before grabbing her own jacket and heading toward the door.

"One of them just ran out and the other is leaving... hang on a sec," the barista said into the phone. "Ma'am, are you all right? I've got 911 on the phone."

Diane didn't respond and was about to open the door when a police car pulled up to the curb. She didn't feel like laughing anymore.

# 20 the Tango Lesson

Martin, Christian, Irène and Sullivan sat in a booth at the back of Café Richard eating dinner and making small talk. Christian and Sullivan's surveillance had been both a waste of time and seemed to add another layer of danger once they were discovered. The silence and tension at rue Rampon had been too much for Irène and she couldn't stand the idea of them all sitting cooped up in her living room for another night.

Sullivan had taken up residence in the spare bedroom, and while she felt safe, it was strange to have him lumbering around the flat and sitting on her sofa with a laptop resting atop his belly. She was at her desk trying to edit a manuscript and he kept making little grunting noises and stabbing at the keyboard until she pulled her glasses off and pinched the bridge of her nose.

"Bernard, what exactly are you doing?"

"Trying to hack the mainframe at the RG," he said without pausing his hunt and peck.

"Renseignements Généraux? That's the French intelligence agency. Are you mad? They will trace it back to rue Rampon."

"I'm using a relay. They'll think it's someone at Interpol."

Irène closed her eyes. "You're using fake Interpol credentials?"

"They're not fake," Sullivan said, offended. "I've done some work for Interpol."

"Oh, really. When was that?"

"Ten or fifteen years ago. If some bored suit doesn't run a backtrace on the credential, we're fine."

Bernard was full of surprises, she thought. Perhaps that's what drew and repelled Diane.

"And what do you hope to find?"

"Something about Lorit. Something about Arnaud. Whatever the hell Christian's father is involved in. Nothing adds up."

Sullivan had given her what he called a burner phone, a cheap untraceable mobile to contact him on. He was worried Arnaud or the government might be monitoring their cell traffic. "Call it an abundance of caution," he said.

Everyone seemed lost in their own thoughts at dinner, going through the motions. It made Irène angry. She was about to speak up, chide them, when she saw Claude come out of the kitchen and go behind the bar. The television mounted there had been silently showing a Catherine Deneueve film she couldn't remember the name of, but Claude reached up, changed the channel and folded his arms over his chest.

On the screen, police were in a standoff with young men carrying bottles and sticks, their faces covered with balaclavas and scarves. In the harsh glow of the wobbly cameras, a Molotov cocktail flew from the crowd, bounced off an officer's shield and exploded on the pavement.

"What are you looking at?" Martin asked between bites of food.

"Trouble," she said.

Claude turned and looked at them. "The police have killed some kids in Clichy-sous-Bois. Now there is a riot."

Christian bolted out of the booth and went to the bar. "Turn the sound up!"

Claude reached up and twisted the knob until the newscaster's voice could be heard all over the restaurant. The chattering of other diners stopped almost immediately as heads turned to watch what was unfolding on the television.

The newscaster reported that three youths being pursued by police for unknown reasons were electrocuted after they hid in a power substation. Irène flashed on the boys she and Martin had seen being arrested near Saint-Sulpice after they had tried to break into the cars.

Martin slid out of the booth and joined Christian at the bar, and Irène nudged Sullivan to move so she could get out.

"Montfermeil will be next," Christian said. "Maybe this was Arnaud's plan all along."

Martin slipped his arm around Christian's waist. "How is that possible?"

"I don't know, but I need to get my father out of there. Sullivan, I need to borrow that Renault."

"You're not going tonight," Martin said. "That's crazy."

"I must get him out," Christian said, a wild, panicked look in his eyes that Irène had never seen before. "I have a very bad feeling about all this."

Irène put a comforting hand on Christian's shoulder. "Phone and see if he is in. He may not even be in Montfermeil."

Christian's hands shook as he dialed the number. Olivier's mobile rang and rang but there was no answer.

"I'm going," he said.

"Wait a second," Martin said. "If you're gonna do this, I'm coming with you. You can't go there alone."

"No. I can slip in more easily and get Olivier out. You

would just attract attention."

"Why?" Then it dawned on Martin. "Because I'm white?"

"Yes," Christian said without hesitation. "A white face, any white face, at a time like this is unwelcome. I do not like it any more than you do, but this is the fact. I need to get Olivier out without worrying you are going to be hurt."

Martin was incredulous. "I'm not afraid."

"I am," Christian said, casting his eyes downward. He hated to admit fear, always wanted to be the strong one, so the admission was startling.

Martin shook his head in frustration and stalked back to the booth.

"Fuck," Christian muttered under his breath and followed him.

Irène turned to Sullivan. "Martin is right. He cannot go alone."

"He won't be. If he thinks Martin's too white, wait until he has me riding shotgun into town."

Sullivan reached into his pocket, pulled out a set of car keys and merrily jangled them. He always seemed ready to charge into any dangerous, impossible situation. Maybe that's what Diane hated about him.

Irène followed Sullivan back to the booth, where Christian and Martin were engaged in a heated argument.

"No, what I'm asking you—if you will just shut up and listen for a minute—is whether Olivier would do the same for you."

"That is not the point," Christian said. "You were the one who told me I had to rise above papa's anger. What was it—take the high road? He is my father no matter what he has done. He is the only family I have left."

"I hate when you fucking quote me," Martin said, sinking back into the booth.

"If your mother was in danger, you would go to her. Even

167

if you dislike her. I know you would."

"Okay, fine. But what if this is some kind of trap, what if…" Martin's words faltered. "I can't lose you."

Christian slid closer to Martin and put his arms around him protectively. "I will come back. I promise."

"Let me come with you. Please."

"I'll look after him. No worries." Sullivan said, twirling the keyring around his finger. Christian started to protest, but the detective jerked a finger over his shoulder. "You need someone with a bit of training. Martin needs to look after Irène. Now get your bony ass moving, lad, before the coppers shut down the roads. No offense, but I don't relish the idea of spending a night in your neck of the woods."

The sidewalks of Montfermeil were filled with people spilling out into the streets and blocking traffic. Angry faces scrutinized Sullivan's car as he drove through the gathering protestors, and hands came out of the crowd to slap at the roof and windows.

"Drive slowly and don't make any defensive moves with the car," Christian said. "We will make it."

"My arse is clenched so tight you couldn't drive a nail into it with a sledgehammer," Sullivan said through gritted teeth. "This is one hell of a chance we're taking. Things are about to kick off here."

Before they arrived in Montfermeil, the radio said that there were running battles between protestors and the police in Clichy-sous-Bois. Unrest was spreading to neighboring banlieues.

The car pulled up to the corner where Olivier's stand was located, but the metal grate was down. Sullivan cursed under his breath and gunned the engine, causing some of the people to jump out of the street. There were shouts of derision, threats, more hands slapping the car. Something hit the trunk hard and Christian flinched, but did not duck or turn back to see where it had come from.

"Are you out of your mind, Sullivan? Don't do that again. They are looking for any reason to start something."

There was the sound of sirens approaching and a police helicopter roared overhead. The street erupted into chaos as fingers pointed toward the sky. Sullivan turned sharply into the car park at les Bosquets just as an explosion sounded from the direction they had come. People hung out of their windows or stood on balconies, youths were gathered in the scrabbled courtyard between the buildings. A group of men stood outside the entrance to Olivier's building. Christian didn't see any guns, but several of the men carried pieces of wood. One, wearing a balaclava pulled over his face, carried a glass jar with a rag sticking out of it—a Molotov cocktail.

"Shit," Sullivan said, pulling a long-barreled .357 Magnum from under his coat.

"Put that away," Christian said. "I know some of them. Just stay in the car and don't do anything."

Christian opened the door, stepped out and spoke to the gathered men in a mixture of French and English. He kept his tone conversational, no hint of fear. "Have any of you seen my father?" he asked.

The men at the entrance had tensed up when the Renault pulled into the car park, but when they saw it was Christian, their postures relaxed, although a few of them stared curiously at the car.

"He's not here," one of the men said.

"I saw him about half an hour ago," another said. "He was going to check on his shop."

Christian turned to walk back to the car and saw two other men were circling the Renault, leaning in close to try and see through the tinted windows. One of them suddenly opened the driver's side door.

"Who's your friend?" the man asked, looking suspiciously from Sullivan to Christian. "He looks like a pig."

At the mention of the word pig, the mood of the group changed again. They seemed to move en masse toward the Renault.

"A mate who gave me a lift," Christian said, getting inside the car.

"Liar," a voice shouted from the crowd, and the men began to surround the Renault.

"Get us out of here!" Christian shouted and Sullivan yanked the car into reverse.

Another helicopter passed low overhead, causing a tornado of dust and dirt. The men who were about to attack the car and the people gathered in the courtyard yelled and scattered as the helicopter hovered above.

A voice boomed from a bullhorn. "Disperse! Retour à votre domicile!"

The helicopter was a timely distraction and Sullivan gunned the engine, but he suddenly slammed on the breaks. The road ahead was choked with demonstrators who had set cars on fire and were breaking windows along the street.

"We're going to have to take the long way around," Sullivan said. "Any ideas where your father might be? Hiding inside the shop, maybe?"

"I don't think so," Christian said. "Maybe he's not even here."

Christian pulled out his mobile and dialed Olivier's number again, but it went straight to voicemail. He was about to return the mobile to his pocket when the text message alert dinged. It was two words from an unknown number: *Youth center.*

It took Sullivan nearly half an hour to find a road unclogged by protesters and police to get them close enough to the youth center. Christian directed him into a service alley that led to the back door. It was dark, but the sky glowed with burning cars and searchlights from police helicopters.

"The youth center is one hundred meters on the left," Christian said.

Sullivan opened the glove compartment and pulled out another gun. He racked the slide and handed it to Christian. "You ever use one of these?"

"Point and shoot, right?" Christian said, taking the gun. It was heavy in his hand and his palms were wet with perspiration. They hadn't gone but a few feet when a kid ran from between the buildings and yelped when he saw Sullivan and Christian aiming guns at him. He couldn't have been more than eleven or twelve and was wearing a puffed jacket that was a size too big.

"Anyone else back there?" Sullivan barked in French. The boy shook his head. Sullivan poked his head around the corner and looked between the buildings. "Lad, if you put your hands anywhere near your pockets, I'll take out an eye."

The kid was trembling and piss darkened his jeans and puddled on the pavement under his trainers. Sullivan and Christian backed away from the boy.

"Scram!" Sullivan yelled, and the kid disappeared between the buildings.

An exposed bulb glowed over the back door of the youth center. Sullivan reached for the door handle, but something else caught his attention. There were crimson streaks on the door, a dark pool at the threshold.

"There's blood here."

Christian grabbed the door handle and it, too, was sticky and wet with blood. He pounded on the door and called his father's name, but there was no answer.

"Stand back," Sullivan said. He fired a round into the lock and kicked in the door.

Weak streetlight filtered through the windows at the front

of the darkened youth center. At the end of the hallway in the main office, a man was standing in profile near Christian's desk.

Sullivan raised the gun and took aim. "Hands where I can see them!"

The man slowly raised his hands. It was Olivier.

"It's my father, Sullivan. Lower your gun."

Even as Christian approached, Olivier did not turn to look at him.

"Why won't you speak?" He stood before his father and saw that his clothes were covered in blood. "Papa! Are you hurt?"

"It's not mine," Olivier said.

"What are you saying?"

"It's not my blood." Olivier pointed down the hall.

Sullivan went back down the hallway and started opening the doors. When he came to the conference room, he raised his gun, but then lowered it and walked inside.

Olivier was staring at the bulletin board on the wall behind his son's desk. Pinned there was a photo of Martin and Christian with their arms around each other, grinning at the camera, haloed by light shimmering off the Seine.

"When was this taken?" Olivier asked.

Christian had not been back long from his exile in Berlin. Irène suggested they go to the quay, have ice cream and watch the dancers. "The light is magic there," Irène said to them, but Martin was reluctant to go. He had gone to the same spot with David and it had ended in disaster. They had promised to start again, but Martin was cautious. Christian would have to prove himself and win back Martin's complete trust.

Irène taught Christian some basic tango steps that she remembered from her nights dancing with Jean-Louis, while Martin watched from a bench. After a few songs, Christian had gotten the hang of it and approached Martin and asked him

172

to dance. Cameras flashed from the bateaux passing along the Seine and from the walkways and bridges above the quay.

Christian held Martin close as they tried to keep up with the fast-paced "Libertango," laughing hysterically as they stepped on each other's feet. Christian lifted Martin and spun him around, and the light was, as Irène said, beautiful.

"I love you," Christian said. "I'll never stop."

Later, Martin would tell Christian that was the night he knew they would be together forever. The past, which had weighed Martin down for so long, lifted away, and the joy he felt when he first met Christian was still there. The crisis was over, and they could settle down and let the days ahead unfurl without regret or fear.

"Say cheese, boys," Irène called, and when they turned, she had snapped the photo that hung above Christian's desk. That day along the Seine seemed both long ago and like yesterday.

"You love him," Olivier said. There was almost a tone of revelation in his voice, as if he finally understood for the first time.

"Very much."

Olivier slumped into Christian's desk chair and seemed to be in prayer. Christian knelt down next to him.

"How did you know we were looking for you?"

Olivier did not answer and wouldn't meet his son's gaze.

"You texted me."

Olivier shook his head and Christian felt his mouth go dry. Something was wrong.

Sullivan called his name and Christian saw he was at the conference room doorway. He motioned Christian to join him.

"Papa said he didn't text me…"

Sullivan pointed into the conference room with the barrel of his gun. Someone was lying on the table, spread eagle. Blood had collected in a pool on the linoleum floor.

"It's Lorit," Sullivan said quietly. "Two gunshot wounds.

And, yes, he is very dead."

There were voices outside the front of the youth center. The door rattled and Sullivan sped past him with the pistol raised and ready to fire. Christian held his breath. A siren wailed close by and there was the sound of running feet along the pavement.

"Fucking pigs have a water canon," someone yelled as the din moved away again. Sullivan's defensive posture relaxed and he went to check the locks on the doors and windows.

Christian knelt again beside his father, who he realized was in shock. "Did you shoot Lorit?"

"No. Lorit thought he was being followed, so we arranged to meet here. When I arrived, Lorit had already been shot in the alleyway. I was able to pull him inside, but I could not revive him."

"Papa, look at me. Try to focus. Why have you been meeting with Lorit?"

"Arnaud is planning a fausse bannière—a false flag operation. He is going to stage an assassination attempt against himself so he can launch attacks in the banlieue."

Christian sat back on his heels, stunned by his father's revelation. "Lorit told you that?"

"No, no," Olivier shook his head wearily. "I gave the information to him. Lorit was a good man. He was trying to protect you and your friends from Arnaud, but he said you did not believe him."

"I don't understand. A few weeks ago, you and your cronies were meeting here to fight Arnaud and now you are passing information to a journalist who is blackmailing Irène and Martin."

Olivier waved his hand angrily. "He had to be sure Madame Irène and Martin were not under Arnaud's persuasion. Arnaud has sent agitators into Montfermeil and other towns to stir up trouble. The meetings held here, the one held in this place, were organized by one of those agitators. I only attended so I could pass on the information to those trying to prevent it."

The revelation that his father was working as some kind of informant made Christian's mind reel. "Is that who was in the Range Rover? Who are the people trying to prevent it? French intelligence? The government?"

Olivier did not answer, but opened Christian's desk drawer and pulled out a silver canister, the kind that held old reel-to-reel tapes. Taped to the top was a flash drive. "Monsieur Lorit said if anything happened to him, I should give these to Madame Irène. She would understand its contents."

Sullivan came down the hall. "We need to get out of here while there's a lull in the action."

Olivier slowly stood up, shaking off Christian's assistance. He reached over and pulled the photo of his son and Martin off the bulletin board and tucked it into his pocket.

# 21 Part of Fortune

Abraham was dozing on the sofa with his glasses hanging off the end of his nose when Diane returned home. It was after five o'clock and the police had kept her sitting in the back of the patrol car longer than necessary, ostensibly to make some point about disturbing the peace. The cops had caught up with David's mother and brought her back to the coffeehouse. Kathy McLaren stood on the sidewalk with her lips trembling pointing at Diane. A couple of the baristas were talking to another cop, but Diane couldn't hear what they were saying.

Eventually, one of the cops came over and opened the back door, leaning in to speak to Diane.

"The staff says that Mrs. McLaren was the one screaming and who turned over the table," the officer said. "Why does she want to take a restraining order out against you?"

"Her son is an alcoholic homosexual, but she refuses to accept it. He's marrying some stupid girl who doesn't know any better. Can I get a restraining order for that?"

"I'm afraid not, ma'am. Sit tight." The cop closed the door and went back to the sidewalk to confer with his fellow officers.

Kathy stood on the sidewalk glaring at Diane in the back of the patrol car until Diane flipped her off.

The officer who'd spoken to Diane returned, opened the door and told her she was free to go.

"What are you going to do with her?"

"Give her a warning about disturbing the peace," the cop said. "I would avoid any contact with her or her family in the future. The drunk gay son is their problem, not yours. Right?"

"Right."

"Have a good day, ma'am."

Diane sat down on the sofa and gently nudged her father, who woke with a snort. He looked momentarily panicked, then smiled and pushed his bifocals back onto the bridge of his nose.

"What time is it?"

"After five."

"Where have you been all afternoon?"

"Just some shopping," she lied. "I need some new clothes and I can't find anything I like or that fits. Did you eat anything? I can cook or we can go out. Or I could order in some Chinese."

"Order in," Abraham said. "Chicken fried rice and potstickers."

The food arrived in half an hour, and Diane opened the cartons and arranged them on the coffee table while her father went into the kitchen to get drinks. She sat down and plucked a dumpling out of the carton and started nibbling the corner. It wasn't the best Chinese in the world, but they had been ordering from the place since she was a kid. It was familiar comfort food.

"Dad, you need help in there?" Diane called out.

When he didn't answer, Diane got up and went into the kitchen and saw her father standing in front of the open refrigerator as if he was in a daze. The harsh light from the fridge made him look incredibly old, and it sent a wave of sadness and a stirring of panic through her. After his violent outburst a few weeks ago, she was more concerned than ever about his mental health.

"Dad," she said softly.

Abraham turned and looked at her, a blank look on his face. "I have no idea what I want to drink. What do you want?"

"A Coke."

"That sounds good. I'll have one, too."

As they sat on the sofa eating dinner, Diane tried to figure out a way to broach the idea of her father going to the doctor.

"I was thinking of going to get a checkup," she said neutrally. "I haven't been to a doctor in ages."

"Are you not feeling well?"

"Just a little tired. When's the last time you had a physical?"

Abraham ate the last potsticker and licked his fingers. "I lost track having to take your mother to her appointments. Not that it did her any good. She went and kvetched, but would never do what the doctors told her."

"We should go together."

Her father glanced at her out of the corner of his eye as he opened another container of chicken fried rice. "I don't have Alzheimer's," he said.

"I didn't say you did, but you've had a couple of off moments lately."

"The last couple of months have been *off*, as you say."

"True."

"Did you ever call Martin back? See, I remembered that."

"I sent him an email."

They ate in silence, the voices of the local news anchors a low hum in the background, still talking about Hurricane Katrina. Business owners and workers were being allowed back into New Orleans, which meant David and his ignorant bride-to-be would be leaving soon. She wondered if David's mother would mention their encounter at Starbucks and how he would react. She hoped it would scare him shitless, but that had never worked before, so why would it work now? It had been a mistake contacting Kathy McLaren, and she vowed to stay out of it from now on. The cop was correct—the McLaren's drunken gay son was none of her business.

Abraham switched over to the CBS evening news. She was only half paying attention to the reports about Katrina and Saddam Hussein's trial, but then she heard Bob Schieffer mention Paris and riots. She grabbed the remote and turned up the volume. Shaky video footage showed cars burning and police clashing with people in the darkened streets in Montfermeil.

"Isn't that the town where Christian works?" Abraham asked, pointing at the television with his chopsticks. "Maybe you should call Martin."

Martin's phone went directly to voicemail as did Irène's and Christian's. It was going on one in the morning in Paris, so why weren't they answering? She felt uneasy as she watched the video play again before cutting to commercial. Diane dialed Martin's number again and left a message asking him to call her in the morning. She scrolled to Sullivan's number, her finger hovering over the button. She hadn't spoken to him in months and suddenly she wanted to more than ever, felt her eyes welling with tears. She scrunched them closed and put her phone back into her bag. Abraham was watching her with a pitying look on his face.

"You should call him, too," he said as he gathered up the empty cartons and took them to the kitchen.

Diane unwrapped a fortune cookie and broke it open, pulling the little slip of paper out before popping a piece into her mouth. As she uncurled the fortune and held it close to read the tiny writing, the sense of uneasiness returned.

~ *What's past is prologue.* ~

# 22 Lorit's Story

Sullivan, Christian and Olivier returned to rue
Rampon in the early hours of the morning. Martin
was stunned when Olivier, covered in dark, dried
blood, shook his hand vigorously before going
into the spare room to shower and sleep. Once
they were in bed, Christian began to tell Martin
what had happened in Montfermeil, but he soon
fell asleep.

When they gathered at Irène's for breakfast
in the morning, Sullivan had already gone to a
pawnshop and procured an ancient looking reel-
to-reel machine. It sat on Irène's desk, Lorit's tape
threaded and ready to play. Martin plugged the
flash drive into his laptop on the coffee table.

Sullivan stood near the French doors, the
curtains slightly parted, so he could keep watch,
smoking rather than chewing a cigar. Despite the
early hour, Irène poured a glass of whiskey for
herself and Olivier, who was sitting rigidly on the
edge of the armchair.

"Monsieur Lorit said to listen to the recording on the computer first," Olivier said, sniffing the contents of the glass before cautiously taking a sip.

"Here we go," Martin said, and clicked on the flash drive to open the sound file.

There was a shuffling sound, paper perhaps, and the squeak of a chair, then Lorit spoke.

"My name is Henri Lorit. I took my mother's surname when we went into hiding after my father was murdered. His name was Yves Dennis. An agent of the French government murdered him. I will tell you my story, which is corroborated by the recording on the reel-to-reel tape. In the process of my investigation into Arnaud and his connection to André Sarde, I discovered that Arnaud has been sending agitators and agents provocateurs into the banlieues—Clichy-sous-Bois, Bondy, Montfermeil and others in Seine-Saint-Denis, Le Raincy and Bobigny. At first, it was a sting operation. The agents would arrange the sale and shipment of guns and the organizers would be arrested. But Arnaud came to believe the operation was too small. Along the way, it was decided, that actual engagement with the residents of the banlieue would be more effective. The plan is to bring in large caches of guns and weapons and distribute them to the hostile immigrants and poor and let the banlieues ignite. A staged assassination attempt of Arnaud would further empower him and the police to quell those riots with deadly force. There will be mass arrests and deportation. And there might even be riots in Paris itself, just to show that the capital is not immune. Again, all this is orchestrated to cause fear, confusion and disruption. It will be like 1968 all over again."

Yves Dennis moved his family from their apartment in the tony west Paris suburb of Saint-Germain-en-Laye back to their large home in Chambéry in the summer of 1968. Even at almost nine years old, Henri instinctively felt there was something off about his father after the spring riots. He seemed distracted, never wanted to play. The days of exploring the woods, fishing or shooting targets with a pellet gun were gone. Dinners were silent and grim, and Henri often heard loud arguments coming from his parents' bedroom.

"Something bad had happened to the world" was the way Henri thought of the May riots and turmoil he had only glimpsed on television or in snatches of confusing conversation from his mother and her friends. When Henri asked about the riots, his father gave him a very simplistic answer, but it stuck with him for the rest of his life.

"Remember what you learned about the Nazis in school, when they invaded and took over France? Well, there was another group of bad people trying to do the same thing, but we would not let them."

"And you helped beat them?" Henri asked, beaming with pride at his heroic father.

"I did my part," Yves said, but Henri could tell he wasn't happy about it. "Remember son, because it will happen again one day, that there are people who will want to take away your freedom. They will try to make you believe things that aren't true, they will lie and kill, but they are the enemy. You may be asked to do things that seem wrong, but you do what you have to do. Does that make sense?"

Henri nodded solemnly, but he didn't really understand, especially the part about doing things that seemed wrong.

As the warmth of summer disappeared, Yves Dennis spent more and more time in his office with the door closed. When he was interrupted, Yves made no secret of his irritation and desire to be left alone. Henri stopped seeking his father's company and was actually happy when the school term began so he could escape the oppressive mood at home. He began to dread coming home in the afternoons, and his mother would often pick him up from school and take him for ice cream, shopping or a drive. She didn't want to go home either.

Some afternoons there would be black sedans parked in the driveway. Henri's mother said they were "business associates" of his father, but he never quite believed her.

Yves' dark wood-paneled office was lined with cabinets topped with bookcases. The cabinets were deep and used to be one of Henri's favorite places to hide. One day when he was home sick from school, Henri heard cars in the driveway. He got out of bed and peeked between the curtains, and saw two of the black sedans pulling through the gate. His father was already walking out to meet them. Henri left his room and went down the back staircase. He was worried the maid or his mother might catch him, but he saw his father had left the door to his office open. Henri raced down the hall and hid inside the cabinet at the far end of the room. There was only an old reel-to-reel tape machine inside that particular cabinet, so nothing to accidently knock over and give away his hiding place.

Henri heard the muffled voices of his father and the other men coming down the hall and held his breath. He heard the office door shut and the men making small talk about the drive to Chambéry, a card game and something about a war in a place called Vietnam. Ice clinked in glasses as Yves poured drinks for the men.

"Messieurs, what is on the agenda for today?" Yves asked as he sat down behind his desk.

At that moment, the tape machine silently whirred to life, and Henri felt urine squirt into his underwear. He put his hand over his nose and mouth, certain that his fearful, heavy breaths could be heard in the office. Why was his father taping the conversation? They were talking about the president, who had been re-elected in the summer after the riots.

"De Gaulle is going to call the referendum in the spring,"

one of the men said.

"It will be the final nail in his coffin," another said. "Did you see the survey results? His own party has lost faith. Too old, too conservative and the anti-American sentiments are not playing well."

"America is a lost country," Yves said. "The negroes, the war in Indochina, the radicalized students and communists... Johnson let the country fall to pieces. Perhaps Nixon will take America in hand."

The talk of global politics continued and Henri understood very little of what they were saying. It was hot inside the cabinet and the mechanical hum of the tape machine was lulling him to sleep. But then the conversation turned to someone named Frederick Dubois who had been in a hospital.

"He's had the final operation, and the doctor said he'll never walk again," one of the men said. "It's time to move him out of the hospital, but he's going to need supervision."

"What are you suggesting?" Yves asked.

"You recruited him, you were his handler. The director has recommended moving him near Chambéry, perhaps Lyon. Somewhere you will have close access while he transitions into his new life."

"I know the boy's father. He's the one who recommended we recruit him in the first place. We could easily send him back to Geneva..."

One of the other men cut Yves off.

"He has to disappear. He can't return to the bosom of his parents as if nothing has happened. No, we will move him here. You're only consulting now, Yves. It's not like you have anything else to do. The boy will need guidance."

One of the men, who had not spoken before and sounded younger, asked a question that made the others laugh. "Does his cock still work?"

"Doubtful, according to the doctor. He will be in a

wheelchair."

"One less faggot with a working cock is good for society," Yves said with disgust.

"I think he has a crush on you, Yves," the young man said and the others laughed again.

"Fuck off," Yves said, but there was an odd tone in voice.

The men continued talking about Frederick. They were going to give him an apartment and he would have a lot of money and the chance to go to school. There was talk of hiring some kind of assistant or minder to stay with him since he was in a wheelchair. Henri felt badly for Frederick and that they kept calling him a faggot. Henri knew it was a bad word directed at other boys on the playground who seemed weak or effeminate. Henri himself had been called the pejorative once, and had responded by punching the kid in the stomach.

Henri felt triumphant that he had not been caught inside the cabinet, but he would never have the chance to listen to another meeting. The meetings continued while he was at school, as his mother referenced their occurrences several times and received a sharp rebuke from his father. Yves began to disappear in the evenings, sometimes not returning until the next day. Henri wondered if he was with the boy in the wheelchair, and felt a pang of jealousy. Yves wouldn't spend time with his own son, but would go to wherever this Frederick was and not come home at night. His mother tried to divert him with games, buying him presents and letting him stay up late to watch television, but Henri wanted his father.


On the first Saturday after the new year, Henri was upstairs playing in his room. His father was downstairs in his office and his mother was away for the weekend to visit her sister in Paris. He heard a car in the drive and ran to the window to see one of the dark sedans screech to a halt in front of the house. Without warning, Yves opened the door to Henri's room and told his son to put on his coat and go outside and play.

"It's cold," Henri protested. "Can't I stay in my room? I promise I won't come downstairs."

"No," his father said angrily. "Put on your coat and take the back stairs. I will come for you after my meeting is over."

"Is something wrong, Papa?" Henri asked, pulling on his coat. "Are there bad people doing things?"

Yves' face softened and he ruffled Henri's hair. "No, son, not right now, but this is a meeting about private things." Henri hadn't noticed until that moment that his father was carrying his briefcase. "I want you to do something important for me. I want you to take care of this while I'm in my meeting. Keep it in your play hut. Can you do that?"

Henri nodded, momentarily elated that his father was entrusting him with his briefcase. The one time he'd opened it before, his father had yelled at him and Henri had never dared to touch it again.

The doorbell rang and Yves took Henri by the hand and guided him toward the stairs. "Quickly and quietly, son."

Henri went into the back garden to the play hut he had lost interest in after they moved to Paris. It was freezing inside, but at least he would be sheltered from the wind. He placed Yves' briefcase carefully in the old chest full of deflated footballs and broken toys. It would be safe there.

Henri sat shivering in the play hut, unable to concentrate on a book, until his curiosity got the better of him. He ran across the garden, keeping low, afraid someone might see him. He quietly opened the kitchen door and crept back into the house. Almost immediately, Henri could hear raised, angry voices.

There was a small storage closet just down the hall from his father's office, the perfect place to hide and listen. As he slipped into the closet, Henri heard the name Frederick Dubois again. They were arguing about the boy in the wheelchair.

"Where else would Dubois have obtained a list of our operatives? You either gave it to him or he stole it from you. He's threatening to sell the list to the highest bidder."

"Eliminate him," Yves roared. "Kill him."

"His death would mean the automatic release of the list. He has somehow been able to arrange all this. So much for your guidance, Yves. God only knows what other schemes he might be up to."

"I cannot be with him every minute of the day," Yves said. "I have a family. I am only a consultant now. Remember? I won't let you put the blame on my back."

Henri heard the door to his father's office open and the men come into the hall.

"Go to him tonight and take care of this, Dennis," one of the men said. "Talk him out of it. Seduce him. Whatever you have to do to get the list back."

"Never make accusations like that again or I will kill you," Yves said.

Henri heard their voices recede as they walked to the front of the house, and he opened the door, ready to run back to his play hut, but he heard the kitchen door open and ducked back inside.

Footsteps padded down the hall and paused in front of the storage closet. Henri held his breath, expecting the door to fly open, but the footsteps moved on. There was noise from inside his father's office: desk drawers being opened, then the cabinet where Yves' stored the tape machine.

Henri cracked the door open and saw his father coming back down the hall toward his office. He paused at the threshold, a stunned look on his face.

"What are you doing here?" Yves demanded angrily.

There was a single, muffled gunshot. Henri slapped a hand over his mouth to stop himself from crying out.

There were more strange sounds from the office, but Henri was too stunned to move. It was nearly an hour later, after he'd heard the scurry of feet back along the hallway and the back door close, that Henri emerged from his hiding place.

Henri peered around the corner of the office door and saw his father lying on the floor. There was a gun in his hand, a pool of blood around his head dripping from a grizzly wound. Henri knew his father was dead even as he picked up the phone and dialed his aunt's apartment in Paris.

Henri's mother screamed and dropped the phone, his aunt urging him to hang up and call the police. Before the police arrived, Henri went back to the play hut and pulled his father's briefcase from the toy chest. Inside was a silver canister containing a reel-to-reel tape.

For years, his father's briefcase sat in Henri's closet. No one ever asked about it, not even the police or the agents who came to ask questions. Henri told them about the men who always visited, the boy in the wheelchair, the man who had snuck in through the kitchen before he found his father's body. Surely an arrest would be made.

A few weeks later, listening from the top of the stairs, Henri heard a policeman tell his mother that Yves' death had been ruled a suicide. His father was a hero, his mother told him, and it was all a terrible accident. But Henri couldn't forget what his father had said: *You may be asked to do things that seem wrong, but you do what you have to do.*

The briefcase and the tape were the only things he had left of his father, and he vowed to protect them. Sometimes, he would cry and hug the briefcase, hoping the leather might yield some lingering scent of his father, but as he grew older, the sadness receded and was replaced with a hollowness he couldn't quite describe.

Henri's grades slipped at school. He began skipping classes, running with older kids and got into trouble for shoplifting and vandalism. The details of his father's murder grew hazier, but he could not blot out the image of his father with the gun in his hand. He just managed to graduate from high school, and was encouraged by his literature instructor to pursue writing, specifically journalism. She said Henri had a knack for writing clear, concise and compelling work that would lend itself well to newspapers. The instructor said being a delinquent and malcontent was no longer fashionable as the 1980s approached, and Henri would have to find a job and a purpose.

"Maybe you'll become a famous investigative journalist," the teacher had said.

Providential words, he would later realize, because he decided that if he was going to be a journalist, the first thing he should do was answer the question of his father's death. Henri's mother died of cancer while he was attending university. Before she became comatose, his mother told him what he had already guessed—his father was a government operative. In the morphine delirium, she confessed that she had planned to divorce Yves before he was killed. Marrying him was a mistake, she said; her friends and family had warned her there was something mentally unstable about him. But she had been young, foolish and in love.

"Go to the attic," she said in a shallow whisper. "You'll find everything you need to know. Just remember that he loved you."

Hidden among his mother's things in the attic was a diary she kept during her marriage to Yves. She raged and ranted in sloppy handwriting, often smudged with what Henri came to realize were tears, about fights with his father, his long absences, his patriotic fanaticism, suspicions that he was having an affair, possibly with another man. The myth that Henri had constructed around his father began to crumble.

Henri took the reel-to-reel tape to a record shop in the Latin Quarter and they happened to have a player in the back room. The owner strung the reels for him, showed him how to stop, start, rewind and fast-forward the tape and handed him a pair of giant headphones.

The tape was a recording of the first meeting held in Yves' office, when all the black-suited men had appeared, including what sounded like a new recruit. He was young with an almost nasally teenage twang to his voice.

"You seem a bit young for this line of work," Yves said. "How old are you?"

"Nineteen," was the terse reply.

"We recruited him right out of baccalauréat," one of the other suits said. "He was instrumental in uncovering some of the radical elements at his school and at the Sorbonne last year. He is a wonderful little actor."

"And more mentally stable than other recruits who will go unnamed," another man said.

There was laughter in the office, but Henri did not hear his father's distinctive laugh among them.

"It is not an easy job," Yves said as the laughter died down. "It takes commitment. The rest of your life will be secondary to the job."

"You seem to have done all right for yourself," the young man said, a cold detachment in his voice. "A beautiful home, a wife and kid. I guess we all choose which commitment is more important."

"I don't like your inference," Yves said.

"There was no inference. You chose to retire and be with your family. I choose to work for France."

"You might feel differently when you are older," Yves said. "Priorities change."

"The future of this country is my priority. That won't change."

"How do your parents feel about that?"

"My father is dead. My mother has remarried and has other

children. Does that answer your question?"

There was a tense silence until Yves spoke again. "I don't believe I caught your name."

"Michel Arnaud."

Sullivan rewound the tape three times to hear the exchange between Yves Dennis and Arnaud. "It will have to be voice matched, but I don't think there's any doubt it's Arnaud," the detective said.

"It is him," Christian said. "I recognize the contemptuous tone."

Irène asked Martin to play back Lorit's narrative of finding the diary in the attic and discovering his father's true identity. The similarities to her discovery of Jean-Louis' journal and the revelation of his secret life were striking.

"He was searching for the truth after years of being asleep, just like I was," Irène said. "We must make this right."

Olivier had been quiet throughout the playing of Lorit's confession and the reel-to-reel tape. "Lorit said that he had devoted his life to exposing Arnaud. It took him years to piece together that Frederick Dubois was this Sarde fellow. It would be a shame if all of that were in vain. Lorit said that if anything were to happen to him, this information must be given to the authorities—someone who could be trusted."

"Aye, that's the problem. Who can be trusted in this nest of vipers?" Sullivan rewound the reel-to-reel tape again. "Bring your laptop over here, Martin. We need to copy this into an audio file for safekeeping."

# 23 Arnaud

A crowd was gathering around the monument at Place de la Bastille. People dashed in front of cars at the busy roundabout, causing horns to honk and traffic to back up along Boulevard Beaumarchais. A demonstration was getting underway to protest the death of the boys in Clichy-sous-Bois and the strong-arm tactics of the police. There were protestors holding quickly made signs showing both support and contempt for the police.

Sullivan kept one eye on the traffic and the other on his rearview mirror. A white Peugeot was following him and Christian as they made their way toward the Paris field office of Interpol to meet an agent Sullivan trusted with Lorit's information.

"We have company," Sullivan said.

Christian glanced into the Renault's side mirror. "Unmarked police car?"

"Looks like it. If Arnaud is onto us, he might try to have us detained."

"And my father."

Sullivan maneuvered the car through the crush of traffic, turned on rue Saint-Antoine and accelerated, but the white Peugeot was still trailing them. Just before the street turned into rue de Rivoli with its arcaded facades full of fashion houses, another white car pulled away from the curb in front of them, forcing Sullivan to slam on the brakes. They were being boxed in.

Christian glanced around the car, twisting to look in the back seat.

"Lad, what are you looking for?"

"Something heavy."

Christian spotted the metal coffee thermos rolling around on the back floorboard and grabbed it, testing the weight in his hand. He was surprised how heavy it was, even empty.

"When we get to the traffic signal, I'm getting out," Christian said. "I'll distract them, you take the information to your contact."

"I highly advise against that. We should stay together. I can outrun them."

The Renault pulled up to the light, and Christian released his seat belt. "It's time to put a stop to all this."

He opened the door and was in the street before Sullivan could say anything else. The unmarked car in front was already through the intersection, and Sullivan gunned the engine as Christian lobbed the thermos into the windshield of the car that had been following them. The Peugeot screeched to a halt as the window shattered on impact.

Christian turned and knelt in the roadway, putting his hands behind his head. Further down rue de Rivoli, Sullivan gunned the car through a red light and was gone, leaving the other unmarked car caught behind a slow-moving delivery truck that had pulled into the street.

Christian lost track of how long he had been sitting in the interrogation room at police headquarters. Three hours or was it six? He had been in rooms like this before at various times in his life: cold, sterile, a table and chair with a tape recorder on the wall to preserve the confession. There was a one-way mirror on the wall opposite him and someone was always sitting behind it. Christian stared at his hands folded on the table, refused to look at his reflection, to meet the unknown gaze of the person behind the glass.

When the police arrested him on rue de Rivoli, the flexicuff restraints cutting into his wrists, he had immediately asked for Arnaud and one of the cops had laughed. They drove Christian to the imposing police headquarters on Île de la Cité and didn't bother with the usual fingerprinting or mug shot, but took him directly to an interview room. His mouth was dry and he had to use the bathroom, but he meditated on his hands folded on the table and tried not to think of his discomfort.

There was the sound of a key in the door, and a middle-aged man wearing a grey suit with slicked back dark hair walked in carrying a manila folder. A thick pair of black-rimmed glasses sat on the end of his nose and he pushed them up as he sat down across from Christian and opened the folder.

"Is your name Christian Kigali?"

"What does it say in the file?"

The man turned the folder around so Christian could see the pages. There was a stack of police reports, but all the information had been redacted with heavy black ink. The corners of the reports were torn where mug shots, once stapled there, had been ripped away.

"Are you an informant?" the man asked.

"Who are you? One of Arnaud's underlings? I won't speak to anyone but him, so save your breath."

"I am Inspector Ruey. I am trying to help you, Monsieur."

"Oh, really? Officers in an unmarked car followed me and

now I've been arrested without formal charge and have been sitting here alone for hours without counsel. Aren't you just following Arnaud's orders?"

"I was given no such orders," the inspector said tersely, pushing his glasses up again. "To be perfectly honest, I have no idea why you have been brought here. Perhaps you could tell me what your connection is with Arnaud."

"I was an informant in 1998. Surely you can tie that year and Arnaud together." Ruey tried not to show any emotion, but Christian could see his eyes light up in surprise. "Do you understand now?"

Ruey allowed Christian to use the bathroom and gave him a small cup of water before returning him to the interrogation room. As he was about to close the door, Ruey stared at Christian, who would not return his gaze.

"Your friend who was driving the car eluded our officers. I thought you might like to know that."

Ruey went out and locked the door behind him. Why had the inspector told him that, Christian wondered. He felt his pulse accelerate and a bead of cold sweat ran behind his ear and down his neck.

Christian stared at his hands and the table for so long that he was beginning to nod off. The sound of a key in the lock roused him, and he turned to see Michel Arnaud in the doorway. He was talking to someone just outside, but his eyes were fixed on Christian.

Arnaud was now in his fifties, his once dark hair now turning silver, the lines on his weathered face had deepened and his rumpled Columbo-style raincoat had become his signature look. He had worn the coat as a cop, wore it now as the police commissioner, was mocked and lauded for it by the media, but his disheveled look had made him seem like an "everyman," and that might play well with conservative and traditional voters if Arnaud ever decided to run for office. He'd captured France's most notorious underworld figure, which made him a hero to many and vaulted him to the position of prefect, despite the questions that still lingered about André Sarde.

Arnaud walked slowly toward the table, his mouth a thin, grim line. He pulled off the raincoat, draped it over the back of the chair across from Christian and sat down.

"Monsieur Kigali. I hoped we would never meet again. Despite your famous boyfriend, nice home, expensive clothes and your good works in the banlieue, trouble still seems to find you."

"My only trouble is you, Arnaud. We had a deal and now you have broken it."

"Come now. I expunged your record for providing information to arrest André Sarde and didn't alert immigration to the illegal status of Monsieur Paige and Madame Jacobs. That is ancient history. The murder of Henri Lorit in the youth center where you work, however, is very much present tense."

"Have they turned off the recording devices in here? Is anyone still watching behind the glass? Because you do not want what I have to say on the record."

Arnaud looked briefly around the room. "Anything you have to say to me will be private."

Christian leaned forward, met the commissioner's gaze. "Fausse bannière."

At the mention of false flag, Arnaud's eyes narrowed and he shifted almost imperceptibly in his seat, but Christian knew he now had the chief's attention.

"Your operation in Montfermeil has been exposed."

Arnaud calmly folded his hands on the table. "I have no idea what you are referring to."

"Of course you do."

"I'd like to see proof."

There was sharp knock on the interrogation room door and Inspector Ruey entered the room carrying a file folder. "My apologies. This was delivered to the front desk by an Interpol courier. It is vital information concerning this case."

Ruey placed the folder on the table and winked at Christian before making a hasty exit. Both Arnaud and Christian looked at the folder.

"Ask and you shall receive, as the saying goes," Christian said.

Arnaud opened the folder and began to scan the documents inside. Christian watched as Arnaud flipped through the pages, which he guessed was a transcript of the tape and thumbdrive. Anger darted across Arnaud's face, his hand holding the paper trembled.

"Your past is beginning to unravel," Christian said, unable to keep the smugness from his voice. "You were sloppy. You thought Frederick Dubois' death would bury your involvement in the death of Yves Dennis, but you were wrong. Then his son comes along and you murder him, too. You should have contained your ambition and bigotry. It's a lethal combination, especially when you have made so many enemies inside your own department."

Arnaud stood up abruptly, the legs of his chair screeching along the linoleum, almost tipping over. There was another sharp knock at the door, which startled them both. It was Ruey again. "Pardon, there are RG agents here to see you, sir. They say it is urgent."

Arnaud never took his eyes off Christian. "Send them to my office. I will be along shortly." Ruey hesitated, lingering in the doorway, until Arnaud barked at him. "That will be all, Inspector."

Arnaud closed his eyes and sighed deeply. "Do you have any idea what is happening in France? Your precious Montfermeil is a breeding ground for jihadists who want to kill the innocent. There are terrorist cells at work right now in this country and we are barely one step ahead of them. The

Muslim scum are planning to blow up our landmarks, airplanes, schools, shopping centers, newspaper offices. If I had my way, I would call up the military and scrub Montfermeil and every place like it from the map."

"And you think your little plot will accomplish that? You're insane, Arnaud."

"Am I? If the people knew what I knew, they would be hiding under their beds in the dark. The people of France want action. Not only do we have the Islamic threat, but we have the Jewish influence to contend with. This country is being given away to foreigners piece by piece. The Jews are funneling our money to their own interests and to Israel. The European Union is a disaster and strips us of our sovereignty. There are those who still believe France belongs to the French and they will fight for the republic."

"According to the tape I heard, you have been preaching that message since 1968 and you're still an all-around bigot. Perhaps it is time to rethink your position now that you are facing charges of murder and sedition. The people, as you say, might want action, but not your kind. You can watch the revolution from your jail cell."

Arnaud shook his head as if the gesture might make all of the unpleasant events go away. He pulled his coat off the back of the chair and put it on, running his hands along the rumpled fabric. He slowly rolled the folder into a tube, twisting it in his hands as if he could make it disappear before jamming it into an interior pocket of his coat. A grin tugged at the corner of Arnaud's mouth as he walked out of the interrogation room, slamming the door behind him.

# 24 Approaching the Void

*She stands on a wooden platform. Light pours in from a nearby window, dances across her half-nude body. There is a series of ropes pulled taut just under her exposed breasts, encircling her legs. Six men appear and encase her in wood, yet she does not look at them. Her gaze remains steady on the window. The men pull the platform along the polished floor down a long, high-ceilinged hall. There are shadows on the wall where paintings once hung, their giant gilded frames discarded on the floor. There is a commotion ahead, the sound of men yelling, terror in their voices. For this, she will turn her head. Through the slats, she sees more men wrestling with another figure, also encased in wood save for her giant wings that flap at the air.*

Irène woke with a start from her nap. She had been having a variation of the same dream for more than a month. The Venus de Milo and Winged Victory being taken from the Louvre, perhaps before the

Nazi invasion, and disturbingly animated and alive, angry about the removal from their home. The sound of wings beating the air, the whoosh and crack, made her tremble even in the dream. Irène had no sense of herself in the dream, only that she was observing from a distance, out of the way. Or maybe she was hidden.

It was late afternoon and Martin sat in the armchair, leaning forward with elbows on his knees to watch the television. Sullivan and Christian had taken the flash drive and reel-to-reel tape to the detective's contact at Interpol, while Olivier was napping across the hall. Christian had been relieved that his father agreed to leave Montfermeil, at least for the time being. The rioting continued in the banlieues around Paris, but Montfermeil seemed to have quieted down.

"You were having the dream again," Martin said.

"Yes, but a different aspect. I saw Venus in a crate and dragged through the empty galleries. She was alive."

"I've had that dream again where Venus was in that grand room, but instead of light, it was filling with water."

"Why didn't you tell me?"

"I was going to, but so much has been going on."

"Was Peter there?"

"No, this time it was David trying to drown me." The memory of the dream made him shudder. "I'm starting to wonder if writing and publishing those poems has conjured him and Peter back up again."

"Our dreams are connected somehow," she said. "We are just missing a section."

"I am not sure I want to know what comes in between," he said.

They sat in silence and Martin channel-hopped to different newscasts, each showing looping video of scenes of burning cars and broken windows in the banlieues.

"I was thinking while you were asleep that we should

be considering our future," Martin said. "Sullivan thinks we should leave Paris—at least for a little while. If the newspaper publishes Lorit's story, we will have reporters camping outside the door. Maybe it's time to call Geoff de Courcy."

Irène sighed. "I already have, and there has been no response. I am sure he already knows about the situation. I believe Geoff has chosen not to get the organization involved. Sullivan is right. We should leave rue Rampon."

"What about the publishing house?"

"I was thinking of Julie," Irène said. "She would do an excellent job. Diane can run the Anglophile and Julie can run the press."

"Diane left a message on my mobile and said the riots made the news in the States. I haven't called her back. She hasn't answered my emails or texts or returned any of my phone calls in weeks. Her dad sounded pissy the last time I called, and he practically hung up on me."

Irène seemed unconcerned. "I think we should talk to Julie soon."

"We should also look inside the publishing house and see who could step up and work with Gerard if Julie says no, which she probably will."

"Poor, Gerard," Irène said. "He will be so upset if we go."

Martin reached over and took Irène's hand, brushing his finger over their shared tattoo. "It won't be forever," he reassured her. "We'll make it a holiday."

She gripped his hand tightly. "I am afraid, Martin. Maybe even more so than when I was going to face Frederick or when I thought you might not return to Paris. I don't want our lives to change. We've been so happy. I thought we would live out the rest of our days here with each other, and then after I'm gone, you and Christian will be here, and Diane and Sullivan."

Martin hated talking about what he considered the distant future. Whenever Irène mentioned she was getting older or said something like "after I'm gone," a void opened up in the future that seemed unimaginable. She reminded him of what a fortune teller in Montmartre had once told them: they were forever linked.

"Remember what she said, Martin? We have been together in some fashion since time began and will be together until there is no more time. I find that very comforting. It makes me less afraid of saying goodbye."

Martin felt a lump in his throat. "I *really* don't want to talk about this now."

"I know. Just promise that you will always come looking for me."

Martin put his arms around her. "Why do I always have to come looking for you?" he said, trying to lighten the mood. "Maybe you'll have to come looking for me next time."

Irène's throaty laugh buoyed him. "Through every mirror and down every rabbit hole until I find you."

On the television, the anchor announced breaking news. Crowds were gathering at Place de la République to protest the death of the boys in Clichy-sous-Bois. The image switched to shaky video from the square where hundreds of people could be seen gathered near the monument, illuminated by headlights. People were boiling out of the metro station entrance and even more stood around the edges watching the scene. Traffic was jammed and angry motorists blasted their horns as protestors darted in front of their cars.

Irène heard the sound of a distant helicopter and immediately looked up at the ceiling. She hated the sound of rotors. It brought her back to the riots in 1968 and the bomb that almost killed Martin. The camera switched again to an aerial shot of the square lit up by spotlights from the hovering news helicopter.

Martin's mobile buzzed and he saw it was an unidentified number. "I shouldn't answer it, but it might be Christian."

He pressed the answer button. "Hello?"

"You and Irène need to leave the apartment. Now." The voice was warped, unidentifiable as male or female, almost computerized.

"Who is this?"

"Arnaud is coming for you. Leave now."

The call disconnected and Martin swallowed hard, trying not to panic. "We have to go."

They tried calling Christian and Sullivan, but neither answered their mobiles. Martin and Irène pulled on their coats and went across the hall to retrieve Olivier. A note was taped to the door saying he had spoken to a friend and that his shop had been looted during the unrest. He was taking a bus back to Montfermeil.

"That stubborn man," Irène said.

A boisterous group of protesters headed toward the square met Martin and Irène as they left the building. Some carried signs denouncing the police. Some were already chanting anti-government slogans, raising their fists. Many had their faces covered with scarves or balaclavas, which frightened Irène. The protestors were in the middle of rue Rampon darting between cars, their headlights blinding. Across the street, guests were standing on the sidewalk under the hotel's awning or leaning out of their windows.

"We won't be able to get a taxi," Martin said. "And the metro will be jammed."

"We can get the Mercedes from the garage. I have the keys in my bag."

Irène held Martin's arm tightly as they walked along the wall toward Boulevard Voltaire. They kept their faces blank, trying not to show fear or panic. At the intersection, a wave of people halted them in their tracks. Police cars and vans were converging on the square, and Irène watched as some of the protestors shouted at the officers inside and banged on the cars with their fists.

"This could get ugly really fast," Martin shouted over the cacophony.

Martin and Irène stayed close to the shops along Boulevard Voltaire, inching their way up the sidewalk. It seemed all of Paris was gathering at Place de la République and they were caught in a strong current. The restaurants, bars and shops— usually packed and busy—had closed signs on their doors and the interior lights switched off.

Martin and Irène were almost to the next block when gunshots rang out. The stampede was almost instantaneous. People were running, yelling, screaming, jostling past, threatening to trample them. They had their backs pressed against the windows of a video game shop, buffeted by arms and legs hurdling past them in the rush toward Republic Square. A hand came out of the crowd and tried to snatch Irène's purse, but Martin swatted it away and then saw a prepubescent boy laughing as he held up Martin's watch that he had stolen instead. The boy was swallowed up by the crowd, the watchband glinting in the headlights and gone in seconds.

Irène felt as if her heart were going to explode out of her chest. She could feel her temples throbbing as a panic attack began to set in. She sagged against Martin and felt his arm slip around her shoulder. He banged on the door of the video game shop, but the two employees inside cowered in fear and shook their heads.

"It is a medical emergency," Martin shouted. "Urgence médical!"

"I think I'm going to faint," Irène said.

Across the street there was the sound of breaking glass. The liquor store was being looted, bottles passed hand over hand into the crowd as cheers went up. Other shops were being looted along the boulevard; even as the stampede continued, people were slipping in and out of broken windows with merchandise of all kinds—clothing, DVDs, food, whatever they could lay hands on.

An armored police van was caught in the middle of the street, revving its engine at the crowd that surrounded it. Protestors were chanting "we will not forgive or forget," while a young woman, holding a sign calling the police assassins, climbed onto the running board and screamed at the officers inside.

A brick paver bounced off the van's windshield, which spider webbed with cracks. The crowd began rocking the police van as if they meant to tip it over, chanting, "Fuck the police." A hatch in the roof of the van opened and a metal canister was tossed into the street. A moment later, it exploded. Tear gas.

"Cover your face," Martin screamed into Irène's ear.

She pulled the collar of her coat over her nose and mouth, but she could already feel her eyes stinging.

"We've got to go back," he said, propelling her forward as he coughed and gagged at the tear gas filling the night air.

They stepped away from the door of the video game store and a rock shattered the window. Youths poured in like ants, snatching and grabbing game consoles and cartridges they held aloft like trophies.

Martin put his arm tightly around Irène's waist and they were swept back toward rue Rampon. She could feel the shoes of others nipping at her heels, pushing past her, knocking her and Martin off balance. By the time they were back at the corner of rue Rampon, Irène's could barely stand, much less walk. The roar of the crowd and the blood throbbing in her ears deafened her. That she was still conscious at all was a small miracle.

Irène opened her eyes, the stinging dissipated, and saw the familiar surrounding of rue Rampon. Fragments of the tobacco shop's window lay in the street, as did several of those of Le Admiral. The small bar that had been installed in the lobby had been looted of its liquor. At the door of the apartment building, just as Martin pulled his latchkey from his pocket, Irène felt something poke her in the back. She turned to see a man in a suit with a scarf wrapped around his face. He was holding a gun.

"Don't shout or do anything stupid," the man said in a muffled voice. "Unlock the door and go inside."

Martin brazenly reached up and snatched the scarf away. It was Arnaud. He raised the gun and put it against Irène's temple, herding them into the lobby and shutting the door behind him.

# 25 Ghost Station

The sound of the demonstration at Republic Square was a muffled hum split by sirens and the roar of helicopter blades. Arnaud had closed all the curtains and turned off the lights except the lamp on Irène's desk.

Irène was slumped on the sofa, her breath still ragged and heavy from the massive panic attack she suffered after Arnaud forced them into the lobby. Irène had fallen to the tile floor gasping for breath and unable to move, but Arnaud said he would shoot them both, so Martin hauled her up the stairs. He could feel the barrel of the gun against the small of his back. Once inside the apartment, Arnaud had taken their mobile phones and smashed them on the floor, grinding them into the parquet with his heel.

Martin fought the urge to lunge and grab Arnaud's gun as he tread the floor to double-check the locks on the door and listen for movement in the hallway before going back to peer between the curtains.

"Irène needs a doctor," Martin said.

Arnaud poked the gun into Irène's shoulder and she swatted it away. "She is fine."

Flashing blue and red lights illuminated the curtains and Arnaud rushed to the window, cursing under his breath. Irène nudged Martin and pointed toward the floor. Martin looked down, trying to adjust his eyes to the gloom. Then he saw it: underneath the coffee table was the burner phone Sullivan had given them. Pierre must have knocked it off the table to play with. He would have to remember to give the cat extra treats. With one eye on Arnaud, Martin inched the phone toward him with the heel of his shoe.

Christian banged on the door of the interrogation room for nearly half an hour before Inspector Ruey freed him.

"My apologies," Ruey said, handing Christian his wallet and mobile. "Arnaud slipped out of the building."

Christian dialed Martin's number, but it went straight to voicemail. So did Irène's. So did his father's.

"You need to send officers to rue Rampon right now."

"There is a riot at Place de la République," Ruey said. "It is crawling with police. Arnaud would be stupid to go there."

"Arnaud has nothing to lose."

Christian ran out of the police headquarters and found Sullivan leaning against a sleek black Mercedes, tapping cigar ash onto the sidewalk.

"Arnaud is gone," Christian shouted. "We've got to get back to rue Rampon."

Sullivan held open the back door of the Mercedes and climbed in beside him.

"Whose car is this?" Christian asked as the car accelerated into traffic.

"I am sorry we must meet again under these circumstances," the driver said.

Behind the wheel was Geoff de Courcy. He wore a black coat, his gloved hands gripped the steering wheel. His slick-backed hair was impeccably groomed and his chiseled features had barely aged in the last decade.

De Courcy drove toward Pont Notre-Dame, expertly dodging parked cars and pedestrians. "This situation escalated much faster than I expected. But you have my word that we will rescue them."

Christian felt a knot in his stomach. "Rescue who?"

De Courcy regarded Christian in the rearview mirror. "Arnaud has taken Martin and Irène hostage at rue Rampon."

De Courcy whipped the Mercedes into a tight space between two cars along a narrow street on the westside of Paris. It was the same street Sullivan and Christian had tracked the Range Rover. Just ahead of them, the narrow street opened into the traffic circle at Place Victor Hugo.

"Go inside the café and tell the maître d' you want to be seated in the private dining room," de Courcy said. "Follow him and wait for me. I'll be along in a moment."

Once inside the café, the countenance of the maître d' didn't flinch when Christian asked for the private room. He hoped there might be some reaction, something in the man's eyes to show surprise or fear, but he showed no emotion as he led them to a small room dominated by a large dining table.

"We were so close the other day," Sullivan said, pulling out a chair and sitting down. "I wonder who's joining us?"

"What are we doing here?" Christian asked. "We should be at rue Rampon."

De Courcy came in a moment later. "Up, up, Sullivan. We're not meeting here."

He pulled a key from his pocket and went to a small door at the back corner of the room and unlocked it. De Courcy swung open the wooden door to reveal the latticework of an old elevator cage.

"You have got to be kidding," Sullivan exclaimed.

"When we get to the bottom, step out quickly onto the platform."

The trio crowded into the tiny elevator, felt it give a little when Sullivan added his weight to the car. Somewhere below, there was a roaring sound, and a gust of warm wind blew up the shaft and buffeted them as the elevator made its descent.

As soon as they stepped out of the elevator, it whirred back to life and ascended again, leaving the three of them standing on the platform of an empty metro station. No, not empty, Christian thought, abandoned. The tracks were still in place and a few harsh, industrial lights illuminated the station, but its walls and ceiling were a sooty black and grey from disuse. The remnants of old advertisements were barely visible behind the grime.

"What is this place?" Sullivan asked over the roar of a train passing in a nearby tunnel.

"A ghost station," Christian said. "There are a few around the city. When I was on the streets, I heard some of the kids talk about living and hiding down here, but I thought they were making it up."

"This way," de Courcy said.

Christian and Sullivan followed the man down the platform until they came to a door marked "Danger - Electrical Equipment." There was a keypad on the wall and de Courcy quickly typed in a long sequence of numbers. There was a buzzing sound and he pushed through the door and motioned for Christian and Sullivan to follow. They walked down a dim corridor alongside rusting control panels, fire equipment and other refuse from the subway system. At a second door, de

Courcy pulled a keycard from his pocket and swiped it over a sensor pad.

There was another buzzing sound and de Courcy opened the door and stood aside. The room was a sterile concrete bunker. There was a long table full of computers. Suspended on the wall were banks of television monitors that were rotating images from cameras placed along streets and at intersections around Paris. There were four people hunched over the computers, typing in commands or looking up at the monitors.

"We've got the feed from the hotel," one of the computer techs said as de Courcy approached him.

"Put it up," he said, standing under the monitors.

A camera was trained on Irène's apartment, where only a sliver of light could be seen through closed curtains all along the balcony.

"Do we have eyes on the back entrances and surrounding streets?" de Courcy asked.

"Yes, sir," the tech said, punching up another series of images from around rue Rampon. The streets were still thronged with protestors.

De Courcy beckoned Christian and Sullivan toward the banks of computers and monitors. "Play back 17:41."

A technician typed in commands and one of the monitors popped up a recorded image of the security camera outside Le Admiral aimed toward the front door of rue Rampon. In the throng of people, Christian saw Martin and Irène at the door and then a man appear out of the crowd and force them back inside. Christian wanted to be sick, tried to breathe deeply to control his panic.

"My father is at our apartment across the hall," Christian said.

"Your father is safe," de Courcy said.

"Interpol is sending agents," Sullivan said, furiously

chewing on another cigar. "They'll get them out."

De Courcy laughed under his breath. "Your support of Interpol is admirable, Monsieur Sullivan, but they are always late to the party. We have an extractor in place."

Sullivan pulled the cigar from his mouth. "An extractor? You mean an assassin."

Christian's mobile phone rang, and he frantically pulled it from his jeans pocket. It was the number of the burner phone Sullivan had given to Irène.

"Don't say anything," de Courcy said. "Let them speak first."

Christian's hand shook as he flipped open the phone. There was a voice, but it wasn't Martin or Irène. De Courcy took the phone from Christian and gave it to one of the computer techs, who attached a cable to it and piped the sound for the whole room to hear.

It was Arnaud's voice.

"Cut the power," de Courcy said.

The screens switched to a series of security cameras in and around Republic Square. The crowd was massive, snaking into the streets that converged at the monument and fountain. On Boulevard Voltaire, the police were in a standoff with rioters, who were carrying bottles and pieces of lumber. As the camera image rotated to another location not far from rue Rampon, a gaggle of men were already engaged with police officers who had formed a line. Then it went dark.

## 26 Just Like a Bright Silvery Mist

The power cut plunged the apartment at rue Rampon into darkness, and Arnaud shouted for Martin and Irène to remain seated or he would shoot them. He parted the curtains over the balcony doors to see what was happening outside, sending a sliver of weak light across the living room. Martin gripped the burner phone he had hidden in his pocket, hoped that it had connected to Christian or Sullivan.

Arnaud grabbed Irène under the arm, pulled her off the couch and ordered her to light candles.

"Don't try anything foolish," he said.

Irène took the pillar candles from the top of the piano and brought them to the coffee table as Arnaud trained his gun on her. She reached into her pocket for her cigarette lighter and Arnaud put the gun to her temple.

"I'll take that," he said, lighting the candles.

"What is your end game, Arnaud?" Martin asked. "Sitting here in the dark all night?"

Arnaud reached inside his coat pocket and pulled out a set of thick documents folded in half and tossed them to Martin.

"My endgame is immunity from prosecution and to see both of you in jail."

Irène began to laugh. It grew in volume until she was choking and cackling.

"Silence!" Arnaud shouted, leaning over her.

"You're delusional," Martin scoffed. "Do you think the government is going to let you walk away from the murders you've committed and the scheme you had cooking in Montfermeil?"

Arnaud smiled, his face lit by the dancing candle flames.

"I have evidence of all the kickbacks and money laundering performed by André Sarde's syndicate for members of the Senate, the police, the intelligence agency and beyond, stretching back to the 1970s. Before I came here, I arranged to have that evidence released if anything happens to me. It would collapse the government—from the president's office to the gendarmerie in every corner of France. The riot happening outside would be nothing compared to the outrage that would follow the publication of what I know. The politicians, the ones in power, would never allow that to happen. They know I am serious, so the deal is being made. Lorit's story will never see print and you will be exposed for colluding with organized crime. No one gets in my way. Did you really believe that I would not have insurance in case something like this ever happened?"

The blast of a police siren made Arnaud jump. He went to the French doors and peered through the parted curtains. There was a sound like ice clinking into a glass, and Arnaud staggered back from the door clutching at his throat. Blood seeped between his fingers and his eyes widened in surprise.

Arnaud staggered toward Irène, his gun raised. Martin sprang from the couch and lunged toward Arnaud, yelling for

Irène to get down. Arnaud fired once before Martin tackled him. They spun around and fell back onto the coffee table, the wood cracking and giving under their combined weight. Books, glasses and lit candles went flying, and Martin heard Irène scream in terror.

Martin was pinned underneath Arnaud's body, which twitched and spasmed as he bled out. He pushed at Arnaud's body and felt a twinge in his abdomen, splinters and glass digging into his back. Martin felt something wet on his face and realized Arnaud's blood was soaking him. The shot through the window had pierced his jugular vein.

"Martin, get up," Irène yelled. "The apartment is on fire!"

With all his might, Martin shoved Arnaud's body off him and struggled to sit up. Smoke was starting to fill the room and the sofa was burning like some strange bonfire. Another candle had rolled toward the French doors and set the curtains ablaze. In slow motion, Martin watched as Irène snatched the burning curtains from the door and stamped on them with her feet. She managed to get the door open and kicked them out onto the balcony.

Martin staggered to his feet, pulled off his coat and started beating at the flames on the sofa. He felt weak and dizzy and his body ached all over, especially his gut. He stumbled backwards, almost tripping over Arnaud's body. He was going to pass out.

"Irène," he called out weakly, and then clutched at his stomach, suddenly wracked with a pain he had never felt before.

Irène caught him as he fell and helped ease him to the floor. "We have to get out, Martin," she said. "Get up!"

As Martin lost consciousness, he tried to reach up and touch Irène's face, which was haloed in the fire that raged above them.

Smoke filled Irène's lungs and the fire singed her hair, throwing hot sparks on the back of her sweater. She, too, was on the verge of collapse. Opening the door to the balcony had only fueled the fire, which was now engulfing the apartment.

Martin had been hit by Arnaud's bullet. There was blood seeping from his abdomen. She managed to stand and reach down to grab Martin under his arms, then summoned all her strength to drag him toward the front door. When she realized the fire was licking at the doorframe, the statues of Venus de Milo and Winged Victory seemed to be strangely in motion, and for a moment she couldn't look away. Irène choked on the smoke, coughing so hard that she saw stars. When she was able to focus again, she tugged at Martin and pulled him down the hallway toward her bedroom. If they could get out onto the balcony, someone would rescue them.

Irène remembered there was a fire extinguisher under the kitchen sink. She lay Martin down gently and stumbled into the dark kitchen, grabbed the dishtowel from the counter and brought it back into the hall. Irène pulled up Martin's sweater, sticky and dark with his own and Arnaud's blood, and could see the wound in his stomach. She pressed the towel to the wound, pushing it slightly into the tiny opening left by the bullet. Irène went back into the kitchen and hefted the fire extinguisher into her arms, having forgotten just how heavy it was. She unhooked the hose and turned on the valve.

Half of the living room was engulfed in flames. The piano and the precious photos of Jean-Louis and her parents were burning, the heat making the strings inside the piano strangely resonate with sound as if some ghost was plucking at them. Arnaud's body was also burning among the splintered remains of the coffee table as if he was on a funeral pyre.

Irène aimed the fire extinguisher toward the door and tried to lay down a line of foam to block the flames from advancing toward the hallway with little success. She hosed down her desk and the books, the walls, spraying wildly until the tank was empty. Her body ached from the exertion and she could feel the muscles in her shoulders and back pulling, but adrenaline was coursing through her.

She dragged Martin through the bedroom door and was about to close it behind her when she felt an odd stillness. Irène looked down the hallway and saw that the dancing flames seemed to be frozen mid-flicker. The roiling smoke collecting at the ceiling and drifting toward her floated like clouds. The sound of distant sirens and voices from the street had gone silent. The only noise she could hear was her own ragged breathing and the pounding of blood in her ears. Pierre ran down the hallway toward the bedroom, suspended in midair, his paws not touching the floor. Irène put her hand on Martin's stomach applying pressure, but even the blood seemed to have stopped gushing from the bullet wound.

"Irène."

The voice startled her so much that she fell back. Frederick Dubois stood above her, holding out his hand. She reached up, expecting him to be ghostly, but his hand was warm and firm.

"There isn't much time," Frederick said. "You'll have to find Martin and bring him back yourself."

"Martin is here. We need an ambulance."

Frederick turned toward her dressing table and the large mirror above it. It took Irène a moment to realize the mirror wasn't reflecting them and the bedroom, but had turned into a silvery mist that, like the smoke, seemed to float motionless.

"Once you go through, there will be wrong turns and distractions," Frederick said, his voice calm and reassuring. "This is going to be difficult, mon cher, but I have faith in you."

"I don't understand..."

"Come," Frederick said scooping Irène into his arms and carrying her to the dressing table. He sat her gently on the edge in the center of the table, her feet not touching the floor. "It will be easier if you simply just push back and let go."

"Where am I going?"

"To the other side of the mirror."

Irène sensed a void was opening behind her, a gentle tugging at her clothes and hair, like a vacuum was pulling her in.

"I don't like your riddles," she said.

Frederick threw back his head in laughter. "Stubborn and defiant until the bitter end."

Irène slowly slid back until she could see the gauzy mist of the mirror in her peripheral vision. There was a piercingly cold dampness against her back that made her wince. Frederick was no longer in the room, and she became aware that time had not stopped but simply slowed to an almost imperceptible crawl. The flames were consuming in infinitesimal degrees; Pierre moved a millimeter closer and the blood that seeped from Martin's unconscious body was soaking the towel one fiber at a time.

Irène took a deep breath and leaned back until the mirror, where she had first seen Martin staring back at her a decade ago, swallowed her up in darkness.

## 27 the Wood Between the Worlds

Voices woke her. They were indistinct and distant as if coming from another room or a great height. Even before she opened her eyes, Irène could sense strong light. It made the inside of her eyelids glow. There was also a gentle current of air dappling over her face and body. It was cool and soothing, and carried with it a familiar scent—a mixture of dust and antiquity she had known since she was a child. And the voices again, closer and urgent, but this time arriving on an echo.

Irène opened her eyes slowly, letting small slivers of light in. She did this several times until she could stand the glare that seemed to be coming from all around her. When she was able to make her eyes focus, she stared up at the high, vaulted ceiling. Irène was lying on some type of bench or divan underneath an arched window. She turned her head slightly and could see that she was in a long corridor full of similar windows. The floor was tiled in an intricate diamond pattern leading toward a grand archway.

Outside the windows, the clouds seemed to move in time-lapse, rushing and slowing down to plunge the hall into dimness or illuminate it with an almost unbearable glow. Irène sat up slowly. There was a pain in her chest so sharp it made her catch her breath, but it passed and she was able to sit with her feet touching the floor. That's when she noticed the empty pedestals along the corridor. There had once been statues lining both sides. The air was filled with motes of dust that shimmered in the sunlight.

"Faites attention!"

They were the first words Irène had understood since she had awoken in this familiar place. She leaned forward to get a better look at what was happening beyond the grand arch and could see a wide staircase. Down the center, a ramp made of wooden planks had been built.

Irène stood up, feeling wobbly on her feet. How had she gotten there? Where had she been before? She couldn't remember. She waited for panic to overtake her at this complete lack of recall, but she stood there, breathing normally, an odd calm enveloping her. She took a tentative step forward, waiting for the sharp pain in her chest to return. When it didn't, she walked slowly toward the grand arch and the stairway beyond.

The ramp was made of five long boards supported with wooden blocks and crossbeams at regular intervals, up the stairs and over the landings. Oval skylights lit the scene like a theatrical production: a dozen men guiding a tall statue encased in a wooden crate on a rolling platform down the staircase. At the very top of the stairs, a pulley and cable dangled from a gallows-like structure that had been built high above the marble prow of a ship where the statue had stood. The men had lifted and winched the statue onto the rolling platform and built the crate around it for safekeeping. Through the top of the crate, two giant wings protruded, thrown back as if ready to fly.

It was the Winged Victory of Samothrace and this was unmistakably the Louvre. Irène felt a wave of relief wash over her that she was still in Paris and in a familiar place, but there was something off about it that she still couldn't quite fathom. It was as if her memory was surrounded by fog. There seemed to be only this moment and nothing else before it.

"Disturbing and peaceful at the same time, isn't it?"

The voice came from behind her and she whirled to find a man standing there. It was Jean-Louis. He looked young, like the first time she had seen him at the hotel through her binoculars, and wore a beautifully tailored suit. A cigarette dangled from his bottom lip, which curled into a grin. Irène gasped in surprise, but his smile and the outstretched hand he offered sent a wave of relief through her body.

Irène took Jean-Louis' hand and he pulled her into a passionate embrace. She melted into him, wrapping her arms around him, feeling the warmth of his body against her.

"Is this a dream or…"

Jean-Louis pulled an ornate cigarette case from his jacket pocket. "I believe this is your brand."

He presented the case to Irène and she pulled out a Gauloises and put it to her lips. Jean-Louis produced a silver lighter from his pocket and lit the cigarette for her. It was strong and unfiltered, yet she did not cough like she expected to as smoke filled her lungs.

"How did I get here?" she asked. "How are you… here?"

"I've been waiting for you. Now we can start again."

Jean-Louis kissed her tenderly, and she happily returned it, lightheaded and giddy as when they first met. The sound of the men as they struggled to bring the Winged Victory down the grand Daru staircase interrupted her bliss. She turned to scold them, but the men and the statue itself seemed to flicker, as if a frame was missing from a film. She looked out the window into the courtyard of the Louvre and saw concrete and a large, empty fountain. That was wrong somehow. She shook her head as if that might clear her memory and, for a moment, she saw something else: a tall glass pyramid, dancing fountains and hundreds of people milling about. It was as if another image was superimposed over the courtyard and, just as quickly as the apparition appeared, it faded away.

"Did you see that?" she asked Jean-Louis, her tongue thick.

"You had a glimpse of something else. The wood between the worlds."

She had heard those words before, not from Jean-Louis, but Frederick. Like some kind of magic spell being broken, her mind was flooded with memories. Jean-Louis cold and dead in the morgue, her years locked inside rue Rampon, Martin's arrival and their shared tattoos.

Martin.

Irène clutched at her skull and felt herself sinking to the floor, but Jean-Louis caught her and eased her back onto the bench where she had woken up.

"Where is Martin?" she gasped. "What's happening?"

"We must go now," Jean-Louis said urgently. "I love you so much."

Irène grabbed at his lapels. "Martin is in trouble."

The museum phased out again and she momentarily could see Martin on the floor of her bedroom at rue Rampon, Pierre curled up next to him nuzzling his face, as the apartment continued to burn.

The present flicked away again, like changing a television channel, and Irène was back in the Louvre. She sat up too quickly and it felt like a knife was turning in her chest. Then it stopped, as if some wire had snapped and she was cut loose from the pain. Irène felt completely in the here and now—wherever that was exactly—and a numbing fright came over her.

Jean-Louis was gone. The men moving the Winged Victory were at the bottom of the staircase and one was walking toward her. He was of medium height, dark hair, dressed in work clothes. The sleeves of his shirt were rolled up to the elbow and sweat stains appeared next to his suspenders and around his collar. As the man moved toward her, he pulled out a handkerchief and wiped at his face and hands before stuffing it back in his pocket.

The man smiled and knelt down on one knee in front of Irène. "Did you fall asleep?" he asked gently. "We're almost done for today."

"I..." Irène's voice faltered. Once again, her tongue felt thick in her mouth and she was incredibly thirsty.

"You must have had a bad dream," the man said. "You are not yourself."

It was almost dark outside and lights had been switched on to illuminate the corridor. Across the hall, she could see herself reflected in the window. She was eleven years old, still wearing her school uniform, her hair pinned back. The man kneeling before her was her father.

"Père," she said, her lips trembling.

Irène's father pulled her into his arms. "What is wrong? You are frightening me."

She flung her arms around his neck and sobbed. He smelled like sweat and the aftershave her mother had bought him for Christmas. Before the Nazis, before the world changed, before her parents disappeared and were murdered in a concentration camp. Irène clung to her father's neck, and he held her fiercely, gently stroking her back as he always did when she was upset.

Irène opened her eyes and could see herself once again reflected in the dark window. And there was someone else there, too. A half-figure, as if he was made of the glass, or coming through it. He held up his hand and she could see a tattoo—the interlocking cross. She looked at her own hand and could see it there, slowly fading away.

It was Martin, calling her back, his face etched with fear. Irène knew if she closed her eyes, she would lose him forever. But how could she let go of her father once she had found him again? Soon they would return to their little apartment near Notre-Dame and dinner would be waiting.

Martin held out his hand and she let go of her father to take it. And as soon as she did, it was like the television channel changed again. There was the sound of wood splintering, glass breaking, urgent voices.

"He has a belly wound. I need that pressure bandage."

She felt a sharp jab in her arm and cried out, but she was about to pass through another mirror. Something was taking shape just beyond it: the silhouette of a building with large, domed towers. Her feet left the floor and she sailed through her own reflection, the building revealing itself as an ornate château surrounded by lush gardens. Martin stood before two great open doors, his arms spread wide in welcome.

From behind him, two shadowy figures appeared and grabbed Martin, dragging him back inside the château before the doors slammed shut. Irène ran toward the château, calling Martin's name, but the pain in her chest returned and felled her. She felt her body convulse, like electricity running through her entire body. Distantly, there was the sound of music—the ascending melody of Barber's *Adagio for Strings*, the same music that had been playing when she met Martin so many years ago.

Irène rose to her feet, approached the doors and tugged at the handles. Locked. She stepped back, far enough to give herself a running start, then hurled herself at the doors. Passed through them like a spirit.

*Through every mirror and down every rabbit hole until I find you.*

# 28 a Rope of Light

He woke in silence, leaning against what felt like a fence. Ahead of him, down a long corridor, a set of double doors was outlined in blazing white light that seeped from around the frame. Through the keyhole, a tiny spotlight sent a beam of light down the long hallway and pulsed against his midsection. Martin ran his hand slowly through the beam of light and felt a sharp pain in his stomach. It made him gasp and double over. As soon as he removed his hand, the pain went away.

Just at the edge of his memory, Martin knew that something had happened to him, but what exactly, he couldn't remember. Was he in danger? His memories were hazy, inconsequential.

Martin pulled himself upright against the oddly textured wall he was leaning against. He was stunned to find that it wasn't a wall, but a tall wooden crate. Through the unevenly placed slats, the light from the other end of the corridor revealed a white stomach, exposed breasts and a familiar face cocked at an angle. The Venus de Milo. Ropes encircled her waist and looped over her armless shoulders.

The doors at the other end of the corridor opened, flooding the corridor with a harsh, clinical light. Someone was approaching, silhouetted in the brilliance coming from the room beyond. There was something familiar about his walk and the curly ringlets of blond hair set aglow from the backlight. It was Paul Richardson. He looked just like he did the first time Martin saw him at the hospital: young, piercing eyes, a strange half-smile on his face. He was dressed in coveralls that were stained with grease and dirt.

"What are you doing here?" Martin asked incredulously.

"I told you I would see you again soon," Paul said.

A memory of Paul and another man surfaced. They were in a bar or a hotel lobby. "I saw you with someone. Recently. Wasn't it?"

Paul reached out and pushed Martin's bangs out of his eyes, a tender and intimate touch. "Yes. I just wanted to make sure you were ready to see me again. So that you would trust my words."

"Why is Venus here? What is this place?"

"You haven't been here yet."

"I don't understand," Martin said.

"We need to finish this. Help me push."

Martin realized that the crate containing Venus was on a wheeled platform. Paul kicked away a block of wood that had been holding it in place and began to tug on the crate.

"Careful. We almost tipped her over bringing her off the truck."

Together, Martin and Paul pulled the crate slowly down the corridor. Martin slipped his hand between the slats and could feel the cool marble against his palm, the rough unevenness of the drapery that flowed around her hips.

As they approached the doorway, there was the sound of

wood splintering and cheerful voices. Clouds moved over the sun and plunged the room into shadow as they wheeled Venus through the double doors. Martin could see more workmen, dressed in the same coveralls, uncrating a statue in the middle of the salon that was unmistakably the Winged Victory. Around the perimeter of the room, other statues stood beside paintings leaning against the wall. It was a treasure trove of art.

"Shouldn't this be in the Louvre?" Martin asked.

"It should be, but here it will be protected."

"Protected from what?"

Paul laughed out loud. "Surely you haven't forgotten your history lessons so quickly?"

One of the workers, a man with a large belly and beard, came up and whispered in Paul's ear. It was the man Martin had seen Paul with in that other place he couldn't quite remember.

"We're done here. The men will finish the uncrating."

They walked back down the corridor, and Paul put his arm around Martin's neck. "I won't see you again after this."

Martin felt anxious, fear rising from the pit of his stomach. He was aware of his heartbeat and the blood pumping in his veins. His whole body felt like it was throbbing.

"I'll see you when I'm home again. I promise."

Paul pulled Martin into an embrace and kissed him gently on the lips. "The next part is going to be very difficult. You'll be tempted by other voices, futures past. Only one voice matters—Irène's."

At the mention of her name, Martin felt a strange sensation wash over him. Like he was waking up. He had momentarily forgotten Irène.

"You're about to find the answer to a question. Most people don't get to know—not like this, anyway—but you and Irène are not like others. It was synchronicity that brought you together and that will keep you together. Remember that."

Martin felt lightheaded. "I'm afraid."

He closed his eyes and let Paul guide him through dark rooms and drafty halls until they reached a giant arched doorway.

"This is the final gate," Paul said, his voice strangely disembodied. It seemed to come from every direction. "Beyond this door is a hall of mirrors. It will look familiar, but it is not that place. Irène is looking for you, but there isn't much time. Follow only her voice."

As if by magic, the door opened, revealing a long hallway full of golden statuary holding candelabras. Along the left wall were archways inlaid with tall mirrors that reflected a row of arcaded windows overlooking a garden.

"Is this Versailles?" Martin whispered, and he turned to look at Paul, but the boy was no longer there.

Martin cautiously stepped through the doorway and looked up. There were rows of crystal chandeliers that should have been suspended from the ceiling that depicted Louis XIV's military victories from the 17th century, but instead the fixtures seemed to float underneath a tunnel of starry night sky. Through the windows, the day-lit garden stretched toward infinity. There were fountains, hedgerows and flowers so dazzling in reds, yellows and purples that the sight of them momentarily transfixed Martin. At the far end of the garden, a white light glowed so intensely that it blotted out what lay beyond.

A distant roaring sound caught Martin's ear and he turned to look for its source. Above him, something streaked the sky. It was a shooting star, or perhaps a comet. It's daylight outside, he thought. How can it be night?

The untold number of stars and the floating nebula that he couldn't name mesmerized him. It was as if the sky was rotating, bringing different galaxies and star clusters into view, like an elaborate planetarium. The roaring noise was emanating from above, too, and Martin realized it was the sound of space—

dark matter resonating across the universe. A planet came into view, a pale yellow ball full of hazy, roiling clouds. A voice from behind Martin identified the orb.

"That's Venus."

Martin turned and saw Peter Davis standing next to one of the mirrors. He wore a long black trench coat like the one Martin had bought him for Christmas at a vintage store in Memphis. When they were still in love. He was young and beautiful, just as Martin remembered him from high school. Before he died.

Peter held out his hand and Martin walked toward him, mindful of Paul's warning that other voices would try and distract him.

"There's nothing to be afraid of now," Peter said gently. "Look."

He gestured at the mirror, and reflected there was the lake outside Memphis where he and Martin had first made love. They had been to a movie, held hands, shared their first kiss and driven to the lake in Peter's jeep. They had held each other's wet bodies in the dark water as a galaxy of stars unfurled above them.

Martin could feel the water, Peter's arms around him and their lips finding each other's in the darkness. It was like he was being infused again with the euphoria of that night, its heady feeling blotting out the future that would come after: Peter's instability, their separation and their duel in the hallway.

"Why are you showing me this?" Martin asked. "I said goodbye to you long ago."

Peter stood before Martin, an almost beatific smile on his face. "We could have that night back again—just like in your poems. A different future."

"That's not possible."

Peter put his arms around Martin and pulled him into a deep embrace. "Oh, you know it is possible. The things you've seen…"

Martin fought the urge to settle into Peter's embrace, the smell of him that had long ago faded was familiar again. The brand of cologne, the clove cigarettes they had both smoked after sex, and the particular scent of his skin that was like vanilla.

Over Peter's shoulder, Martin could see that the scene in the mirror had changed. He and Peter were older, walking along a street in Paris, and they held the hands of a young, blonde girl who walked between them. Their daughter.

"You see," Peter said. "Things should have been different. It would be a beautiful life."

Martin buried his head in Peter's shoulder. The desire to say yes was strong. The word bubbled on his lips. Inside the mirror, he watched himself, Peter and their child turn a corner, and he realized it was rue Rampon. They were walking toward the hotel. Across the street, on the balcony above, a young man was sitting at a table reading the newspaper. A woman came out carrying a baby and sat down across from him. That's not right, Martin thought. What are they doing there?

Martin let go of Peter and held him at arm's length. "Where is Irène? Why isn't she on her balcony?"

"Different choices," Peter said.

Martin felt heat on his back and turned to see that the light at the far end of the garden was moving closer, enveloping the landscape.

"We have to hurry now," Peter said, a note of desperation in his voice. He held out his hand again.

Martin backed away. "I loved you so much. I wanted to be with you. Marry you. Have children. But that's not what happened. There's no going back. Not for me."

A look of resignation clouded Peter's face and he walked back toward the mirror. As he stepped into the silvery mist that appeared there, he turned back to Martin. "Goodbye." And then he was gone.

Martin heard a frantic voice call his name. It was Irène searching for him. He called out to her just as a current of pain flooded through his abdomen. Martin felt like he might pass out and started to sit down, but two hands under his arms pulled him back up.

"Don't sit down. I know you're tired. So am I."

David McLaren stood before him, also dressed in black— baseball cap, jeans and a baggy sweater all dripping with water, which pooled around his feet on the marble floor.

"Why are you here?"

"To show you something."

"I've seen enough," Martin said, backing away from him. "You shouldn't be here."

David grabbed Martin's arm. "Come on," he said, exasperated.

Martin felt as if he were gliding above the floor as David pulled him along. There was also an odd tugging from above. He looked up and Venus was now directly overhead. They passed directly underneath the southern pole, the inky blackness of space only visible at its edges. The gravity of the planet seemed to be pulling at him.

At the other end of the hall, David stopped in front of a mirror and pointed at it. Inside, Martin could see himself and David at the Memphis airport. It was the day they had returned from Paris, in love and planning their lives together. They pulled their luggage from the conveyor belt and it was in that moment, Martin remembered, that they both saw David's parents waiting in the arrival hall.

"I don't want to see this again," Martin said, his stomach churning with anxiety. "I was there. I know what happened."

"Just watch," David implored.

David's parents approached, their faces grim and determined to rescue their son, but instead of walking to them,

David grabbed Martin's hand and told him to run. The scene shifted and they were at a ticket counter. The departure board behind it labeled "Paris." The vision shifted again and they were getting out of a taxi at rue Rampon. Irène was waiting to meet them.

Martin felt a surge of happiness that made his entire body tingle.

"This is the way it was supposed to be," David said, his voice trembling with emotion. "It's still waiting for us."

David pulled him closer until their noses were practically touching the mirror, which seemed to be dissolving into an opaque mist. The desire to step through the mirror with David was overwhelming. It was burning the edges of his memory, erasing what had come after that day at the airport: his return to Paris alone to live with Irène at rue Rampon, his relationship with Euan, Diane and Sullivan, and meeting Christian.

Christian.

Martin stepped back from the mirror so quickly that he tripped over his own feet and fell hard to the floor. "What happens to Christian?"

"It doesn't matter," David said. Water streamed off him like he was in a shower or a rainstorm.

Martin was on his knees, struggling to stand. "I want to see."

The mirror shimmered, almost like a body of water flattening out, and another scene appeared there: police clashing with a group of youths, rocks and bottles thrown, buildings on fire. Gunfire erupts and the youths retreat behind a hastily assembled barricade of burned out cars, shopping carts and smoldering furniture dragged from houses. As tear gas and smoke swirls, Christian appears in the middle of the street dragging a wounded boy toward the sidewalk. A riot officer, truncheon raised, breaks from the police line and strikes Christian across the back of the head. He falls lifeless to the pavement beside the boy as their blood mingles and runs into the gutter.

Martin's scream was soundless, the polarity of the mirror reversing to show him kneeling on the floor of the hall of mirrors, the blazing white light engulfing the windows behind him.

The great doors at the end of the hallway opened, swinging on screeching hinges, the sound combined with the great roar of noise coming from above. Venus was so close that Martin could see through the layers of atmosphere to its rocky, grey surface.

"Martin!"

Irène was running toward him down the hall. He felt a wave of relief wash over him, but as she drew closer, Martin could see the terror on her face. He stood up, clutching at his stomach as another bolt of pain coursed through him, and felt something warm and sticky. It was blood.

Irène grabbed Martin's hand and saw that their shared tattoo was forming and reforming, the ink appearing and disappearing like ripples under the skin. Then the white blazing light blotted out his vision. He felt Irène's arms around him, tugging at him, and they were falling into some void. If this was the end, at least they were together.

And as if a switch had been flipped, the light disappeared and he was standing with his arms wrapped around Irène in her bedroom at rue Rampon.

"I found you," Irène said over and over again, as if in some kind of trance. She rained kisses on his forehead, cheeks and mouth.

"What's happened to your room?"

The room seemed narrower somehow and he couldn't quite see the edges of it from his peripheral vision. It was like looking at the room through a tube or a telescope. They looked in the mirror above Irène's dressing table, but they had no reflection.

"This isn't real." Martin was drowsy, wanted to go to sleep.

Irène shook him hard. "Stay awake."

A face appeared in the mirror so suddenly that it made her cry out in fear before she recognized that it was Frederick Dubois looking back at them.

"Ah, there you are," he said, a jolly tone in his voice. "That was something, wasn't it? The Yolngu people in the Arnhem Land of Australia call it the Barnumbirr, a very important ceremony. They wait for Venus to rise and as she approaches, she draws a rope of light behind her that allows them to talk to their dead loved ones. It's quite spectacular."

Martin felt Irène's arms tighten around him. "What is this place?" he asked.

"Alice called it the Looking-Glass House." He considered his words and then nodded with a smile. "Yes, I like that."

Frederick's countenance changed and he looked back over his shoulder.

"I'm afraid, Martin, that the return trip is going to be... well... painful. Like being shot, actually."

The memory of Arnaud firing the gun and the apartment on fire materialized in Martin's brain.

"Irène, you are to be commended for your bravery and selflessness. Because, just like Martin, the crossing will hurt. A lot. But the good news is, you'll both live."

"I'm ready," Irène said.

"That's my White Queen. Okay, now both of you just let yourselves go limp. Don't try to fight it. Irène, you come first. Oh, and Martin—when you come to, tell Sullivan or Christian to call Diane. She needs to get to David McLaren's house as quickly as possible. There's still time to avert a tragedy."

Irène kissed Martin on both cheeks. "Don't be afraid. I'll see you soon." She sat down on the edge of the vanity, swung her legs around and disappeared into the mirror.

Martin felt pressure against his body, as if he were lifting off the ground, as he approached the mirror. Like Irène, he sat on the edge of the vanity and saw the glass turn a shimmering opaque. Martin closed his eyes, let his body go limp as Frederick said, and fell back into darkness.

Martin came to with a start, his entire body racked with pain. He gasped and tried to sit up, but two hands held him firmly back. He was able to open his eyes and see Christian hovering above him. Martin felt something covering his nose and mouth and tried to pull it away.

"Don't take off the oxygen mask," Christian begged him. His face was streaked with black ash and tears. "We've got to get him out of here."

"The defibrillation did the trick," Sullivan said. "Irène's pulse is steady. We can move her."

Martin turned his head and could see Irène on the floor next to him. Sullivan adjusted Irène's oxygen mask as he checked her pulse.

Martin reached out for Irène's hand and squeezed it tightly. Irène's eyes popped open and she turned her head slightly to look at him. A weak smile darted across her face and Martin felt her hand tighten around his. They were both safe. Christian was here. Sullivan was here. Everything was okay.

Then he remembered Frederick's words.

## 29 Against Fate

Diane accelerated through the intersection, running the red light and causing a barrage of horns to honk in complaint from other cars that narrowly missed colliding with her. Abraham sat in the passenger seat, holding onto the handle over the door and both feet pressed into the floorboard, his body slightly lifted off the seat. He didn't speak, but made little grunting sounds as Diane broke every speed limit and traffic law.

When she pulled up in front of David's house in Germantown, there were no cars in the driveway and no lights were visible from the street.

"Stay in the car, Dad. I'll be right back."

"It doesn't look like anyone's home."

"Dad... just stay in the car."

Abraham waved her on. "Fine, fine. Just go."

Diane ran across the lawn and up onto the front porch. She put her hand to the small, octagonal window and could see light coming from under a door at the end of the hallway.

Diane rattled the door handle, but it was locked. She thought about going around the back, but instead reached into her pocket and brought out the lock-picking kit Sullivan had given her for Christmas one year. She equated it with a washing machine, but it had come in handy before and she was fast. Faster than Sullivan, she reminded him several times when illegal entry had been required for a case.

She picked the lock in less than a minute, even in the dark, and came through the door calling David's name. No sign of his parents or the fiancée; the burglar alarm had not been set. Diane rushed down the hall toward the light coming from the door. As she was about to push it open, she felt water squishing under her feet.

David was in his underwear submerged in the overflowing bathtub, the water crimson with blood and pooling on the tile. He had cut both wrists and there was a deep slice along the femoral artery of his left leg.

"Motherfucker," Diane cursed under her breath. "You motherfucker."

She caught David under both arms and pulled him from the tub onto the tile floor and checked for his pulse. It was weak but thready, and the wounds appeared fresh, as if he had only made the cuts a few minutes before. She dismissed the bizarreness of Christian's urgent phone call, and snatched towels off the racks to wrap the wounds. The leg cut was the worst and she tied the towel tight to stem the flow of blood.

"Oh, my god..." Abraham was standing in the doorway. "Oh, why did he do that?"

"There's a phone in the hall. Call 911."

She wrapped David's arms near the elbow and started slapping his face. "Wake up! You fucking coward! I am not going to let you do this." She raised her hand and slapped him so hard that it left a mark.

David coughed and sputtered, his eyes popping open,

glazed and unfocused.

"All right, there you are," she said. "That's more like it. Yeah, take a look, asshole. Here's your worst nightmare back again."

"They're coming," her father said. "They said an ambulance was close."

David closed his eyes again, but Diane cradled him on the floor, rocking him like a mother would a child. She looked up into the face of her horrified father, who was saying the prayer for healing in broken Yiddish, with tears streaming down his face.

*HaKadosh Baruch Hu yimalei rachamim aleihem, l'hachalimam ul'rapotam ul'hachazikam, v'yishlach lahem m'heirah r'fuah, r'fuah shleimah min hashamayim, r'fuat hanefesh ur'fuat haguf, hashta baagala uviz'man kariv…*

May the Blessed Holy One be filled with compassion for their health to be restored and their strength to be revived. May God swiftly send them a complete renewal of body and spirit…

The hospital emergency room was crowded and hot. A dazed looking mother comforted a crying infant; a frat boy who had sliced off part of his finger in a drinking game was telling racist jokes to his buddies; a reeking homeless woman snored into her chest in a corner of the room. There was shitty cell reception in the waiting room as Diane tried to find a flight. Scenarios danced through her head about what had happened in Paris. Christian had given her only basic information: Martin shot, Irène's heart attack, the apartment partially destroyed in a fire. Christian had reeled off this information so quickly that Diane didn't have time to process it all before running out the door to David's house.

When she stepped into the ambulance, she flashed back

to the horrible Sunday in Paris when David had been injured in the terrorist attack. She had ridden to the hospital with him that day, too. Rescuing David McLaren seemed to be her only profession. Diane half expected to see Martin and Irène through the oval windows in the back doors of the ambulance, but instead she saw her father giving her a little wave as he got into the car to drive home. Images on the television mounted near the ceiling of the waiting room caught her eye and she watched, a feeling of panic rising inside her again. The sound was turned off, but the scenes of riots in Paris needed no soundtrack.

A commotion at the entrance to the emergency room distracted her as she typed a text message to Sullivan. She looked up and saw David's parents, his fiancée and her dyke friend coming toward her down the hallway. They moved in formation, led by Jim McLaren, his face red and twisted in rage. Before he even got to the waiting room, David's father pointed an accusing finger at Diane.

"I'm going to get a restraining order against you," McLaren shouted.

"You should be more concerned about your son. He's alive, by the way."

Jim McLaren loomed over Diane, his fist drawn back as if about to strike. She surprised herself by not flinching or ducking away. She stared up into his face, saw in exacting detail the toll the last ten years had taken on him.

The waiting room went silent, the sick and injured staring at the scene unfolding before them. The nurse behind the admittance desk held a walkie-talkie and whispered into it before closing the glass partition. Diane gripped the armrest tightly, prepared to kick David's father in the groin again or deliver a disabling punch to the voice box, just like Sullivan had taught her.

Before she knew what was happening, Jim McLaren

crumpled to the floor, his body racked by great, heaving sobs. His head rested on Diane's lap, arms tightly clutching at her waist. She instinctively drew back, wanted to push the crying man away, but she looked up and saw David's mother and fiancée clinging to each other, also in tears. Only Miranda's friend Kari was unmoved by the scene; she stood back, a smug, knowing look on her face.

Diane tentatively stroked Jim McLaren's hair, almost like petting a dog she was afraid might bite her. "He's going to be okay," Diane said, summoning up the closest approximation to a soothing voice she could find, but David's father only clung to her tighter, his body convulsing with emotion. Diane felt her eyes well up, but she blinked back the tears. Perhaps Jim McLaren's public meltdown was the breakthrough, the cathartic moment needed so that his family could move forward with their lives.

Kathy McLaren tugged at her husband's arm gently, urging him to stand up so they could go see David. He slowly staggered to his feet, his face wet and pale. He slumped against his wife and she led him toward the nurse's station where a security guard had been watching with his hand resting on his taser.

Diane sat back in her seat. She shrugged off her jacket and pulled the damp t-shirt away from her skin. That's when she noticed Miranda and Kari were still there.

"Is David really all right?" Miranda asked. Her face was smeared with mascara and she looked incredibly young.

"He's in surgery," Diane said, fanning herself with a magazine. "He's gonna make it. Don't worry."

Miranda sat down next to Diane. "I know why he did it."

Diane held her breath, waiting to hear what Miranda was going to say. Maybe she had finally wised up, or Kari had finally persuaded her that David was "fagging out" as she had put it that night at Wal-Mart.

"Why do you think he did it?" Diane asked.

"Well, I mean, it's kind of obvious." She tried to laugh through her tears. "They're kinda religious nuts and his dad… well… he's just nuts. Everything David does is wrong. They've been ragging him really hard about moving back to Memphis and working here instead of us going back to New Orleans. And his mom's a sweetheart, but she's all over my ass about the wedding and when we're having kids. David said they've always been like this. Sometimes I wish he'd never gotten back in touch with them…"

Miranda's voice trailed off and she dabbed at her eyes.

Diane put her hand on Miranda's shoulder. I should tell her right now, she thought. I should tell her so David won't wind up ruining her life, too.

Diane glanced at Kari, who was standing with her arms folded over her chest just behind Miranda.

Tell her the truth, Kari mouthed to her.

Diane started to speak, but Miranda cut her off. "I know you're going to tell me about David and that guy Martin, but he's already told me, so save it. And I know a lot of people think you seduced him, but I know that's not true either."

"Yeah, I'm old enough to be his mom," Diane said sarcastically, rolling her eyes.

"Well, yeah… I mean… I know David's gone through some rough shit, but he's been honest with me."

"Telling stories is one thing, but being honest about his feelings…" Diane caught herself. She had promised to stay out of David's business and here she was wading back in again. "You seem like a nice girl, and David needs someone to be nice to him. If you can make him happy, go for it."

Kari's face fell, disappointed that Diane hadn't spoken the truth she obviously knew about David. But Kari's motivation was designed to get Miranda back in her bed, and Diane decided she wasn't going to interfere with that either.

A nurse approached and said David was out of surgery and

in the recovery room.

"He's asking for someone named Martin," the nurse said. "Is that a family member?"

A mocking little laugh escaped from Kari's throat.

"Fuck you," Miranda said to her friend before turning back to the nurse. "I'm his fiancée."

Miranda followed the nurse, leaving a dejected Kari in the waiting room.

"Why the fuck didn't you tell her that David is gay? She needs to hear it before she marries that dumbass."

"I'm getting out of the McLaren family business," Diane said. "I suggest you do the same."

"Thanks for nothing, bitch." Kari walked away, headed for the emergency room exit.

"You'll thank me later," Diane called to her.

Diane pulled her jacket back on and stood up. She needed to go home and pack a bag and figure out her flight plan to Paris.

"Excuse me, ma'am." The security guard who had been watching from the nurses station was hovering by her seat. "Your father is trying to reach you and says it's an emergency."

Diane felt the color drain from her face. "My father? I've got my cell phone right here." There were no missed calls or voicemails.

"Thank you," Diane mumbled at the officer as she dialed her father.

The answering machine switched on and she was about to leave a message when someone picked up the receiver. "Dad, are you there?"

"Is this Mr. Jacobs' daughter?"

She felt a flutter of panic. "Who is this?"

"Memphis Police. Are you Mr. Jacobs' daughter?"

"I am. What's happened?"

"Your father called 911 and said you had disappeared. He

243

was in a very agitated state."

"Can you put him on the phone?"

"We've had to sedate him." There was an accusatory tone in those few words. "We're going to take him to Memphis General for observation. You might want to meet us there."

"I'm already here."

Diane leaned forward and put her head between her knees to stop the nausea that crept into her stomach. She covered her mouth with her hand and ran into the ladies room. Diane managed to make it to the toilet before she vomited up the contents of her stomach. She knelt on the floor, her entire body heaving and throat burning with bile. Then she screamed, a wounded howling sound that had been trapped inside her for months.

# 30 Recovery

Christian lay on his side in the hospital bed next to Martin watching him sleep. He hadn't left Salpêtrière in days, watching as Martin floated in and out of consciousness. The bullet had nicked a large vein and the small intestine, but Martin was expected to make a complete recovery. Irène was recovering in the cardiac wing, already walking again, shuffling down the hallway with her IV drip to check on Martin twice a day.

The television suspended from the ceiling in Martin's room showed that rioting had spread to other parts of France. In Paris, Place de la République was filled with the debris of hastily made barricades, burned out cars and looted shops. There was a quick shot of Irène's burned out apartment on rue Rampon, the walls outside the windows scorched black.

What hadn't been reported on the news was the rescue of Martin and Irène from the burning apartment. In Christian's recounting, he and

Sullivan had arrived at rue Rampon to find the apartment on fire and managed to get inside and save them.

"Who shot Arnaud?" Martin asked after he had been brought back to the recovery room from surgery. "There was a sniper."

Christian and Sullivan didn't have an answer to that question. De Courcy had ordered a helicopter, which had landed in Place Victor Hugo and took Christian and Sullivan to a wide intersection near the canal not far from rue Rampon. Six men dressed in paramilitary gear and carrying first aid satchels and collapsible stretchers met the helicopter. They led Christian and Sullivan on foot to rue Rampon, where smoke was curling into the air.

Once at the apartment, the men quickly suppressed the fire with quick-acting foam, while Christian and Sullivan found Martin and Irène on the floor of the bedroom. They were quickly stabilized and removed from the apartment on the stretchers. Before he went back into the hallway, Christian saw the other men lifting a charred body from the living room floor.

Henri Lorit's exposé on Arnaud appeared on the front page of *Le Monde*. The bombshell of Arnaud's plans to destabilize the banlieues, the fake assassination attempt and a laundry list of questionable arrests, violence and kickbacks reverberated around the country. The police named Arnaud as the only suspect in Lorit's murder. According to the head of the RG, Arnaud's body was found in his apartment a few days later, dead from a self-inflicted gunshot wound. There was no mention of Arnaud's body being consumed by fire and the events at rue Rampon. Despite Lorit's threat, there was no mention of Irène or Martin in the article, either.

Henri Lorit was hailed as a hero. Even as rioting continued, thousands attended a candlelight vigil at the Bastille monument and there was talk of a posthumous award of the honor medal for courage.

Christian dozed off and when he woke, Martin was watching him.

"Hello," Martin said. "I was being creepy and watching you sleep."

"Super creepy," Christian said, kissing him on the cheek. "What time is it?"

"I think it's about six-thirty. I couldn't reach my glasses."

Christian shifted so he could roll over and see the clock. "Oh... it's morning. Did I keep you up?"

"No. I would have kicked you if you were bothering me. I like waking up and finding you here. Even if it is the hospital."

Morning light began to fill the room and they watched in silence as day broke over Paris. The nurses and doctors would soon be making their rounds.

"My father is coming by today before he leaves," Christian said.

"He's going already?"

"Geoff thought it was best that he leave the country now. It's all been arranged. He'll have an apartment in Brussels and enough money to start up whatever business he chooses. He could even open another newsstand."

"I'm glad," Martin said. "You should be proud of him."

Christian kissed Martin again on the cheek and his forehead. "I want to tell Olivier something, but I need to ask you first."

"What?"

"That we're getting married." Christian reached into his pocket and produced a tiny box and opened it to reveal two simple silver bands. "I wish we were someplace romantic."

Martin grinned at him, his eyes glistening. "This is pretty romantic, actually."

Christian pulled one of the bands from the box and held it between his fingers. "Martin Paige, will you marry me?"

"Duh, who else would I marry?" he said, rolling his eyes

playfully before kissing Christian softly on the lips.

"Just promise that you'll tell me about any strange things you see in mirrors."

Christian had been shaken by the story Martin told about his encounters with Paul, Peter and David as he hovered between life and death. He was, at first, angry and jealous, but he knew it was driven by the realization that Martin could have made a different choice. Time would have reset itself and they would have never met, and perhaps he would be dead.

"I chose you," Martin had said. "I'll always choose you, Christian. Don't ever wonder."

They slipped the rings onto each other's fingers and then stared at their hands, the cold metal around their fingers warming up, beginning their slow imprinting into the skin. They kissed, gently, looking into each other's eyes and not speaking. It was something they did often and would do for the rest of their lives. Unafraid of the silence, learning to read each other's thoughts and moods without saying a word.

Olivier was waiting in the hospital commissary, sitting at a small table in the corner. He was dressed in the second suit he had ever owned, and Christian thought he looked distinguished, almost like a doctor. He sipped from a hot cup of coffee, but refused Christian's offer of food.

"I should buy you food," Olivier said. "I am a man of means now."

Christian nodded. "Have you decided what you will do?"

"A small shop of some kind. Something to keep me occupied. How are Madame Irène and Martin?"

"Recovering." Christian paused, still nervous about telling his father about his engagement. "I want to tell you something, and I do not want you to get upset. I don't want to fight with you anymore."

Olivier closed his eyes and sat up even straighter in his chair. He tugged at the collar of his shirt. "What is it?"

"I know you do not approve of how I live my life and my relationship with Martin, but I love him very much. I have asked him to marry me and he has said yes."

A deep breath escaped from Olivier and he seemed to deflate. "You are free to do as you like. You are a man. I know you think I dislike Martin, but that is not true."

"Papa, I do not think you like *me* very much."

Olivier looked stricken by such frank words from his son. "No, Baptiste... Christian... you are my son and I love you. I may not agree with your choices, but I must respect you and Martin. You have been together for many years now, and I see that he is loyal. He is very brave."

Those were the kindest words his father had spoken in years. "Thank you for saying that. I am glad to see you are more tolerant."

"There were homosexuals in my village, but no one spoke about it. Those who were either kept quiet or they faced being shunned. Things have changed. Now everyone seems to be a homosexual."

Christian laughed, but his father did not. "I am sorry, Papa. I know you are being serious. But you are right—times have changed."

"It is still a sin."

Christian sighed. "I will worry about that when it is time to meet my maker. Perhaps he or she or it will have changed their mind as well."

Olivier raised an eyebrow at his son, but did not respond. He drank the rest of his coffee and shifted in his seat as if about to depart.

"Your mother would have liked Martin," Olivier said.

"I think so, too. They have the same sense of humor and a very clear-eyed view of the world."

Olivier's voice choked with emotion. "She would be glad that you are happy."

Christian reached across the table and put his hand on top of his father's. "I hope you are happy for me, too, Papa. I am very proud of you. You are the brave one."

A tear rolled down Olivier's dark cheek. He patted his son's hand and then stood up. "Yes, happy."

Christian bit his lower lip to stop it from trembling. "I will come and see you once you are settled in Brussels."

"I would like that. Bring Martin and Madame Irène." Olivier pulled his long dark coat from the back of the chair. He reached into the jacket pocket and pulled out the photo of Christian and Martin he had taken from the youth center. "I am keeping this."

"By all means," Christian grinned.

Olivier put on the matching fedora and made a production of positioning it just so and smoothing out the brim. This was the father Christian remembered as a child—at ease, funny and smiling.

"Papa… was it you?"

"I do not know what you mean."

"Yes, you do. Did you shoot Arnaud?"

Olivier laughed heartily. "I told you, I was in Montfermeil cleaning up the shop."

"I am not sure I believe you. At the very least you could tell me who you were working with to expose Arnaud."

Olivier pursed his lips and twisted an invisible key before tossing it away and waggling his fingers.

Christian held out his hand and Olivier squeezed it tightly before turning and walking away. At the door to the commissary, Olivier paused at the door, turned back and winked at his son.

# 31 | Leaving Paris

Irène and Martin lay side-by-side in his hospital bed watching the news. A state of emergency had been declared as the rioting spread to other towns around Paris. The images of burning cars, youths hurling rocks and police with raised batons made Irène's heart race, but she couldn't turn away. It was like 1968, just as Lorit had predicted. There was even tension and fear among the staff at Salpêtrière. More than once, Irène had caught a doctor or nurse staring at the television in her room when they were taking her temperature or pulse. When she walked up and down the hallways, there were huddles around the small television at the nurses station and visitors were glued to the screens in the waiting rooms.

The riots had been going on for more than a week and there seemed to be no sign of them stopping, even as the politicians stepped up their rhetoric and threats. More incidents in the city itself—cars set alight and stores broken into—had even the most hardened Parisian on edge. There had been more demonstrations at Republic Square and Christian said there had been some vandalism along rue Rampon—spray-painted windows and walls, rubbish bins knocked over and leaflets from various radical causes tucked under windshield wipers. The shops around Republic Square had started closing early or not opening at all as it seemed more violence could kick off at any moment. The police kept their distance, but they were in full riot gear with helmets, shields and batons.

"You should take a holiday," a voice said from the doorway.

It was Geoff de Courcy. As always, he was immaculately groomed and dressed in a camel coat and matching leather gloves. His ability to appear without warning and in total silence gave him a supernatural air that unnerved Martin and Irène.

"I'm not sure we're up to a holiday," Martin said.

Geoff came into the room and stood by the bed. "Irène's doctor says she needs rest and you still have healing to do, Martin. I am afraid that rue Rampon is unlivable at the moment. We were able to recover many of your belongings and they are in storage. Of course, you could rent another apartment, but there is the issue of the media."

"The media?" Irène asked. "Lorit kindly left us out of his story, so why would they seek us out now?"

"Unfortunately, while we were busy elsewhere, an enterprising journalist reporting on the riots discovered that the burned apartment on rue Rampon was owned by the associate publisher of Éditions Resolvere. That same reporter phoned your office and spoke to Gerard, who claimed that he hasn't seen you or Martin in weeks and was worried about your welfare."

Irène put her face in her hands. "Oh, my god. I spoke to him last week and said we were away on an extended holiday while the apartment was being repaired."

"Will they call the hospitals?" Martin asked. "What if they start checking around?"

"You are both here under assumed names and there is protection, so you should not worry. We took the liberty of sending the journalist a note from Madame Irène's email account explaining that the fire was an accident started by a candle after the power cut and that she and Martin were out of the country. With the ongoing riots and coverage about Arnaud, it should not go any further, but you could have press show up on your doorstep and at the publishing house. That's why leaving Paris for a period might be beneficial."

"For how long?" Irène asked. "We have work to do at the publishing house."

"You will be able to continue that work without interruption via computer and teleconference. The staff also believes you are both out of the country. You're reading new manuscripts, Martin is working on a new book. It is all very plausible."

"Too plausible," Martin said. "Where exactly do you want us to go?"

"It is being arranged. I promise you will find it extraordinary. It is a small token for what you have endured. Like Frederick, I pride myself in always being one step ahead and this time I was not, and you were both injured."

"We are alive thanks to your intervention," Irène said. "And to the marksman at the hotel."

"Hidden bases in abandoned metro stations," Martin mused. "That doesn't seem like Frederick's style."

De Courcy smiled courteously. "The organization has transitioned in the last few years. Some would even consider us legitimate."

"Oh, really? I'd like to hear about that," Martin said.

"Of course, I cannot be specific. Let's just say—security and information."

De Courcy reached into his pocket and pulled out a sealed envelope. He hesitated before handing it to Martin. "Monsieur Sullivan said you had requested this."

De Courcy walked out of the room, giving a sort of royal wave as he went. Martin turned the envelope over in his hands.

"What is it?" Irène asked.

"I asked him to find Paul Richardson. I had to know."

Martin slipped his thumb under the flap and opened the envelope. Inside were photocopies of a police report and death certificate. Paul Richardson and his partner, Mike, had been killed in a car accident in Nashville on September 16—the day before they appeared in the bar at the Peabody Hotel in Memphis.

"I already knew he was dead, but I just had to be sure," Martin said blinking back tears.

"I am sorry for Paul and his partner, but also thankful," Irène said. "Paul helped save your life. He must have cared about you very much. Just like you cared enough about David to save his life."

A fresh wave of emotion washed over Martin at the mention of David's name. Diane had called and given him a progress report. Physically, David would recover, but she was convinced he was still in danger if his parents didn't answer the wake up call of their son's attempted suicide.

Irène touched Martin's face. "I've been thinking about something. I want to tell you, but it will sound insane."

Martin nestled his cheek against her hand. "When has it not?"

"We were always going to be at this moment in our lives. As terrible as the last few months have been, we are supposed to be right here. Together. It's like a pattern emerging—all these things that seem to have no connection *are* connected."

"Synchronicity."

"Yes. I have faith in the truth that nothing is random.

Every event of our lives has meaning—some kind of message for us. We just have to listen closely."

On the muted television, the screen was filled with the image of a rocket launching into space. The fireball of ignition and liftoff faded as the camera followed the spacecraft into a darkening sky. Words appeared at the bottom of the screen: *Venus Express Begins Two-Year Mission*. Animation appeared showing the orbiter moving into position beneath the polar cap of the planet. It looked just like the vision of Venus that Martin had seen in the mirror hall.

"What do you think that means?" Martin asked Irène.

She looked at the screen wide-eyed as a mixture of exhilaration tinged with uncertainty washed over her. "How do we go back to the life we were living before?"

"It won't be the same."

Irène squeezed Martin's hand tightly. "Time to leave."


Pierre the cat ran down the stairs of the Anglophile as soon as Irène and Martin stepped inside the door. Irène picked him up and he burrowed into her neck purring loudly. Julie came around the counter and hugged them both. She was the only person who knew any details about what had actually happened at rue Rampon, but Martin trusted her with the secret.

"You've been sprung!" Julie said.

"I never want to see a hospital ever again if I can help it," Martin said. "That was the longest two weeks ever."

"You both look well. Come upstairs and I'll make some tea. Where are Sullivan and Christian?"

"They've gone to pick up some things from our apartment," Martin said. "We're taking a holiday."

"Good idea. Where?"

"It's a surprise, apparently," Irène said, a hint of sarcasm in her voice.

"That could be fun," Julie said.

"I will be the judge of that," Irène responded.

Once they were seated in Julie's office with cups of hot tea and Pierre sleeping on Irène's lap, the conversation turned to business.

"We aren't sure when we will return to Paris," Irène said, "and we need to make sure the publishing house is in capable hands. You have been wonderful acting as our liaison these past few weeks, so we would like you to take over day-to-day operations at Éditions Resolvere. At least for the next few months."

"If you have time," Martin chimed in. "I know you want to make some changes to the store and you're still trying to get settled here."

"The changes can wait," Julie said. "It would be an honor."

Irène visibly relaxed. "Thank god. I was afraid you would say no."

"Next year's books are in production, the catalog is out, so it shouldn't be too stressful," Martin said. "Maybe you could read some poetry submissions."

"Do I get to publish what I select?"

"Of course," Irène said. "We could build a campaign around it—collections selected by award-winning poet Juliette Lacombe."

Julie topped off her cup of tea. "That has a ring to it, and at least it would be something I'd actually like to read."

"Do you think you will be able to handle Gerard?" Martin asked.

"Gerard and I get along just fine. He's a horrible old flirt, so I just let him take me to lunch, flirt back and he's happy."

Irène raised her cup of tea in salute. "A woman after my own heart. Yes, things will be just fine."

"The publishing house will help anchor me," Julie said. "I have to admit, giving up my life in the States was a little more difficult than I expected. I wanted to be in Paris, and I thought things would simply fall into place, but it's never what you think. I have to keep reminding myself that Paris is my home and I now have something tangible with the Anglophile. After moving around so much with my father, settling in one place has never been my thing, but I think I'm ready to nest."

As Irène and Martin were preparing to leave, Martin noticed a guitar case sitting against the wall of Julie's office. "When did you take that up?" he asked.

"Oh, please, you know me better than that," Julie laughed. "I can't even keep a beat. Someone left it in the shop this morning. I'm sure they'll be back to collect it."

Julie walked them back downstairs. With the holidays approaching, the Anglophile was busier than usual. She had hired two more part-time booksellers and set up an ambitious slate of events. The open mic was on hold until Martin was ready to return.

"Send me a postcard when you get to where you're going," Julie said, hugging Irène and Martin and scratching Pierre under the chin. "And don't worry about anything in Paris. I've got you covered."


Martin awoke in the back seat of the car, his head resting against the cool window glass. Irène was dozing beside him with Pierre still on her lap. Sullivan drove and Christian was in the front passenger seat. Sullivan was talking about train schedules to places called Gièvres and Vierzon. Martin looked at the time on his phone. He had been asleep for two hours, which meant they were at least three hours outside of Paris.

"Where are we?" Martin said stretching. His abdomen was still sore, and sitting in one position for an extended period made it even more so.

"The dead have arisen," Sullivan said, and Christian shot

him a look. "Oh, lighten up."

They were passing through a small village of stone buildings with high gabled rooftops, the bottom floors containing restaurants and shops.

"I think we were supposed to go east at the roundabout," Christian said.

"The GPS is taking us west," Sullivan insisted. "I didn't program it, remember?"

"Who did?" Irène asked, her eyes still closed.

"The sat nav was waiting for us when we arrived at rue Rampon," Sullivan said. "Mr. de Courcy, I presume. He's probably hiding in the trunk."

Irène laughed. "I would not doubt it, Bernard."

They drove up a winding road that looked out over treetops on one side and was lined with a whitewashed stone wall on the other. Eventually, the sat nav indicated that they had arrived at their destination: a tall wooden gate set into the wall.

"What is this place?" Irène asked, looking out the window. "How do we get in?"

As if by magic, the gate swung open. Waiting inside was an old man wearing coveralls and a flatcap, which he pulled off as Sullivan rolled down the window.

"Bonjour," the old man said. "Welcome to the château."

Martin rolled down his window. "What château is this?"

The old man smiled. "Valençay."

For a moment, everything went white just like it did in the hall of mirrors as the rope of light passed overhead. Martin could feel Irène grasping his hand.

"Are we awake?" she whispered to him.

Sullivan drove over a rise and the large domed towers of Château de Valençay revealed themselves.

"I don't know," he said.

Irène pinched the back of Martin's hand so hard that he yelped in pain. "I think we are," she said.

The gardens were just as Martin remembered them from his vision, ornate and beautifully pruned for the coming winter. Sullivan drove them around the L-shaped château into a large courtyard dominated by a circular gurgling fountain.

"It's a castle," Christian marveled as he helped Irène out of the car.

"Surely, Geoff doesn't mean we are to stay here?" Irène said. "Isn't this a private home?"

"Parts of it are private, apparently." Sullivan was squinting at his mobile phone. "It says here the Château de Valençay is a public park and historic site in the Loire Valley." He whistled loudly. "One hundred rooms and forty hectares of gardens. I'd hate to be the one who had to keep this place up."

There was the sound of gravel crunching under tires and a sleek black limousine pulled up behind them.

"Who is this, then?" Sullivan asked, reaching under his coat for his gun.

The back door of the limo opened and Geoff de Courcy stepped out. "Holster your gun, Monsieur Sullivan."

"Bernard!" Irène scolded him. "I've had enough of guns."

De Courcy led them toward the main entrance of the château while his driver removed their bags from Sullivan's car. "This was one of Frederick's favorite retreats. We spent many happy days here."

"Only Frederick Dubois would have the power to commandeer a private home and historic site as his own personal palace," Irène said.

"No commandeering is required when you are the owner," de Courcy said without ceremony. "You, Martin and Christian may stay here as long as you like. And even you, Bernard."

"Thank you, but no," Sullivan said. "I'm a city mouse, not a country mouse."

De Courcy pointed out artwork and statuary to Sullivan and Christian, who were in awe of the giant house. Irène and

Martin paused at the doorway, uncertain whether to step inside.

"What if we're dreaming?" Martin said to her. "What if we never woke up to begin with?"

"No, we are awake," Irène said, tightening her grip on Martin's hand. "We're supposed to be here. We will just have to figure out why."

Together, they stepped across the threshold.

Inside the entry hall was a large, round mahogany table holding a vase full of white tulips flanked by the statues of Venus de Milo and Winged Victory rescued from rue Rampon.

Martin watched as Irène touched each statue, then delicately ran a finger over one of the budding tulips.

"We had these brought from the hothouse at the château in Chambéry, which I am sure you remember very well, Madame Irène. White tulips were Frederick's favorite," de Courcy said. "He liked the symbolism."

"Le pardon et l'espoir," Irène said.

Forgiveness and hope.

# 32 One Year Later

The cab pulled up in front of Diane's father's house and Martin hesitated before he opened the door. The front lawn was overgrown and the house could do with a coat of paint. He hadn't seen Diane in more than a year. Her communication was infrequent and not forthcoming, but he knew that Alzheimer's disease was robbing Abraham of his memories.

Martin climbed the steps to the porch and was about to knock when Diane opened the door. She'd put on weight, had strands of silver in her hair. She was wearing a baggy sweatshirt over cut-off jeans and flip-flops.

"The prodigal son returns."

Diane turned and walked back into the gloom of the house, letting the screen door slam. Martin pulled it opened and followed her inside. The house looked even shabbier on the inside and there was a medicinal smell he couldn't quite identify. Diane had never been a great housekeeper, and she seemed to be in over her head.

"Don't say a fucking word about the house," she said from the kitchen. "I can feel your judgment all the way in here."

He moved a stack of *People* magazines and tabloids and sat on the couch. It was dark and cool in the house. A small tray filled with bottles of pills sat on the coffee table. Out of the corner of his eye, he saw that a chair lift had been installed on the stairs to the second floor.

Diane returned from the kitchen carrying two glasses of lemonade. "It's from a carton," she said, handing him the sweating tumbler before flopping down in an armchair on the other side of the room.

"Is your dad asleep?"

"He's at therapy. The vegetable wagon will toss him back on the porch shortly."

"How is he?"

"Dying, thanks for asking."

Martin sighed loudly. "Are we going to have a conversation or are you just going to be a bitter bitchhole?"

Diane laughed harshly. "I've earned my bitterness, don't you think? This is my worst nightmare come true. Trapped in Memphis in this house with a man who used to be my father."

"That's not my fault," Martin snapped back. "You could have brought him to France. Arnaud is dead, so no more problems there. De Courcy could arrange a visa…"

Diane sloshed her drink toward him, the lemonade spilling on the carpet. "You know I couldn't. He freaked out. He thought Hitler was personally coming to take him to Auschwitz."

"But he wouldn't know the difference now… would he?"

Diane was silent.

"The last time we spoke you said he was starting to confuse you with your mom."

"Yeah. Then I was his sister, then his mother and then I

was some woman from the bowling alley he obviously had an affair with," Diane said. "It's been a real learning experience."

"I'm sorry," Martin said gently. "Maybe it's time to start thinking about alternative care."

Diane shook her head. "No nursing homes. Absolutely-fucking-not. Even the nice ones are gross. They all smell like piss and the staff is a bunch of abusers and molesters."

"That's not true."

"Would you put Irène in a nursing home?"

Despite her age and the heart attack, Irène was still alert and lively, but she was always joking about a broken hip being the beginning of the end. She was taking calcium and other pills to fight off an osteoporosis diagnosis and Martin had noticed Irène was more careful about going down steps and walking on uneven ground at the château.

"No, I wouldn't, but I would at least get some help in," Martin said. "It's not like you can't afford it."

Diane slapped the chair arm and snorted. "We've had a parade of morons in and out of this house over the last year. Lazy, incompetent, thieving fucktards ignoring the most basic instructions. Don't get me started. You really have no idea what's been going on around here because you've been too busy being an artiste and living in your fancy château."

They sat in silence for a moment, unsure what to say next. Diane finally got up and went over to a window, opened it and pulled a pack of cigarettes from her pocket.

"Want one?"

Martin shook his head.

"You and the old woman still on the patch?"

"I haven't smoked in two years."

Diane blew smoke out the window. "You do look like you've put on some weight."

"I could say the same about you."

"Except I have an excuse," she said, tossing the half

smoked cig out the window into the yard. "I guess now that you're all settled down with loverboy you'll get the middle age spread and he'll have to go looking for some hot, skinny ass. Is Christian still ministering to the disaffected youth?"

Martin stood up. "Okay, I'm outta here. Now you're just being mean for no damn reason."

Diane was still staring out the window. There was the sound of doors opening and closing. "Dad's home," she said flatly.

She walked back towards the kitchen and Martin heard a screen door open. He heard Diane talking and another indistinct voice before the screen door closed again. Diane returned, walking Abraham slowly toward the sofa. Martin hadn't seen him in ages, but he didn't remember him being so tiny and shrunken.

"Dad, Martin is here," Diane said, easing him into a sitting position on the couch. "Do you remember Martin?"

The old man looked at Martin, looked through him, his eyes glazed over. Then his face changed and he smiled. He spoke in a phlegmy voice: "Have you moved back from Paris?"

"Uhhh…" he looked at Diane unsure what to say. "No, I'm just visiting, Mr. Jacobs."

"Is my daughter with you?"

Diane leaned over from the chair she was sitting in and put her hand on his arm. "I'm right here, Dad."

He turned to look at her slowly and laughed. "Why didn't your mother tell me you were coming to visit? She's still pissed at you for marrying a goyim, you know. We'll never hear the end of it."

"You know how mom is," Diane said, her voice thick with emotion. "It's good to see you, Daddy."

Diane's father leaned toward her conspiratorially. "Do you need any money? I'll write you a check before you go. Just don't tell your mother. I'll never hear the end of it."

"I'm fine," she said and patted his hand.

Abraham turned and looked at Martin again. "I hope you're taking care of my daughter, Mr. Sullivan. I know she's a handful and has a mouth on her, but she gets that from her mother." Abraham laughed and coughed. "But she's a good girl. Always has been a good girl."

Diane turned her face away, brushing tears from her eyes.

"She's the best, Mr. Jacobs," Martin said. "I don't know what I'd do without her."

"Are you still doing that detective work?"

Diane stood up. "Dad, it's time for your lunch. Do you want a sandwich?"

Abraham's face clouded and he looked up at Diane. "I can make my own goddamn sandwich. I'll eat when I'm hungry. I was having a conversation with..." his voice trailed off.

"Martin," Diane said softly.

"Martin? I thought he was dead." He turned to Martin. "Weren't you dead?"

"Recently resurrected," Martin said, but Abraham looked even more confused. "I had an accident, but I'm fine now. I'm visiting for a few days."

"That's good, that's good. Always nice to see a familiar face."

Diane reached down, picked up a remote control and switched on the TV. "It's time for Judge Judy. You don't want to miss your girlfriend."

Abraham was instantly mesmerized by the show and Diane motioned for Martin to follow her into the kitchen. She pulled a loaf of Wonder Bread and a jar of peanut butter from the cabinet.

"So, that's my day in microcosm," Diane said, smearing the peanut butter onto the bread, then opening the fridge and pulling out a jar of grape jelly. "That was one of his most lucid moments in months."

Martin was sitting at the kitchen table, picking at something dried on the formica countertop. "I had no idea he was so far advanced."

"The old bastard lied to me and mom. He'd been having symptoms for a while and denied it. He flat out told me he didn't have Alzheimer's and he was already stage four. Now he's probably between five and six." Diane licked jelly from her fingers. "The doctor thinks he might have had a small stroke, which makes the decline worse. They've got him hopped up on pills to help him sleep and control his wandering."

"Jesus. Why didn't you tell me?"

"It is what it is. Now you see why I don't want to move him. He's too fragile. The doctor said a sudden change in location might cause a more rapid decline. Moving him to France would probably finish him off." She returned the jelly to the fridge door, pulled out a gallon of milk and poured a glass. Diane put the sandwich on a tray with the milk and took it to her father.

"PB&J—your favorite," she said.

"Shhhhh," her father said. "Judge Judy is about to rule."

Diane came back into the kitchen and went to the cupboard. She pulled a giant bottle of Jack Daniels from the top shelf along with two glasses and brought them to the kitchen table. She hefted the half-empty bottle and said, "I'm buying in bulk."

Diane filled both of the glasses halfway and clinked hers against Martin's. "To détente."

They both downed the whiskey in a couple of long gulps and set the glasses back on the table. Martin reached his hand across the table and gently touched Diane's hand. A sob rose in her throat and she slapped her hand over her mouth to stifle it.

"We'll get through this," he said softly. "I swear."

Diane nodded, but kept her hand covering her mouth. She didn't want her father to hear her crying.

Martin circled the Memphis airport baggage area twice before he saw Sullivan lumbering out the door with his bags, his face flushed from exertion. The detective had called and awoken Martin at four in the morning to announce he was at De Gaulle and was on his way to Memphis.

"What?" Martin asked groggily.

"After you rang yesterday, the situation has been weighing on my mind. I have to talk some common sense into Diane about her father. I thought face-to-face would be best. At least she can't hang up on me."

"Ummm… okay."

"I should arrive around five your time. I'll call you. They're boarding my flight."

Martin thought about telling Diane that Sullivan was coming, to let her rage and get it out of her system, but maybe seeing her husband would be a comfort. That's the way it should be, he thought, but this was Diane.

Sullivan opened the back door of Martin's rental car and threw his bags in and then crammed himself into the passenger seat. He awkwardly leaned over and half hugged Martin, crushing him against his shoulder.

"I cannot believe I'm back in this hellish place," Sullivan said, pulling a handkerchief from his pocket and mopping his brow.

"I'm glad you're here."

Sullivan grunted. "Have you told the missus I was coming?"

"No. I thought maybe this should be a surprise. A joyous surprise."

Sullivan shook his head. "That woman does not like surprises and joy hasn't been part of her vocabulary for many a year." He took a deep, rattling breath. "How is she holding up?"

"At the end of her tether, as you always say."

"Has she run off all the nurses?"

"All of them. She's doing it all on her own."

Sullivan grimaced. "Stubborn woman."

"She needs you."

Sullivan let out a roaring sound that made Martin flinch. "Like hell. She made it clear that I wasn't needed in any way, shape or form. I bent over backwards to mollify that woman and nothing was ever good enough. We should have never married. Things were jolly when we were traveling together and working on cases. We were like Nick and Nora. That is until I made the stupid mistake of asking her to marry me and trying to settle down. It ruined everything."

"You can get that back."

"She's had a double blow with her mum dying and now her father losing his faculties. She's not in her right mind."

Martin smiled. "Diane has never—and I mean ever—been in her right mind. That's part of her charm."

Sullivan roared with laughter. "You do make me laugh, lad."

They pulled up in front of Diane's house and Martin shut off the engine. "Sullivan, you dropping everything and coming here is a big deal. It's what I call a grand gesture. I do think she'll get that."

Sullivan harrumphed loudly. "I could have been spying on some lady with her knickers around her ankles dallying with the husband's boss. I was getting a huge per diem."

"I wouldn't mention that to Diane. Okay, sit tight. I'm going in."

The door to Diane's father's house was ajar when Martin reached the front porch. He pushed it open and saw Diane sitting on the fireplace hearth with her head in her hands. Abraham was lying on his back on the living room floor tossing M&Ms into the air and trying to catch them in his open mouth.

"He started yelling at me because I wouldn't give him the candy," Diane said. "I thought he was going to hit me."

Diane's father tilted his head back and looked up at Martin, a wide smile spreading across his face. "Martin. Would you like an M&M?"

Martin knelt down next to him and Abraham put a handful of the multi-colored candies into his hand. "Diane and I used to have contests to see how many M&Ms we could catch in our mouths. Do you remember that?"

"I do, Dad," she said. "I always beat you."

"It's because you have a big mouth," Abraham teased. "You got that from your mother's side of the family."

"Would you like a pillow, Mr. Jacobs?" Martin asked.

The question seemed to befuddle the old man and he raised his head and looked around. "How did I get on the floor?"

"Would you like me to help you up?"

Abraham rose up onto one elbow and winced. "Yes, my back is killing me."

Martin helped Abraham onto the couch and placed the bag of M&Ms in his lap. "It's almost time for Judge Judy," Martin said, patting him on his shoulder. He picked up the remote on the coffee table and switched on the TV as Abraham continued to toss candy into his mouth.

Diane got up and walked into the kitchen and Martin followed her. She leaned against the sink staring out into the backyard. "Thanks," she said.

Martin leaned on the counter next to her. "When's the last time you left the house and just went out to dinner or to do something for yourself?"

Diane laughed. "Are you fucking kidding me?"

"Why don't you? I'll stay here. Go to a movie. Go to dinner. Go get a massage. Go talk to your husband."

"You almost had me there until you mentioned Sullivan."

"He's in the car."

At first, Diane didn't react, but then she slowly turned to look at Martin.

"Who's in the car?"

"Sullivan. He's worried about you, and your dad. I was going to arrange some movie-style chance meeting to reunite you, but… well… fuck it, I'm tired."

"He couldn't haul his fat ass out of the car to come in and be a decent human being?"

"He wasn't sure you'd actually see him. It's not like you two have been on speaking…"

"Well, he could have at least made the fucking effort."

Diane pushed away from the sink and marched out of the kitchen, past her father, who was happily enrapt in Judge Judy, and out the front door. Martin trailed after her and could see the look of horror on Sullivan's face as Diane came toward the car. He shifted over into the driver's seat as if about to flee, but Martin held up the car keys and twirled them around his finger. Sullivan's face fell and Martin couldn't help but laugh. He didn't even notice that Diane had turned around and was standing in front of him. Diane slapped Martin hard across the face with one hand and snatched the car keys off his finger with the other. She ran toward the car, and then turned back. Martin was sure she was going to hit him again. Instead, she grabbed him by the shoulders and kissed him on the lips.

Martin could taste blood in his mouth as he watched Sullivan repeatedly relock the door as Diane opened it with the key fob.

"I'll break the goddamn window," Diane shouted.

Sullivan reluctantly slid back over to the passenger seat and let Diane get in the car. He shot Martin a withering look as Diane started the car and peeled away from the curb, tires squealing on the pavement. Martin noticed that several of Diane's neighbors were standing on their porches or in their yards staring at him.

"Nothing to see here," he called out, trying to keep a cheery tone in his voice. Martin walked back into the house and shut the door. He sat down next to Abraham and poured M&Ms into his hand and started tossing them into the air and catching them in his mouth.

Diane intended to drive Sullivan to the fleabag motel on the interstate, but wound up fucking him in the backseat of Martin's rental car in a cul-de-sac. She didn't care who saw her or if the police caught them—she felt totally out of her head.

Sullivan was, at first, frightened as Diane threw the car into park and lunged at him across the center console, grabbing his fat face and shoving her tongue into his mouth. She felt the gearshift scrape her shin as Sullivan pulled her onto his lap. As soon as Sullivan's sausage fingers grabbed her ass, she felt wet for the first time in a year. She fumbled for the release handle, planning to do him right there, but Sullivan's weight made the seat fly back and catapulted her over his head into the back seat. The seat cracked as Sullivan crawled back to her, as he strained to unbutton his trousers.

They both came like teenagers, too soon and in a rush of moans and groans worthy of a porno movie. Diane lay beached on top of Sullivan's belly, sweat pouring from her entire body. Sullivan's breath sounded labored and his face was the color of a tomato.

"Don't you fucking die on me," Diane said, struggling to sit up.

"Well shift over, woman, you're crushing me."

"Fuck you, you fat fuck."

Sullivan grinned and slapped her on the ass. "You love it."

She did love it. Diane tried to hide the grin, but Sullivan saw it and pulled her back down on top of him, running his hands softly up and down her damp back. It raised chill bumps all over her body and she shuddered with pleasure.

"Don't think for a second that everything is okay between

us," Diane said.

"I wouldn't dare. But it seems to me there is just one obstacle standing in our way—the care of your father."

Diane frowned. "He's not your *obstacle* to worry about now, is he?"

"You know what I mean. I love the old bugger, too. He's as decent a bloke as I've ever met, and you love him more than you love anyone else."

She sat up, straddling Sullivan again. "If, and I do mean if, I consider moving Dad anywhere, I'll be making all the decisions. I don't want any lip off of you."

"That's a start."

"And you know it's more than just Dad," she said, softening her tone. "You annoy the living fuck out of me."

Sullivan reached up and stroked her face. "So do you, but we've had a hell of a lot of fun, too."

"Maybe I don't want to always go running off on cases with you. Maybe I just want to hang out at the château with the gay boys and the old woman. I'm pissed off that I haven't gotten to mooch off that deal. I might even go back and harass Empress Lacombe to give me a job at the Anglophile."

"Sounds reasonable."

"Or maybe we just stay in Memphis for a while."

"Whatever you like, my sweet."

"You are pouring it on thick, fat bastard," Diane said, but felt a wave of calm pass through her. "We should go before someone catches us."

There was a loud tapping on the window. Diane looked up and saw a policeman standing beside the car with a woman who was pointing and gesticulating wildly. A younger woman stood next to her, arms folded smugly over her chest. It was Esther and her Picasso-faced daughter.

Even through the glass, Diane could hear Esther's screeching voice. "Oh, my god… you're a disgrace to your mother's memory."

## 33 You Must Set Its Worth

The bar was dark and smoky, and the high-backed booths were perfect for a private conversation and not being noticed by other patrons. Martin wondered if that was why David had chosen it for their meeting. He ordered a glass of red wine and fought the urge to ask someone for a cigarette—the combination of the smell of smoke and rattling nerves only intensified his craving. He self-consciously touched his stomach, still smarting over Diane's comment about putting on weight. But he had gotten a little flabby since moving to the château. Hours at his desk writing and the sumptuous food from the kitchen made him overindulge. He'd felt skeletal and sickly after being shot and the operation, but his appetite had returned with gusto and he replaced his desire to smoke with salty and sweet treats.

Martin had thought about contacting David numerous times to see if he remembered their meeting in the hall of mirrors as their lives ebbed away, but Diane said David had left Memphis and was presumably back in New Orleans. Martin had started a dozen emails, dialed the number of the Blue Parrot, but always changed his mind before hitting send or call. Then David left a message for Martin at his father's house on a Sunday afternoon, the same day that the notice of David's impending nuptials appeared in the newspaper. Maybe David wanted to be talked out of it or maybe he was feeling guilty and needed to clear his conscience.

Martin sensed someone approaching the table and looked up to order another drink. Instead of the waitress, it was David. He was wearing a long-sleeve polo shirt that seemed slightly too big, faded jeans and a baseball cap with the Saints logo on it.

"Hi," David said, and leaned down for an awkward half hug. Martin was so taken aback that his arms became tangled with David's and he found his face momentarily smashed against his shoulder. There was the scent of old pot smoke, beer and sweat in that instant and Martin drew back, trying to smile as David took a seat across from him.

Here was David again at last. Skinny, overly tanned, the hair peeking from under the cap bleached and brittle and, even in the dim light, his teeth yellowed from cigarettes. He'd already ordered a beer at the bar and as he put it to his mouth, Martin noticed David's fingernails were bitten down and ragged. The pretty boy he had once been was long gone and he wasn't quite thirty.

"I'm glad you agreed to meet me," David said. "I know it was kinda weird leaving a message with your dad, but I wasn't sure how to get in touch."

"It's okay," Martin said, trying to focus and not dwell on David's appearance. "You must be busy with the wedding. My dad showed me the announcement in the *Appeal*."

"Yeah, it's pretty crazy. Maybe not the best time to be

getting married, but our folks have been dogging us for years now, so we decided to get it over with." There was a tone of resignation in David's voice, and Martin desperately wanted to steer the conversation elsewhere.

"You're still in New Orleans?"

"Yeah, managing the bar. Holding Mardi Gras helped. The tourists are coming back now, so we're doing okay."

"That's good. I still can't believe it's been a year since Katrina."

"It's still weird. There are only a couple hundred thousand people in the city now and there was nearly half a million pre-K. It still feels empty and there are parts of the city that look like war zones. But it's home now, so I can't imagine being anywhere else."

"It always reminded me of Paris."

David smiled. "Part of it does, yeah. But, hey, you're still in Paris being all famous and successful. I knew you would be."

Martin felt color rise to his face. "I don't know about famous. It's poetry after all."

"You were in the *New York Times*. That makes you pretty famous, if you ask me."

"So, you read the book?"

"I always thought I was the first to read it."

Martin flashed on the manuscript sitting in his old apartment with the statue of Venus de Milo resting on top of it.

"Oh, right... right. Of course."

"I'm not pissed or anything, if that's what you're worried about," David said. "You were pretty much honest, so I can't be mad about it."

"Has your fiancée read it?"

David swirled the rest of the beer around in the glass and averted his gaze. "Maybe she saw some online," he mumbled. "I don't know. I mean what happened was a long time ago."

"We've all moved on. Obviously. You're getting married and so am I."

David's face clouded. "You're getting married?"

"Civil partnership. Same difference."

"Wow," David said, drawing out the word. "I gotta admit it's really weird that you wound up with that Christian guy."

"Why?" Martin tried not to bristle, but he could feel the conversation starting to take a turn.

"Well… you know. He was a hooker and drug dealer."

"That's what he did survive. It's not who he was."

The waitress brought David another beer, and Martin realized David was already tipsy. He'd obviously been drinking before he arrived at the bar.

"He even put the moves on me," David whispered. "Did he tell you that? Was trying to grab my junk in a bathroom stall."

"He did tell me. A long time ago. We don't have any secrets from each other."

That answer seemed to irritate David and he changed course. "You totally owe me for getting y'all together. If it hadn't been for me, you would have never met. And now you're getting gay married."

Martin sat back in the booth, folding his arms over his chest. "And you're getting straight married. Do I owe you for that, too?"

David couldn't meet Martin's gaze.

"Why did you want to see me, David?"

There was a hint of panic in David's eyes; he wanted to say something, but a decade later he was still unable to be honest with himself or Martin.

"I saw online you were guest lecturing at the college, and I thought it would be cool to grab a cold one and catch up. That's it, man."

"Really? You thought it would be 'cool' to see your old

lover before you get married? Did you want me to give you head in the parking lot for old times sake, too?"

David's face flushed red and with shaking fingers he pulled a cigarette pack from his pocket and started trying to light it. Oh, fuck, Martin thought. Was that what this was about?

"Wait, is that what you really wanted?"

"Keep your voice down," David said through clenched teeth. "I didn't say shit."

Martin finished his glass of wine and started to slide out of the booth.

"Don't go yet," David said, reaching for Martin's hand, his sleeve sliding up to reveal a raised scar on his wrist. Martin could feel David's calloused yet familiar fingers brush against his hand.

Martin took David's hand in his and ran his thumb over the scar. David tried to pull his hand away, but Martin held it tightly. The look of panic on David's face had been replaced by one of despair.

"Why are you marrying that girl? Why would you do that to her? To yourself? After what happened…"

"She's pregnant," David said, a quiver in his voice.

"Oh, Christ."

"It's not like I don't love her. I do. I do love her. When I first came back to America, I didn't have any contact with my family and was living under that fake name. I thought I was going to lose it. I was so lonely. Miranda saved me. She never asked any questions and supported me."

"And she's still not asking any questions."

"She loves me!"

David's voice cracked with emotion, and tears were dripping onto the table. Martin looked around uncomfortably and could see faces glancing in the direction of the booth as David's gulping sobs became audible over the football game on the television behind the bar.

"Ooookay," Martin said. "Let's go outside. You've been overserved, as usual."

Martin left money on the table before helping David out of the booth. All eyes were on them as he gently propelled David toward the back door and the parking lot beyond. After the darkness of the bar, the bright sunshine was intense and Martin shaded his eyes with a hand, momentarily blinded by the light.

He felt arms slip around his waist, lips pressed against his. David pushed Martin against the rough brick wall of the bar and pinned him there.

"Get off me!" Martin shouted, and shoved David away. "What the fuck?"

David stumbled backwards and tripped over the curb. He sat on the pavement with his face in his hands trying to muffle fresh sobs. This isn't happening, Martin thought. What kind of bad movie is this?

Martin reached out a hand and David reluctantly took it. He pulled David up to standing position. "I think you need to go home and sober up," Martin said. "I'll call you a cab."

"I'm sorry," David said wiping his face with the back of his hands. "I'm sorry, man."

They waited in silence for the cab, leaning against the hood of Martin's rental car.

"It takes forever to get a cab in this town," David said.

"Yeah. I remember."

David had pulled the brim of his cap low over his face and now it was in shadow.

"Remember that letter you wrote me from New Orleans?" David nodded.

"You told me to try and be happy. And I am happy. I wish that for you, David. It's all I've ever wanted."

David took Martin's hand and held it. "I really blew it. If I hadn't been so scared. If I wasn't…"

"Don't beat yourself up about that now. We can't go back, so we go forward. If you haven't figured yourself out and what you want, for fuck's sake, don't marry that girl and ruin her life. And your kid's life."

"I'm so scared," David whispered.

The cab pulled into the parking lot and Martin waved to the driver.

"Promise me you're not going to do anything stupid."

"I won't. It was just a bad day…" David's voice trailed off.

"I don't want to have to send Diane to your house again."

Another sob escaped David's chest, his shoulders quivering. "How… how did you know what had happened?"

"I woke up with a bad feeling," Martin said, putting his arm around David. "You don't have any memories of what happened after you cut yourself?"

David pushed up the brim of his cap and wiped at his eyes. "No. Just Diane in the bathroom giving me shit as usual."

David opened the door to the cab and got inside. He rolled down the back window and motioned to Martin.

"If I hadn't gone with my parents that day at the airport, we'd be together, wouldn't we? If I'd just made another choice."

A strange sensation rippled through Martin's body, a feeling of displacement and lightheadedness. The memory of David begging him to walk through the mirror, to put their lives on another course, pulsed in his mind.

"Don't look back, David. Our lives are littered with what-ifs and second-guessing. You'll never find happiness if you dwell on it."

"Thank you for saving my life," David said. "I thought for a long time that you hated me and wanted me dead."

"If you're ever having another bad day, just remember that I don't hate you," Martin said. "You saved my life, too. You just don't remember."

"Maybe you'll write a poem about it," David said as the

cab started to pull away.

"Count on it."

"Don't forget me," David said, his composure starting to crumble again.

"Not likely."

David gave Martin a thumbs up as the cab pulled out of the parking lot.

Martin watched as the car disappeared down the street. He remembered putting the box of matches next to the manuscript in his empty apartment.

*Tuck it away or turn it to ash.*
*But you must set its worth.*

He realized David was still in that apartment, hand poised to strike the match, uncertain of his future. Had been there for a decade. Might always be there.

# 34 the Transit of Venus

Irène sat at her desk overlooking the château's gardens, her elbows resting on the pages of the completed manuscript. Her manuscript. The three hundred pages felt solid, substantial. She lit her second cigarette of the day—she could never go cold turkey at her age, even with the doctors and Martin badgering her about it—and opened the window to let in the fresh air. It was a cool, crisp day and she still thrilled at the sight of peacocks roaming the grounds, the glint of sunlight off the distant Nahon River, the sound of children laughing and the muted voices of tourists speaking in every language as they strolled the gardens. Pierre was asleep in his new favorite patch of sunlight beside her desk, his furry belly rising and falling with contentment. He had his run of the château and was more active and curious than ever.

The corner of the château she shared with Martin and Christian was twice, maybe three times as large as their combined apartments on rue

Rampon. While they were essentially hidden in the private wing, Irène never felt restricted or claustrophobic. After the tourists were gone for the day, they could wander the house and property at their leisure. They made few demands, often going to the cavernous old kitchen to make their own food or eat at the large communal table with the staff. Their nights were spent going into the village for dinner, walking by the river, watching films in the château's cinema and exploring the library. If she read a book from its shelves every day for the rest of her life, she would never be able to finish them all. Although they had been living at the château for more than a year, the art and décor fascinated her and she often found herself contemplating a statue or painting for an hour or more.

Martin was busily working on a new collection of poems and his acceptance rate in literary journals all over the world was staggering. He'd begun to accept invitations to guest lecture again—in Memphis, New York and London. He was teaching a weekly writing workshop for teenagers at the youth center in the nearby town of Vierzon, where Christian was working as a counselor. Christian was also reading the young adult novels that were now being submitted regularly to the publishing house after Julie convinced them that the genre was becoming more and more popular. Christian had a sharp eye and a sense of what kids wanted to read. Some nights, as the three of them sat in the lounge discussing books, passing pages of manuscripts back and forth or reading parts aloud, drinking wine, jazz playing softly in the background, it was as if they had been transported to another era. The days and nights at the château were happy and peaceful.

As blissful as their lives were, it was a long period of adjustment at Château de Valençay. Irène was recovering from her heart attack, unable to smoke, eating a bland diet and taking a round of pills. She felt the strange sensation of statelessness again, as if she didn't belong anywhere, and the château was merely a way station. Martin was weak and unable to focus, spending many of his days in bed or wandering aimlessly around the château. Christian traveled back and forth to Paris every other day, acting as their emissary to the publishing house, meeting with Julie and even returning one day a week to the re-opened youth center in Montfermeil. Martin didn't like it, but Christian said it would only be for a short time. He needed to go there. It was closure for him, fully letting go of his past and all that had happened in Montfermeil.

As the days passed and the shock of what had happened at rue Rampon dissipated, the charms of the château began to reveal themselves. There was no pressure to be anywhere, do anything or be interrupted by city life. Irène's novel began one day after observing Martin and Christian in the garden. They were on a bench in the sunshine, Christian reading a manuscript, Martin's head resting on his lap staring up at the clouds, their fingers interlacing, touching or caressing in an absent-minded way. They had learned to be comfortable with each other in silence, something Irène and Jean-Louis had cherished about their relationship. She picked up a pencil and wrote the first paragraph of what would be a roman à clef about her life on rue Rampon. In a few days, she had filled two legal pads and started transferring it to her laptop.

At the château, they were also isolated from the media speculation over what had happened at rue Rampon and Irène and Martin's whereabouts. Julie dismissed all the rumors, telling journalists that they were traveling and working on projects. Martin was sure reporters would turn up at one of the schools where he was guest lecturing, but they never did. Eventually, the media lost interest. There was a Senate investigation into Arnaud's schemes, but no agents or police ever came to call at the château.

They all missed rue Rampon, or at least they thought they did, until Christian snapped a photo with his mobile and showed it to them one night over dinner. The boarded-up, soot-ringed windows should have brought her to tears, but Irène felt only a hint of wistfulness for her old home.

"I should be crying," she said. "Shouldn't I?"

"I'm in no hurry to return," Martin said, handing Christian's mobile back to him.

Christian looked at the photo again. "I had a dream the other night that we never went back."

"You didn't mention that," Martin said. "Where did we go?"

"We were walking across a wet, grassy field at dusk... or maybe it was early morning. There were rock formations silhouetted against the sky. The moon was up and there was another bright star that shown just as bright."

"Venus," Irène said.

"Yes, it could have been," Christian said, his brow furrowed as he tried to remember all the details. "I just had this sense that we were not going back. We were going toward something else. There was... I do not know how to explain it... an expectancy in the air. As if something was about to happen."

"Good or bad?" Martin asked.

"Something wonderful," he said with a smile.

Irène and Martin exchanged a knowing glance. Martin leaned over, kissed Christian. Then he took Christian's mobile and deleted the photo of rue Rampon.

*Seven o'clock in the morning. A sound wakes her. Something familiar. A rustle of feathers, a flap of wings. Irène bolts up, adrenaline pumping, ears keen. She slides out of bed and goes to the window. She sees Christian walking toward the garage, calls to him, but no sound comes out of her mouth. Irène waves her arms hoping Christian will see her as he pulls the car out of the garage, but he takes no notice and his car disappears down the long drive toward the main road into the village. Irène turns back to the bed and stops short. She is still in bed. Sound asleep, nestled under the duvet, her breath steadily rising and falling. Irène moves toward the bed, horrified and fascinated, and she feels her feet lift from the floor, the tug of wakefulness pulling at her sleeping body. She backs away and the strange gravity dissipates. Irène realizes she's having an out-of-body experience, a waking dream, not unlike when she went through the mirror to find Martin. The rustle again outside the bedroom door. Without even thinking, Irène runs toward the door, passes through its wooden solidity, momentary darkness like a blink, and then she is in the hallway. Just like a ghost. She runs down the hall, feels faster, more agile, as if she's skimming above the wooden floorboards, almost flying. At the end of the hall, Martin's door is cracked. He, too, is asleep. Irène calls his name, feels the shape of it in her mouth, but no sound. The beat of wings again. Irène takes the stairs two at a time, leaps until she is on the main floor, and the sound is coming from the grand salon at the end of the long hallway. The doors are open, the salon filled with the dazzling morning light, prisms of color bounce from the chandeliers and rainbow across the floor. Irène is on the threshold in an instant. She shields her eyes, looks up at the ceiling for the source of the flapping wings, but the sound is not above but directly in front of her, coming from behind the arched mirror over the fireplace. Irène stands before the mirror, but cannot see her own reflection. The paintings and furniture are gone and the salon is empty, except standing behind her, between the two Doric columns that divide the salon, is the statue of Venus de Milo. It seems larger than life, fills the room. Irène turns and looks, but the statue is not there. Venus is only visible through the mirror. She reaches out, her fingertips about to touch the glass, then another sound. Her name. She turns and sees Martin standing in the doorway of the salon. Irène's feet lift off the floor and in another blink, she is back inside her body, sitting up in bed, heart racing. Seven o'clock in the morning.*

Irène and Martin stood before the mirror in the grand salon contemplating their reflections. Somehow, they had crossed into each other's subconscious in their dreams. Martin had also heard the beating of wings, saw Christian leaving to go into Paris for the day, found he couldn't speak. He had followed the sound to the grand salon and was stunned to find Irène there, her hand reaching toward the mirror while the statue of Venus stood like a monolith in the room. He'd found his voice, called her name, and then he was sitting up in bed. Even without his glasses, he could see the digital clock on the bedside table read 7:00 a.m.

"We are obviously supposed to be here," Martin said to Irène's reflection. "This all began when I was in Memphis, when I saw you in the mirror before the reading."

Irène nodded. "And that is when I began having the dreams about watching Venus and Winged Victory being taken from the Louvre. Then you…"

"Died."

"I hate when you say that," Irène said, turning to look at him.

"But it's true. We both did."

"Not quite. Almost. We survived."

"Now we have to find out why."

Martin brought his laptop to Irène's room and they read every article available on the web about the Venus de Milo and Winged Victory being removed from the museum and hidden at the château. With the Nazi invasion imminent, the decision was made to move the treasures of the Louvre in early September 1939. Boson de Talleyrand, the Duke of Sagan, leveraged his descendancy from German nobility and declared his château a neutral zone during the war, which spared it from occupation. That made Valençay the perfect place for hiding the statues and other artwork coveted by Hitler and the Third Reich. Both statues were returned to the Louvre after the end of World War II and the museum reopened to the public in 1947.

"It says here that members of the Resistance helped intercept art stolen by the Germans," Martin said, reading an essay about the work of the men and women who risked their lives to preserve France's art treasures. "Your father was in the Resistance and you saw him at the Louvre after we... after whatever happened to us."

"It was a distraction to throw me off from finding you," Irène said. "I don't remember my mother or father saying anything about art or the Louvre as part of their work. My father was a courier and helped supply food and my mother did some work with one of the underground newspapers. That's what I remember."

"But they took you to the Louvre, you told me that before."

"Oh, yes, I remember going as a child and playing in the Tuileries."

"Do you remember anything your father said about the art?" Martin pressed her.

"He loved it. Both of my parents did."

They could find no list of the Resistance members who had helped move the art from the Louvre to the various hiding places around France. There was one grainy image of Venus being put inside her crate, but the faces of the men were not visible. Irène studied the photo, marveled at how closely it resembled that of her dream, but she could not identify her father as one of the men. She zoomed in and out for half an hour until the photo became nothing but pixilated black and white dots.

They were still glued to the computer when Martin's mobile phone rang and they both jumped at the sound of it echoing in the high-ceilinged room. Christian had missed the first train from Gare d'Austerlitz to Vierzon, so would be late.

He urged Martin and Irène to have dinner and he would see them in a few hours.

They had dinner at the long wooden table in the kitchen, a small fire snapping and crackling in the giant stone fireplace, and made small talk about manuscripts over their steaks. As they were about to go back upstairs, a maid came in carrying a plate of small cakes and a white envelope and placed it on the table in front of Irène.

"What is this?" Irène asked her.

"Madeleines," the maid said. "The curator said I should bring them in after you were finished with dinner."

Irène turned over the envelope in her hand. It had no stamps or address, but the stationery was expensive, like the kind Frederick used when he was alive.

Martin picked up one of the shell-shaped cakes and bit into it. "Mmmm... now all I need is a cup of tea."

"The inseparableness of us from the past," Irène said, sliding her thumb under the envelope flap.

Inside the envelope was a small note card. In neat block letters was printed: *Your presence is requested in the theatre.*

Inside the ornate little theatre, a movie screen covered the stage curtains. About halfway down the aisle, two seats in the center were marked reserved.

"Okay, this is creeping me out a little," Martin said as they took their seats.

The house lights dimmed of their own accord and a clacking sound, like that of an old movie projector, came from the back of the room. Martin and Irène turned to look and see who was in the screening room as a beam of white light appeared over their heads.

A silent, sepia image of the number five appeared in a circle and began to count down to one. There was a ragged jump cut followed by a black and white image of the grand gallery inside the Louvre. The camera panned in a slow, halting motion showing giant, empty frames lining the walls. There was another jump and Venus de Milo was shown being hoisted onto a wooden flat by a group of men. Martin felt Irène's hand on his and they both leaned forward. The film cut again, and the camera was pointing down to the Daru staircase from one of the mezzanines. A group of men were easing Winged Victory down the wooden ramp.

"Where did this come from?" Martin asked aloud, but Irène was too mesmerized by the images on the screen to answer. She had propped her elbows on the back of the seat in front of her, staring intently at the film unspooling before them.

There was another jump, and the camera focused on the staircase as four men moved the Venus de Milo. The camera zoomed in clumsily onto the statue's face, peeking from behind the slats of the crate she was being moved in—just as she appeared after Martin was shot and transported to the other side of the mirror. As the camera zoomed out again, the men moving Venus were shown posing around her on the stairs. The camera panned to each man, the first three looking exhausted and staring gravely into the lens. Then the camera came to the last man. He was tall, wearing coveralls and a cap, which he quickly removed and stuffed in his pocket. He ran a hand through his sweat-soaked hair to smooth it back and grinned at the camera before giving a little salute.

Irène gripped the seat in front of her and slowly stood up. "Father."

The moment she uttered the word, the film froze. Her beloved father, who had disappeared one night and never returned, was looking back at her. Her entire body shook with emotion as tears coursed down her face. She felt Martin's arms around her and sank weakly into them, but she couldn't look away from the screen.

The film started up again and her father's face disappeared. "No, bring him back!" she cried out.

There was one final scene. The crated Winged Victory and Venus de Milo being removed from a canvas covered truck outside the Château de Valençay. And there was Irène's father again, guiding Venus through the open doorway before pausing to look back at the camera and wave goodbye. The scene lingered on the doorway for a moment, until a figure in a long, dark coat appeared and blocked the view. The figure backed away for a moment to reveal a woman who looked almost exactly like Irène with her deep-set eyes and downturned mouth. She bent down a little to make sure she was in frame and smiled for the camera before she too waved goodbye.

"My mother," Irène said, brushing away tears.

Irène reached out toward the screen as the image cut away, the film making a whisking sound against the reel. The projector switched off and the screen began to retract back into the ceiling.

"I want to see it again."

Irène started toward the back of the theatre, but Martin was distracted by what was being revealed on the small stage: a tall, wooden crate lit by dim spotlights.

"Irène…" Martin called out.

She was standing in the aisle looking back at the stage, a hand covering her mouth. "What is this?"

Martin moved into the aisle and took Irène's hand. "The reason we're here."

They walked to the front of the theatre and climbed the stairs at the side of the stage, approaching the statue cautiously and in awe.

"I don't believe it," Irène said, reaching through the slats to run her hand over Venus' smooth abdomen. "Could this possibly be the real Venus de Milo?"

"I believe it is." Martin touched Venus' face, traced the curve of her breast with a finger. This was no cheap plaster cast, but solid marble. "I guess Monsieur Talleyrand was so taken with Venus that he couldn't let her go. If the real Venus is here, does that mean the Winged Victory at the Louvre is a copy, too?"

"Perhaps that is our next mystery to solve." A throaty laugh escaped Irène's lips. "Look at this, Martin."

She pointed to the side of the crate holding Venus. Written there in painted, flourished script was a message.

*For Irène and Martin,*
*The transit is complete.*
*Love, Frederick*

# Lighting Out
## epilogue: for the Territories

Julie Lacombe flashed a quick smile to the maître d' at Café Victor Hugo before she slipped into the back room. The guitar case bumped against her leg, its heavy familiar weight would soon no longer be a burden. She put her key into the elevator door and descended to the platform. She soaked in every vibration, every sound, the smell of diesel and rot. It would be her last trip on this elevator.

She paused on the platform to watch a distant metro train rumble and flash by, leaving a gust of warm wind in its wake. Julie tapped the entry code into the keypad without looking, then went down the corridor to the final checkpoint.

Inside the command center, all the computers and monitors had been removed. There was just a large metal table where Geoff de Courcy sat waiting for her. As she approached, he stood up— impeccably dressed in a Savile Row suit—and greeted her with a firm handshake. She sat down, placing the guitar case between them on the table.

"Well," he began. "We have come to the end of the line."

Julie nodded. "We have."

"Thank you for your assistance as we close up shop here. I know you are busy with your other life now. The bookstore is doing well."

"Well enough."

Geoff reached into his coat pocket and pulled out an envelope. "This will ensure that it stays open as long as you like."

Julie accepted the envelope without opening it and slipped it into her bag. "And the other?"

Geoff cocked an eyebrow. "You don't want to know how much you've been paid?"

"I'm sure it's very generous. You always are. All I've ever wanted is information."

Geoff reached down and pulled a thick folder from his briefcase. It was tied with a cord to prevent the pages from falling out. "The dossier on your father, his work, his medical condition, photographs and maps." He pushed the folder across the table and tapped it with two fingers. "Very unexpected."

"You've read it?"

"I paid for it, so I thought I should have the privilege."

"Is it a disappointment?"

Geoff looked thoughtfully at the folder. "Unbelievable is the word that keeps coming to my mind."

Julie began to untie the cord, then stopped. She picked up the folder, surprised by how heavy it was, and put it into her bag. She wanted to digest her father's past and his death from the strange cancer alone with a bottle of Scotch.

"Will you be content at the Anglophile?" Geoff asked. "After all these years in service, going back to a normal life will be difficult."

"It's time. When Henri Lorit died, I knew it was time to

get out of the business. I failed to protect him."

"You are too hard on yourself, Juliette. Lorit knew he might not survive tangling with Arnaud."

"I'm tired and ready to be a civilian again," Julie said. "The shop and the publishing house will keep me busy. I'll continue to write and travel."

"Be sure to add Wyoming to your itinerary," Geoff said.

Julie fought the urge to pull the folder from her bag. Those tantalizing clues were buzzing around her brain. Her father's secret life and death would finally be revealed, and she hoped it would bring closure to that part of her own life.

She had been pressed into service by the French government while she was still at the Sorbonne, approached by an RG agent who had known her father. Once she returned to America, she had briefly worked as an operative for the CIA, but she left after becoming despondent over the country's late move to stop the horrific war in Bosnia. She became a gun for hire, extractor, fixer—whatever the government or entity she was working for at the time wanted to label her. She only took jobs that she thought were for the greater good. The black op to prevent Arnaud's war in Montfermeil was worth the danger, even if Lorit had died. She would have to live with it. Martin and Irène were alive. That was what mattered most.

Geoff's mobile beeped and he picked it up from the table. "Well… after nearly two years, the intelligence agency has completed its investigation into Arnaud's death. Nothing like government efficiency. A ruling of suicide, as expected. Martin, Irène and Christian should be able to come back to Paris whenever they like."

"I'm not sure they want to," Julie said. "The city has lost a bit of its light."

"They've become quite the travelers in the past year. America, Germany, Belgium, Italy, Greece and now Australia."

"Christian emailed a few months ago that they were leaving

Sydney and headed north into the Arnhem Land," Julie said.

Geoff ran his hand over the guitar case. "Are you ready to surrender this?"

"Yes."

He flipped open the clasps of the case to reveal a sniper rifle beside a telescopic sight and silencer. Julie reached into her pocket and tossed the encrypted pager to Geoff, who caught it with one hand and placed it in his own pocket.

"And the Range Rover?"

"Scrapped for parts in Calais."

Geoff stood up and extended his hand to Julie. "You are home free."


Julie walked across Paris to clear her head. It was late afternoon and autumn was fast approaching. The air was crisp, the sun glinting off buildings and passing cars. The streets were alive with people on their way home from work. The bag carrying her father's secrets weighed heavily on her—literally and figuratively—but she walked until she was in the Tuileries. Children laughed and played while their parents watched from nearby benches. The trees lining the garden's pathways were a spectacular shade of gold.

Julie walked on toward the Louvre, Pei's pyramid glowing with light from the courtyard. She hadn't been inside the museum in years, but the thought of a glass of wine and the chance to put down the bag and rest her aching feet in the lobby café was a grand idea. She wasn't quite ready to go back to the Anglophile, to the rest of her life.

Off-season tourists lingered in the Louvre's courtyard, snapping photos and sitting on the edge of the triangular reflecting pools consulting maps. Julie descended beneath the pyramid and joined the short queue to buy a ticket. Instead of going to the café, she found herself wandering down the long galleries, not really looking at the art, but remembering the night Arnaud died on rue Rampon. She rarely lingered on her work, had disciplined herself long ago to keep her emotions at bay, but her closeness to Martin and Irène had made this job personal. For the first time in years, as she had knelt in front of the window at her room in Le Admiral surveying Irene's apartment through slightly parted curtains, Julie was frightened she might fail again. The image of Lorit dead on the conference room table at the youth center loomed in her mind. As she cracked the window, making just enough space for the rifle barrel, she became hyperaware of the weight of the stock on her shoulder, the sterile coldness of the trigger under her finger, the perfect black crosshair etched into the scope. She had to shut out the sound of thousands of voices, sirens, honking car horns seeping through the crack and filling the hotel room. Then Arnaud had appeared at Irène's balcony doors, candles perfectly outlining his silhouette behind the curtain. One shot.

Julie found herself in the long gallery of sculptures. Ahead of her, a temporary barrier had been erected with a neatly worded sign with apologies from the Louvre for the temporary closure of the exhibit. Julie walked around the tall screen until she found a slender gap where it met the wall. Peering inside, Julie could see a large, wooden crate suspended over a pedestal. Four men—two in workman's coveralls and two more strangely dressed in white lab-style coats—were carefully removing the crate's slats. Inside was, unmistakably, the Venus de Milo.

"She's beautifully preserved," one of the white coats said reverently as he used what looked like a jeweler's loop to inspect the famed statue's draped legs and feet.

The two workers were muscling another statue onto a small loader for removal, and although covered with a long, white drape, it was obviously another version of Venus. The fake one that had been photographed millions of time by unknowing tourists and art lovers for nearly sixty years.

Julie felt a presence behind her and looked over her shoulder to find one of the museum guards with his arms folded over his chest.

"Pardon, madame, but as the sign says, this exhibit is closed to the public. Please move along."

As she walked back toward the lobby, Julie felt her spirits lift. She could handle whatever was in the report de Courcy had given her. No matter how far afield the search for the truth about her father took her, she would always return to Paris.

Julie came onto the mezzanine overlooking the Daru staircase and Winged Victory sitting majestically at the top of the landing. The last visitors were slowly heading down the stairs, their footsteps and hushed conversations echoing up to the high ceiling. As the crowd dispersed, Julie noticed that a man and woman remained on the landing, their backs to her, looking up at the statue. They were both wearing long dark coats and stood so still that they, too, seemed like statues. Julie reached into her bag and pulled out a small camera. She was so struck by the image of the man and woman juxtaposed against the statue that she wanted to capture it. As she was focusing the camera, the woman reached for the man's hand and he took it. Julie zoomed in and her eye caught something on the back of the woman's left hand. A small tattoo where the index finger and thumb met, two interlocking crosses.

Julie readjusted the lens, pulling the camera away from her eye for just a moment. When she raised it again, the man and woman were gone. She ran to the landing, Winged Victory towering over her on its pedestal, but there was no sign of them in the dwindling crowd of tourists at the foot of the staircase. Maybe they were never there at all.

Julie took a cab to rue Rampon, but she already knew Martin

and Irène would not be there. The apartment had been renovated and repaired. Save for a slight differentiation in the brick and stone, it was impossible to tell that the flat had been almost destroyed by fire. All that was left was for Irène to return and plant new flowers along the balcony.

Julie planned to circle back to the square and take the metro to the Anglophile, but then she remembered the little café around the corner that Martin and Irène frequented, and thought it was definitely time for a glass of wine.

The tables outside Café Richard were full of couples chatting and smoking over their meals and coffee. She ducked inside and was met by an old man who asked if she wanted a table or booth. It didn't matter.

"You look very tired, madame," he said. "There is a booth opening in the back. One moment."

A delivery boy came into the café and put a bundle of *Le Figaro* by the door. A formal portrait of Arnaud stared back at her from the front page with headlines about the ruling on his death.

The old man returned with a menu, introduced himself as Claude, the owner, and led her to a booth in the back of the café. Julie ordered a glass of red wine, but Claude returned with a bottle.

"A small token from absent friends," he said, pulling the cork out with a loud pop.

Julie started to ask Claude if Martin and Irène had been there, but decided against it. She drank the entire bottle and felt light-headed, almost drunk. The folder sat on the table before her, but she wasn't ready to read it. Not just yet.

She reached into her bag and pulled out the new issue of *Resolute* literary magazine. Martin said in his last email that a new poem would appear in its pages. She flipped to the table of contents and saw it was the final poem, "Three Light Out for the Territory."

*Leaving now. Again. Always.*
*Departures and arrivals, constant motion.*
*We are nomads unleashed on the world, stateless.*
*Answer to no one but ourselves.*
*Cut ties, lifelines, comfort zones.*
*Future sight: a low brick house in the Outback.*
*Simple rooms. Life uncomplicated.*
*Open arms that embrace. Let go. Embrace again.*
*Or disembodied. Fast forward. Into the dreamtime.*
*Not just one place, but all sights unseen.*

The poem felt like a message. Perhaps she would never see Martin, Irène or Christian again, their communication reduced to messages bouncing off towers and satellite relays. Or maybe she would cross paths with them again during her own travels. They would share a drink and stories in a dark bar in some far corner of the world. Or maybe they would only come to her in dreams.

Julie put a tip on the table and was about to depart when Claude reappeared. "Please come with me, madame. There is a package for you."

"What?"

"A gift," he said.

She followed Claude cautiously into the kitchen, half expecting to see Martin and Irène standing there, but instead the old man led her into a tiny office where a large box was sitting in the middle of a cluttered desk. He opened a drawer and pulled out a pointed letter opener and handed it to Julie. As he left, Claude smiled and patted her gently on the shoulder.

Out of habit, Julie put her ear to the box and listened carefully for any sounds. The box was new and freshly sealed and, when she picked it up, was surprisingly heavy. Julie carefully ran the letter opener under the tape and released the tabs.

Inside the box, buried in packing pellets, was the statue of the Venus de Milo that Frederick Dubois had found on the street during the riots, which had been taken by Jean-Louis as a final gift for Irène, who had sent it to Martin as a call to return to Paris when everything went wrong with David McLaren. Julie imagined the statue sitting in Martin's empty apartment with the manuscript that became his collection of poetry, David putting it into the locker at Gare du Nord, Martin and Christian bringing it as a trophy back to rue Rampon.

Inside the box was a folded piece of paper. Julie pulled it out, surprised that her hands were shaking. She unfolded the paper, but there was no note—only the symbol of interlocking crosses Martin and Irène had inked into their hands. The thing that bound them together. Equal but opposite. Reflecting hands.

FIN

# NOTES / ACKNOWLEDGMENTS

I was supposed to write these notes and acknowledgments in Paris, sitting in the lobby bar of the hotel on rue Rampon that inspired the Bel Air/Le Admiral that has been a main setting for The Venus Trilogy. However, life intervened.

My mother was involved in a car accident that forced me to postpone my return to London and Paris for what would have been the 20th anniversary trip to the cities that originally inspired this trilogy. While my mother was on the mend, terrorists attacked Paris. For the second time in less than a year, events unfolded in the City of Light that were eerily similar to scenes I'd written for this novel. The attacks on the restaurants and the Bataclan music hall took place in the 10th and 11th arrondissements not far from rue Rampon. I had to pause in the editing process to grieve for those innocent people, just as I had to stop earlier in the year when terrorists murdered staff members of the satirical magazine, *Charlie Hebdo*. The magazine's office was also located in the 11th. This was "my" neighborhood in Paris and had been since 1995, so the attacks struck especially close to home.

The weekend after the November 13 attacks, I considered rewriting some of the scenes and dialogue, especially where Christian confronts Arnaud. The devious Arnaud sounds incredibly prescient (and bigoted) about the future of France, but Christian's response still rings true despite what extremist politicians might say. The people of France want safety and security, but they have not abandoned the country's motto: liberté, égalité, fraternité. My continued hope is that Paris and France will continue to embrace immigrants and refugees, especially those fleeing war-torn countries who look to France as a beacon of hope.

*Leaving Paris* took three years to write. While it was in process, I left the original press that had published *Conquering Venus* and *Remain In Light* and put the trilogy into the capable and loving hands of Bryan Borland and Seth Pennington at Sibling Rivalry Press. Their encouragement and excitement about the adventures of Martin and Irène kept me motivated, while the trilogy's inclusion into the Rare Books and Special Collections Vault of the Library of Congress put a big cherry on top.

*Leaving Paris* was the most difficult book of the trilogy to write. I veered wildly off the outline in the summer of 2014 and just allowed the characters to dictate where they wanted to go. Reining them back in wasn't easy. They weren't quite ready to say goodbye. Giving Martin, Irène, Diane, Christian, Sullivan and David a proper sendoff weighed heavily on me. But just like with the first two books in the trilogy, Martin and Irène steered me toward the unexpected, but inevitable, conclusion. There's a very good chance that you'll see Diane, Sullivan and Julie Lacombe in their own book sooner than later. My one regret about this book is that Diane and Julie have no scenes together, so I'll have to remedy that or I won't be fit to live.

This novel was inspired by a disparate list of television programs and films, and you'll see obvious and subtle references throughout—from sci-fi shows like *Ashes to Ashes* and *Fringe* to French classics *La Femme Nikita* and *La Haine* to *Close Encounters of the Third Kind* (did you figure that one out early on?) and *The Dark Knight Rises* (also the final installment of a trilogy). Lewis Carroll's *Alice in Wonderland* and *Through the Looking-Glass*, Marcel Proust's *À la recherche du temps perdu* and C.S. Lewis' The Chronicles of Narnia (especially *The Magician's Nephew*) are also echoed in *Leaving Paris*.

This book would not have been possible without the love and support of Karen Head (poet assassin and hand model extraordinaire), Colin Potts, Donna Kile, Agnes Meadows, Tina Miller, Malory Mibab, Joy Thomas, Kate Evans, Julie Bloemeke, Peter and Krystyna FitzGerald-Morris, Dave Cross, Joy Borazjani, Ken Cloudt, Bo James, Steven Reigns, Anderson Rodriguez, Lisa Allender, Cecilia Woloch, C. Cleo Creech (for the Paris paperweight on the cover), Rachel Ann Lisi, my mother, my colleagues at *Atlanta INtown*, John Carder Bush and Kate Bush (who I saw twice in concert in the autumn of 2014 while I was writing this book in London).

Extra thanks must go to my longtime editor Kathy Dean, who kept these books on course, and to Sarah Rawlinson, who polished up this one with great care; Elizabeth Holmes for her gorgeous design work on the trilogy covers; and the music and friendship of Vanessa Daou and brokenkites. Be sure to check out iTunes and YouTube for the "Leaving Paris" song and music video that Vanessa and brokenkites collaborated on as homage to this book and the trilogy. Seriously, how cool is that?

And thank you to all of the readers of The Venus Trilogy. Letting Martin and Irène go hasn't been easy, but as Ood Sigma said to the Doctor in the final moments before his regeneration in *The End of Time*—this song is ending, but the story never ends.


Collin Kelley
November, 2015

# BOOK CLUB QUESTIONS

1. How have the main characters—Martin, Irène, Christian, Diane, Sullivan and David—changed or matured since their last appearance in *Remain In Light*? What surprised, delighted, angered or disturbed you about their lives and attitudes in *Leaving Paris*.

2. Talk about the book's structure. Were you able to easily pick up the plotline and characters originally introduced in *Conquering Venus* and *Remain In Light*? Does the tone of the writing and trajectory of the story arc remain consistent throughout the trilogy?

3. The "magical realism" and supernatural aspect of the trilogy continues and is heightened in *Leaving Paris*. Discuss the symbolism of Irène and Martin's psychic connection and how it affected the story and other characters in their orbit.

4. Is the ending satisfying? If so, why? If not, why not? How would you change it?

5. *Leaving Paris* ends with some of the characters' storylines still unresolved. What do you think happens next for Diane Jacobs, Bernard Sullivan and Julie Lacombe?

# THE AUTHOR

Collin Kelley is the author of the novels *Conquering Venus* and *Remain In Light*, which was the runner-up for the 2013 Georgia Author of the Year Award in Fiction and a 2012 finalist for the Townsend Prize for Fiction. His poetry collections include *Better To Travel, Slow To Burn, After the Poison*, and *Render*. Kelley is also the author of the eBook short story collection, *Kiss Shot*. A recipient of the Georgia Author of the Year Award, Deep South Festival of Writers Award, and Goodreads Poetry Award, Kelley's poetry, essays, and interviews have appeared in magazines, journals, and anthologies around the world.

# THE PRESS

Sibling Rivalry Press is an independent press based in Little Rock, Arkansas. Its mission is to publish work that disturbs and enraptures. This book was published in part due to the support of the Sibling Rivalry Press Foundation, a non-profit private foundation dedicated to assisting small presses and small press authors.

www.ingramcontent.com/pod-product-compliance
Lightning Source LLC
Chambersburg PA
CBHW020540020726
47494CB00006B/1844